THE STEEP

Richard Freeborn

Dynasty Press Ltd.
36 Ravensden Street
London SE11 4AR

www.dynastypress.co.uk

First published in this version by Dynasty Press Ltd.

ISBN: 978-0-9553507-71

Cover artwork design by **Rupert Dixon**

Typeset by **Biddles**, Blackborough End, Norfolk.

Printed and bound in the United Kingdom.

Also by Richard Freeborn:

Academic Studies

Turgenev, A Study
A Short History of Modern Russia
The Rise of the Russian Novel
The Russian Revolutionary Novel
Dostoevsky
Furious Vissarion: Belinskii's Struggle for Literature, Love and Ideas

Translations

Ivan Turgenev, Sketches from a Hunter's Album
Ivan Turgenev, Home of the Gentry
Ivan Turgenev, Rudin
Ivan Turgenev, A Month in the Country
Ivan Turgenev, Fathers and Sons
F.M Dostoevsky, An Accidental Family.

Fiction

Two Ways of Life
The Emigration of Sergey Ivanovich
Russian Roulette
The Russian Crucifix
American Alice
The Killing of Anna Karenina
Mr Frankenstein
Watching the Accident Happen
The Grand Duke's, er, Great Idea
The Girl in the White Fur Hat

I

When Jim Nordon said goodbye to his lodger after they'd shared the same apartment for three years, he realised he'd grown very fond of Dave. After a fashion he'd been in love with him, he supposed, though it had never really occurred to him that there would be anything more than a warm, rather boisterous, jovial, untidy friendship between them. Anyhow, Dave had gone. He had finished his degree course and left for the continent with his lovely girlfriend Francesca who wore green nail varnish and had a torrent of long auburn hair and the neatest round bottom. Dave had always attracted girls like that. Jim had envied him. The secret, if one can call it a secret, was worn as openly to the world as the badge sported on his woollen jersey or his leather jacket: it was religious. Dave had become religious during the three-year exposure to the shade of Jeremy Bentham within the confines of University College and had talked about God and salvation and rebirth to more than half-a-dozen girls to Jim's certain knowledge, with prodigious results. Francesca had especially enjoyed the rebirth and salvation bits. Dave had done a lot for her, that was clear, which Jim envied him for, though he took less readily to all the earnest pamphlets Dave left about the place. Printed on poor paper, they merchandised God and salvation and rebirth like so many weekend bargains.

'Look,' said Dave reasonably, in a tone more pitying than hot-gospelling, 'you're just not ready for it yet, are you? I mean, you're in the wrong job for one thing, and you haven't had the guts so far to make up your mind to pursue your true vocation – now be honest, have you? No, well, you see, I'm right, aren't I? And you've got this place at the top of this building, which is the nearest thing to a noble ruin within walking distance of the Elgin marbles, and it's full of a lot of human wrecks who'll most likely fall down sooner than Victorian Mansions gets pulled down. Which we all know is due for demolition next year – so why you don't get out now while the going's good, I don't know. The trouble with you, Jim, is that you're like the rest of them here, you've come to recuperate from the twentieth century and found yourself straying into the twenty-first, when you ought to be enjoying *this* century by being reborn again in the Lord God. You ought to look for salvation here and now. Well, it's been good fun being here for three years. You've put up with me and I'm really grateful, I mean that. I'll be going to Aussie-land for the winter and after that I hope to get to the States. So I'll probably not see you again before the old apartment is pulled down and you're off on your own somewhere. But you've got to stop bloody recuperating, you know what I mean, and start living again. The Lord be with you!'

It was a relief for Jim to know he had the place to himself. He immediately moved his easel and painting things into the second bedroom. For the first time since his occupancy of the apartment he realised how spacious the sitting-room or main room was, with its large Edwardian marble fireplace and its pretentious plasterwork on the ceiling. Two of the walls were given over to his paintings, chiefly portraits. The only windows were on either side of the fireplace and at the far end of the room nearest to the entrance to the apartment was a small kitchenette. A small hallway divided the main room from the two bedrooms (both had basins) and the bathroom and loo. It was spacious by comparison with others in Victoria Mansions. Jim had rented it relatively cheaply because the leasehold had had only a few more years to run before demolition would put an end to it. He knew he had to leave in a few months. With this in mind, three years previously and for the companionship, he had allowed Dave to lodge in the second bedroom. He had had other lodgers previously but non as companionable as Dave. All he had to contemplate now that Dave had left was the problem of finding other accommodation. It would mean having to find somewhere he could afford much farther out of London than Southampton Row.

Victoria Mansions was by any standard a decayed edifice of late-Edwardian design that had been renovated and refronted more than once in its more than century-long existence, but little had been done save necessary maintenance to the top floor that provided housing for lift machinery and water tanks and what grandly called itself 'The Apartment'. Because it was half-a-dozen floors above street level 'The Apartment' could be considered quiet, but nowhere in Victoria Mansions could claim to be beyond the reach of street noises. On either side of it further structures of the same vintage had already been demolished to make way for new hotels, office buildings and shops. It had long been recognised by all the occupants that their days were numbered – and in more senses than one. With the exception of a young couple on the second floor, Jim and his lodger had been the youngest occupants for the past three years. Most had lived there thirty or more years, or, if they were new arrivals (like Dora Pratts-Morris, for example), they were invariably elderly.

Jim had never discovered to his satisfaction why this was so. The firm of estate agents that managed the property had an elderly staff, but that hardly seemed to explain why so many of those in Victoria Mansions were widows or retired or near retirement or certainly elderly and all determined, it seemed, to be regarded as rightful occupants of what, in their childhoods, had been recognised as a fashionable place to live. It had become rundown, for sure, and rather neglected. It had been unfair of Dave to describe it as a place to recuperate from the twenty-first century, yet there was some truth in it. Victoria Mansions in its final years bore a resemblance to what in a religious sense might be called 'a retreat'. It was a home for lives seeking spiritual refreshment and a rekindling of hope. Elderly though they might be, they preferred to behave as if the metropolitan world had kindly offered them a Calypso's isle as a refuge from the stormy seas of the capital while not denying them the possibility of enjoying its zest. The only real occupant of Victoria Mansions who had gone there to recuperate from both the twentieth and the twenty-first centuries was Jim Nordon.

Jim Nordon had several problems. He found difficulty in giving them an order of priorities. He could usually manage to single out one or two of them as on the whole rating greater prominence than the others. The first was a fact of his past life: he was divorced. He had been divorced for about five years, the same time roughly as he had been an occupant of Victoria Mansions. If the fact constituted a problem for Jim Nordon it was because the other problems of his life accrued round it and tended to exaggerate it. His wife Vicky had been an attractive brunette schoolteacher whom he'd met at a Christmas party not long after he'd first arrived in London. They'd married in the summer after his twenty-fifth birthday. Through the death of an uncle, his father's bachelor elder brother, he had been fortunate in acquiring a modest capital, enough to help him plus a mortgage to purchase a semi-detached house in Harrow where he and Vicky set up home. For six months he had been happy, or he thought he was. He had been as much in love with Vicky as he imagined he could ever be in love with anyone. Then certain things that he attributed to selfishness on his part spoiled the marriage bliss.

They had been such ordinary things. It seemed absurd his marriage should have come to grief on such ordinary things. There was his fondness for painting, for instance, that Vicky could not stand, although he persisted in doing it. They quarrelled over it. She liked practising to run a half-marathon, but he was no runner and fretted over the times he was expected to make supper after coming home from work to a dark house while she was away on some overnight running event in the country.

Then there was his sex life. He discovered quickly enough after marriage that he couldn't achieve an erection unless he fantasised. When he fantasised he had always to think of Vicky as a girl called Megan with whom he had lived for a while as a student. In the beginning when he thought of Megan he could easily persuade himself that Vicky was as loving and expert. Soon he found she wasn't and they both knew it. He blamed himself for being too demanding while she more or less insisted that sex spoiled her running. It quickly became hard for them to keep up the sort of pretence that their intelligence – Vicky talked a lot about the need for them to have an intelligent approach to all their problems – obliged them to maintain. This was true especially in regard to their parents. One day, when her parents came to lunch, they had a row in front of them. Looking back, he knew that was the moment when their marriage ended.

The cause of the breakdown had actually been Vicky's relations with one of her colleagues at school, an older man whom she had been meeting before she knew Jim. Perhaps their marriage had been based on a self-congratulatory belief that they would always be intelligent enough to understand each other's individual needs. But Jim simply wasn't intelligent enough to understand the old-fashioned cuckolding. However much he blamed himself, he was bitterly hurt and angry, bottled up though these feelings were in long silences at mealtimes with radio or television supplanting the need to talk, and when they had to say something to each other the exchanges were curt and rude. So Vicky's sexual nervousness ended in frigidity and his sexual frustration became a humiliating impotence. Their life in the cramped, semi-detached house facing a main road became as neat and bloody-minded a hell as two people can unintentionally create for themselves.

The breakdown of his marriage made him mistrustful of himself. He had never been over-confident. If responsibility had come his way, he had accepted it, but he had never sought it. At games, particularly soccer, he had been confident of reasonable skill, and he had been good at school work, though not outstanding. In personal relationships he had always been a little uneasy, as though there were always parts of human behaviour that remained inscrutable and incomprehensible and would never yield their secrets to him. It was only with his elder brother Sam that he felt completely at one. This was because they had been united as children in their opposition to parental wishes – not a serious opposition, just enough of an opposition to stop parental ideas being imposed on each of them separately. Mind you, their parents had not tyrannised in any strict sense. They had simply laid down what was right in their opinion – 'right and proper', in fact, were the words often used in laying down the rules. Brushing teeth, of course, keeping finger- and toe-nails clean and cut, having baths regularly, having one's hair brushed were part of the catechism; also watching one's language, being decent (meaning no masturbation or having sex) and making sure one kept with one's own kind, a refined kind of person, people of one's own class. Old-fashioned, Victorian, healthy precepts, outdated perhaps in the late twentieth century, let alone in the twenty-first, yet deriving from the sure, middle-class, instinctive conviction that good families brought up their children to obtain good jobs and make successes of their lives.

Then there was *Cotswold House*, the rather grand name given to the home in the southern suburb of Manchester where Jim Nordon had been born and lived out his adolescence and where his parents still lived. There was nothing distinguished or even pretentious about it. It was ordinary, self-effacing, middle-class and conventional, though no more than a million others. All his boyhood and adolescence he had dreamed of escaping from *Cotswold House*, his first day school (Mrs Leonards Infant School), his primary and secondary school and sixth-form college and all the streets of the suburb, if not including the wide area of public parkland called *The Steep*. He simply had no idea why he had developed such a loathing for the place. It was irrational, petty, futile, ignoble, arrogant and stupid of him to think that the place was to blame rather than his own immaturity, or that so many bricks held together by so much mortar, or so many tiles on so much roof timber, could somehow acquire a quality of such menace and spiritual threat that he, Jim Nordon, would make it an aim of living to be rid of it, perhaps forever.

After the experience of the semi-detached house in Harrow he had transferred his dislike to all forms of suburbia, subtopia and metroland. He loathed the very conformity of the houses, the constraining neatness of the many lives housed within them and the tiny self-importance of mock-Georgian front doors and coloured porch lights. Even so, secretly, in pitiful awareness of the treason committed against himself, he could not help having a perverse inquisitiveness about those self-confident, formidably respectable, suburban houses. The imaginary excesses of eroticism and licentiousness he called into being behind their curtained windows! The lusts in those first-floor bedrooms! The splendours of fleshly passion with which he invested the glimpsed interiors of rooms in the moonlit glow of television screens or the bright white gleam of frosted glass in upstairs bathrooms! No, he swept it all aside, consigning it all to the past. When Vicky left and a divorce was finally agreed, he sold the Harrow house very profitably, but resolved never to live in suburbs again. He was lucky, of course. Indeed he had been called a 'Lucky Jim' because he had saved his money even if he knowingly spent a fairly large amount furnishing and even repainting the rented apartment in Victoria Mansions. That was part of the cost of returning to bachelorhood. It was part of swearing a silent oath that he would never go back to marriage and semi-detached respectability.

But of course, being so much bricks and timber, it was all still there. He could revisit it whenever he wished. Except he didn't wish, he preferred to stay in Victoria Mansions. Naturally there was no denying that *Cotswold House* was where his past began. He was still loosely attached to it if only by the slight northern inflexion or resonance he gave to certain words and phrases and which his mother's monthly letters always recalled to mind as if, in some atavistic way, he was being drawn back to visions of a world inhabited by dinosaurs and pterodactyls. His mother could have phoned him or sent an email or texted had she wished. Instead she preferred to write, just as she kept in touch with Sam and scattered relatives in the United States and Australia by writing short, chatty letters (accompanied by suitable pics) that roamed haphazardly up and down a spectrum of domestically newsworthy items. To Jim she had lately written:

My darling Jim,

I'd been looking forward so much to receiving a letter from you but you must have overlooked it this time. We have been enjoying some nice weather in the last few days. Your father's cucumbers are coming on very well. I hope you're not feeling too lonely. There was a bring-and-buy sale the day before yesterday in aid of Christian Aid for which we made over thirty pounds. When you think how small our little group is that is really quite an achievement! You may remember that Mrs Walton, I think you used to play with her boy Stephen (he's now working in a Manchester office in what she says is a very good job), she made a beautiful lace dress, it must have taken her a very long time. It sold quite well. Mrs Jennie Smith who lives just four doors from us is very clever in making little clay figures. They were very popular. I made some biscuits and did the refreshments. Dr McGregor thinks your father will have to go into hospital for an exploratory operation, probably in August or September. He has complained of pains. He is all right now. Generally we are in good health. I heard from Aunt Marjorie in Adelaide. Her grandson's won a life-saving award and she's very proud of him. I do wonder sometimes what the Russians are up to. They're being so odd, aren't they? When will you be coming up here? Your father was saying yesterday that the last place he'd want to live would be London. I think life is quieter up here. But of course we've had our atrocities too. We are enjoying the garden a lot in the recent fine weather. There are likely to be a lot of apples on the big tree this year. Well, my dear, I must end.

The letter had the curious effect of emotionally diminishing him to a five-year-old. It had occurred to him often enough, if he wanted an easy explanation of his problems, to blame the relationship with his parents. The argument would have run that, despite his and Sam's opposition, they would have dominated him as a boy and prevented him from allowing his one talent to flourish. On the other hand, his inherent distrust of jargon, like his distrust of easy explanations, obliged him to work out the answers for himself. There was one answer, sure, that Vicky had been attractive and he had loved her, but she had unmanned him and made him mistrustful and yet the experience had shown him that he had sufficient natural strength and resilience to overcome even a disaster of that kind. Because he had a talent that his parents had dissuaded him from using at a crucial moment and that talent had come to his aid when he most needed it.

As a boy he had been skilled at drawing and painting. Art lessons had been among the most enjoyable of all the items in the school curriculum. After leaving school with two good A Levels he had opted for an art course. The year at art college had brought him into contact with Stanley Worthington. Stanley was an unremarkable man to look at, with rimless spectacles and a lined, dry-skinned face that seemed either mummified or somehow tautened against the underlying bone structure, so that his lips were thin, his eyebrows little pronounced and his cheeks very straight. He was rather tall, a little over six feet in height, and thin, with a way of heaving at his belted trousers to draw them back over his bony hips, but he had an affectionate, winning smile and extraordinarily bright brown eyes. Jim never knew how old he was. He had once heard it said that Stanley had looked the same since his early twenties. He looked unusually inconspicuous, withdrawn, a background figure turning aside in a photograph, forever seeming to be on the point of leaving. It was only when he looked directly at you that his strength of personality, his warmth, his devotion as a painter and his power as a teacher became apparent. It was then that he appeared to be concentrating fully on your needs to the exclusion of anyone else's or his own. This show of commitment to individual problems was the secret of his remarkable influence as an art teacher, as it was of his own talent as a painter, which expressed itself in detailed, intricate studies of landscape or collections of *objets trouvés* or portraits so small in scale they were barely more than miniatures. He was an enthusiast, and if he became enthusiastic about a student's work it was not far short of impossible for the student in question to avoid becoming enthusiastic about his own work. Jim felt the infection of that enthusiasm during his first two terms at art college.

He assumed that there was nothing else in the world he wanted more than the opportunity to paint. Then, through illness, Stanley Worthington was absent and Jim was confronted by other teachers. One in particular took a dislike to his flowing, inventive, arrogant assumption of confidence in his own powers and tried to make him pay greater attention to accepted procedures, to draw more carefully and follow rules in the use of paint. Jim regarded such things as not having the first priority. After a term's readiness to acquiesce, if only for the sake of Stanley Worthington, he grew stubborn. Contending with what he considered to be schoolroom pedantry and engaging in petty strife with his teacher, he was reminded of Stanley's quotation from Hazlitt: 'In writing you have to contend with the world; in painting, you have only to carry on a friendly strife with Nature…' He realised that he would rather contend with the world after all. There was also the fact that his parents disapproved of the art course and wanted him to go to university. So notwithstanding Stanley Worthington or his hatred of convention, he left the art college and was admitted into the Department of Government of the University of Manchester to read for an honours degree in political science.

The friendships he made with fellow students who had since become civil servants or like himself had joined local government (there were one or two, of course, who began the long rung-by-rung ascent of executive power in a multinational) had proved reasonably durable so long as marriage had not intervened. After his own marriage had come and gone and theirs had flourished into families, he had been left with barely more than a couple with whom he exchanged Christmas cards. All he had left over were a number of memories, one of which concerned a girl called Megan.

He had met her in his last year at university. Looking back on the relationship, she had made all the running to start with. There had been a lot of drinks one night in a Salford pub where he'd gone with one friend (male) to talk about politics. Afterwards, abominably drunk, he remembered being taken down a street, and then the next thing were Megan's gorgeous bare breasts leaning towards him and his sudden realisation that he was not as fully dressed as he supposed. Her hair descended over him, finally blurring an overhead light. Glistening eyes and parted lips and sweet winey breath were in exact focus, exact immediacy, above him. Then he folded his arms round her, feeling her bosom pressed down on his chest and her hair all over his face like a delicate cobwebby mask so that when he breathed in he felt strands of it enter his mouth. Whether he was clutching her or she was pressing herself to him, he could not be sure. He remembered feeling for his trouser zip and finding only his Y-front underpants, while she was still wearing her tight jeans. They executed a slow prone dance motion of lifted thighs which somehow reversed their positions. She was laughing through it all, he realised, and mentioning some silly joke he had made about her eyes looking like opals (or Opels?), the joke seeming giggly tremendous. They were floppily hitting each other with stray limbs in what might had been a fight but was also a struggle with clothing. And then he knew he was making love to her, he could hear the long sizzling silence growing into a single prolonged, high-pitched note in his ears and feel the tremendous racing of his body and hers with it, though when he tried to remember back to it he knew the drunkenness made it seem as if he were doing it by remote control, in amused surprise and crazy delight. In the morning she had left for her work and he could hear only loud street noises.

A day or so later he moved himself into Megan's one-room studio. His parents had been furious with him, especially his mother. Their principal objection was the classic one that she was socially inferior to him, though they never put it as openly as that. What's more, though, she had a local accent which she could make sound real mock-genteel if she wished; and she was clever and pert and great fun and completely unreliable, so he'd never be sure she'd be back from work or off home to Liverpool if she felt like it. She relied on him to pay the rent, which he did with money from his father (who was the less censorious of his parents) and she tolerated him with a certain fondness as she might an oversize dog that had strayed into her bed and her life. But she tolerated him; it was never a binding commitment. By good fortune, he found the days spent in her room allowed him to work harder and more consistently than he had done in the hall of residence or at home, and so... and so he did well in the final university examinations, to his surprise.

Of course, there were evenings and weekends when he kidded himself into thinking it was only sexual experience, student-fashion. It would end with an exchange of kisses and they would go their separate ways. At least, he was sure, sure as he could be, that they'd never be able to stay together. The stupid bloody arrogance of that certainty amazed him forever afterwards. How he could have been so sure never ceased to surface in his heart like some stream of bubbles rising from the hole she had made in it, the useless thing. When, annoyed at her casualness and her talk of another man, he did finally walk out on her, he knew he loved her. He had been in love with her all the time and that had made the hole in his heart. He described the experience just like that: 'You made a hole in my heart.' Not that he described it to anyone except her, in the only letter he ever wrote to her, after he'd left her. Though she never answered it and he was ashamed of what he'd written.

He had of course been applying for jobs. Counsellors' advice suggested he should try in local government, which he did, and to his astonishment his application to a London borough brought him an interview. He travelled south, hardly daring to suppose that he, a Manchester boy, would be given a job close to the heart of government. As it turned out, he was not only offered a job in one of the departments concerned with house planning but of his own volition he decided to stay in the south. His brother Sam had long since snapped the umbilical cord connecting him to *Cotswold House* by joining a firm of solicitors in Reigate and transforming himself into a good, subservient husband to his intelligent wife Debbie and a splendidly indulgent father to two small daughters. Jim uncharacteristically followed in his footsteps, since, used as he had been to bossing his elder brother in all their boyhood games, in the game of life he found himself second-stringing along behind Sam with his transfer to the south and his 'good' job (as his mother insistently called it). At the age of twenty-two Jim moved into a bed-sit in Islington and shortly afterwards met Vicky at one of several Christmas parties and married her a couple of years later.

His career as a junior administrator or administrative assistant working under the supervision of Charles Ball in one of the planning sections grew by stages into something more mature and responsible. In fact, he could reasonably have expected promotion to a higher grade by the age of thirty-one, had he not been caught in the toils of Charles Ball's ambition and his own rather confused self-doubt. Charles Ball had received what passed for a remit from the Housing Policy Committee, through the Housing Management Committee, through the Housing Programme Board (as a result of political decisions taken in the Council, of course), to propose effective ways of achieving an 18% cut in staff and a 20% improvement in efficiency, not to mention financial savings amounting to not less than 25% over a three-year period (allowing for inflation, etc., of course). Charles Ball had summoned Jim to appear before him.

It would be unfair to describe Jim's attitude to his superior as hostile or even unfriendly. He had a devotion to Charles Ball that was scrupulous in its loyalty and yet completely unserious in its amazement at his skill in bucking the system. Jim knew how incompatible these two things might be. It was deeply painful for him to confront such duplicity and so he made every effort to conceal it, even from himself. He had been given a number of projects on which he had worked successfully, most recently on the issue of privatising some aspects of consultancy in the planning process. That matter was still under consideration and would no doubt require more attention from him later. As for the new proposals regarding cuts (there had been annual exercises of this kind more than once, but without much effect), Charles Ball, looking grey from a prolonged recurrence of the winter's influenza, peered over his reading spectacles, rested his elbows on his desk and clasped his hands.

'We are going,' he said, 'to box very clever over this one, you know, so I'm going to propose something rather unusual to you. Everyone knows someone's got to be made redundant. We can go on freezing this post and that, but in due course we'll find there's no such thing as Father Christmas and we'll have to lop off a few heads. We are aware of this, I think. What I'm not aware of is what I'm now going to propose. It is this. If we can hide the identity – I'm speaking in confidence, you are aware – if we can hide the identity *of the source* of the report – I repeat, *of the source* – then people will very likely suppose it came from upstairs, wherever that is, or fell off a milk float or was brought in person by the Archangel Gabriel. It's only when there's a lot of wringing of hands and appointing of committees and drafting of this and that that people get stirred up and bothered. The worst thing is when a report is named after the chairman. Then people go round talking about 'Atkinson said' or 'Atkinson's put the lid on that' and so on, and Atkinson, whoever he may be, earns notoriety and a New Year's honour and perhaps receives the ultimate accolade of a mention in the Guinness Book of Records. That's what we don't want. But what we do want is a nice, tidy report, written lucidly and with an air of compassionate understanding, rather sanctimoniously, that will spell out the unacceptable fact, the inevitable fact, that almost a quarter of the staff must go over the next three years. We've got to make it seem virtually equivalent to an Act of God. Are you aware what I'm saying?'

Jim said he was.

'Well, I don't think you are. I'm sorry, but I don't think you are aware. Because what I'm saying is that we need a new section or mini-department or an objective agency of some kind to make it seem the report is not of our doing, something like that. We'll have it put on the next agenda and approved at the next meeting – it may even get by on the nod if we're lucky, especially if we concentrate on the 25% reduction – and then there'll be a bit of funding from our own budget for it and we'll say we're appointing the agency under the auspices of the Council. But the point is it'll be around long enough for people to know it exists, but not long enough for anyone to get really interested in it. And then, by the autumn meeting, there'll be a report ready about redundancies, the source of which is this little fictitious agency or whatever, at which very time – are you aware what I'm saying? – the approval of funding will be granted because everyone'll be so interested in the report that they'll probably not notice that the fictitious agency has quietly disappeared. I think we should give it a code name, something like Z10, but the supposed host agency will be situated in New York with a name like Plath and Siegfried Corporation or Plath and Siegfried Enterprises. And I think you ought to be in charge of it.'

Jim knew he was innocent in comparison with Charles Ball. He also knew he would never learn the proper skills of duplicity and deviousness required for ultimate success in administrative work. Lacking a natural talent, he surreptitiously admired Charles Ball's boyish delight in such fiendishness. It had about it something of the skilfully devised hoodwinking associated with avant-garde art, the kind of thing Jim had often seen at the Hayward Gallery: self-conscious, contrived, often funny and harmless, though whether it was worth doing or looking at depended to a great extent on its title (Solo VIII, Fastidious Sculpture 16, etc., for instance). Z10 seemed as good a title as any.

'Well, I don't think I'm really the sort of person…'

'I'll fix you up with one of those rooms overlooking the river. In my experience they're always the best ones for writing reports in. Rowney's retiring next week, you can have his. It's got a lovely plastic Italian chair in it. I've had my eye on that some time. And another thing.' Charles Ball took off his rimless spectacles, dangled them from his long fingers and let them descend slowly to the surface of his desk. He ran his hand in a slow washing motion over his eyes and nose. 'Get another PA. That Miss Jacobs is bound to cause problems. If she's associated with Z10 or whatever it's called people'll be bound to suspect something, ever since she did that manpower thing with the last lot.' (Meaning that she provided assistance for the report on manpower ordered by the last leader of the Council.) 'Get someone from an outside agency who doesn't know anything about how we've done things here or how we're likely to do things. Someone who won't be noticed. In any case, Z10 will be outwardly concerned with coordinating interdepartmental planning and you'll need someone who looks pretty. In my experience it can make all the difference.'

'Miss Jacob's been unwell.'

'So much the better, in that case. But the main point of the exercise is that you'll be able to study the departmental files and get a clearer picture of what's needed, so as to ensure fewer squeaks of protest and complaint when the report comes out. And since they won't know you've done it, they won't suspect you. Okay?'

It was outrageous and silly and Jim knew it. But he had enough respect for Charles Ball to recognise that subterfuge of this kind had to be used, otherwise the wheels of administration could become clogged by paperwork and feuding and the chaos of power-grabbing. Charles Ball's approach had about it an etiolated, grandiose sleight of hand, as though the insufferableness of human nature deserved to be mocked. Therefore, the most sensible way to deal with it was by humour, deception and indifference, though never in sufficient quantities to make his attitude seem cynical.

Where Jim found himself at odds with Charles Ball was exactly at the point where their personalities came into conflict. If Charles Ball enjoyed his own small exercise of power in an amused and supercilious way, Jim couldn't. Maybe, he had to admit to himself that Charles Ball knew this and had chosen him for this very reason. The trouble was that Jim Nordon had a serious mind. It was a grave handicap to him and he knew it. Perhaps it was really a flaw in his personality, he often thought, and when he thought about this likelihood he recognised something else, a thought that had often sneaked up on him recently: his personality wasn't suited to administration, let alone administrative reports, especially those of the kind Charles Ball was suggesting. But if he turned down the offer of working for this subterfuge, what else was he fitted to do? A serious mind was not of itself a very marketable commodity. More important, had he the courage to leave the Borough that gave him employment? And if he did have the courage to leave, did he have the courage and strength of personality and confidence in his own talent to give himself over completely, as he most wished, to the real passion of his life, which was painting?

Dave, his lodger, had never doubted. Only Jim had doubted. For most of the years of his marriage to Vicky he had doubted, if only in the sense that he would come back in the evening to an empty house and find no meal ready (Vicky developed a habit of coming home at nine o'clock, making her own supper, saying nothing to him, going to bed and leaving early for school the next morning), so at last he had reverted to his earlier passion, bought paints, brushes and easel and started painting. It saved him. Selfish, self-absorbed, the act of painting induced forgetfulness and a gentle recuperative pleasure. To his astonishment, it also brought him by chance into contact with Stanley Worthington again. His former teacher had moved south also, to an organisational job in a North London art centre, and it was there Jim had met him. Stanley Worthington had organised evening classes of his own for some three or four of his most gifted part-time painters on two days a week. Jim joined them. Throughout the last year of his marriage he spent most evenings either at these classes or in the small spare bedroom at the back of the Harrow house, engaged in painting – or, to be more correct, engaged in learning to paint and slowly acquiring a genuine proficiency.

When he left Harrow and moved to Victoria Mansions, he devoted one end of the main room of the apartment to his 'studio' while Dave, his lodger, occupied the second bedroom. By this time he had begun to paint portraits. Dave sat for him. His first attempt was unsuccessful, but later he was to do a very striking portrait of him. He also persuaded several elderly inhabitants of flats below him to become his models. They were all good sitters, busy with knitting or reading or listening to music or watching the telly, heads half turned or bent forward; gentle, comfortable faces betraying dignity and a kind of wisdom, due as much to their pose as his skill (not by any means always sure) in suggesting a faint bloom to their complexions and making the light soften, even blur, the detail of their features.

Some of course were aggrieved by this, others flattered. His most successful portrait was that of his cleaning lady, Mrs Rogers. She had wanted to be painted in her wedding dress. He obliged. He had painted her fifty-year-old plump smiling face in her white wedding veil of thirty years before, carefully avoiding any hint of caricature, and shown her ample figure clad a bit awkwardly in a noticeably large wedding dress. The result made her look slightly like royalty. She was delighted. It hung in the front room of her little flat off Queen's Square. It made her Jim's willing cleaner, though she would have done anything to look after Dave. She doted on him as fondly as any mother. Working largely from photographs and sketches, Jim also did portraits of his parents and of Sam and his family.

It had always been his desire to paint nudes. Some of the evenings under Stanley Worthington's tuition had been devoted to life classes. Now he felt sufficient confidence in his talent to work on his own. During the past year, particularly in vacation time when Dave was not there, he had begun. He had hired two models. The decision was hard and the first result was only a partial success. The girl who offered herself for hire and sent him a short video was in fact black and an art student. She had a charming small face, with wide-spaced brown eyes, a pretty nose, a tapered chin that had the effect of accentuating her high cheekbones, brown fuzzy hair and a body that was trim, almost wiry, with most delicate tints of flake white and ochre and umber in profuse riot on the uppermost surfaces and deeper shades, even with ultramarine, in the clefts and hollows, or so he amateurishly supposed in his initial attempts at capturing her allure. He could have added all the brightest colours in his palette to her full-length portrayal in homage to the beauty of her figure, except for one thing. Being an art student she wasn't content to be a model. She began to offer advice and make suggestions. He soon found the emotional strain of the relationship too great and he paid her off, though they parted as friends.

The next model was white in her mid-thirties, co-operative and sensible. He employed her on several occasions. The trouble was that he could portray her face without too much difficulty and even continue the characterizing process to her entire figure, which was graceful and well-proportioned, but he never succeeded in overcoming a certain woodenness and stiffness in the overall effect. He felt intuitively he would have to relate sexually to the woman he was painting. That would be the only way to achieve the lyrical, soft, flowing manner he needed to make the figure truly vital, truly alluring.

There was one example of this – almost. The 'almost' was of course the all-important distinction between success and failure. In this case he never painted her though he frequently saw her nude. She was Rachel Wallace. Rachel had been one of Vicky's friends. He often thought he should have married her rather than Vicky and it was only because Rachel had suddenly found Steve Wallace that Jim had broken off the relationship. That marriage had followed the same pattern as his. Rachel and Steve were married for four years and than parted. Steve remarried. Rachel didn't. She took a flat in Orpington, close to where she worked. One weekend, after Jim and Vicky had been divorced, he received an invitation from her. He had intended returning home that evening at an appropriate time, but the dinner and the drinks were good, and Rachel had laughed a lot, and he felt happy and suggested – casually, as it were, almost for a joke – that they slept together, and they did, and for the first time since he had known Megan he enjoyed sex as much as Rachel as something delightful, natural and uncomplicated.

This relationship became the one sure emotional solace of his recent life. They met perhaps once or twice a month, on every occasion in her flat in Orpington. Sometimes they were lovers. They did not ask more of each other than such companionship. That and trust. They trusted each other to tell the truth. He told her the truth about Vicky and she told him the truth about Steve. Their mutual trust was firm enough to ensure they did not violate the separate anguish of this shared knowledge by turning their own relationship into a copy of what each had known before. They were not always successful. Each knew that the former partner kept them apart. They were lucky to have a kind of sixth sense between them that made it relatively easy to share wave-lengths, just as Rachel herself was never shy about stripping naked when she felt like it and he followed suit out of sheer respect for her candour. They attempted nothing more sophisticated.

Theirs was a vulnerable, adult sharing of emotions designed for pleasure without commitment.

His fondness for Rachel had grown bit by bit, as a mosaic, but patternless. Her brown soft curling hair. Lines in fine waxing smiles about her eyes. Their colour – a hazel tint lightening to some pastel shade, he never knew what, never stared in them long enough to discover. They were fringed with delicate lashes that he had watched once while she slept and flickered like tiny antennae answering to the slightest tremor of her dreams. Her brisk walking beside him up a street. Always the quick movements, fingers quickly moving in flour, crumbling the mixture in a bowl, lifting dishes from soapy water and lightly slanting them under a tap to remove the suds, sewing quick stitches and snapping the cotton between white teeth. Bite. These bits of memory had one frame into which their higgledy-piggledy patterns merged.

The frame for him was partly the very sureness of this relationship, and partly it was a mysterious combination of masochism and curiosity and a very insecure feeling that through Rachel, in a literal as well as emotional sense, his life had continuity, was not broken, possessed from start to finish at least one thread. For Rachel had kept in touch with Vicky. She was not close, simply in touch at intervals. Through Rachel he knew of Vicky's two children and the Bristol home. He could trust Rachel not to tell too much, even if she knew more than she told. In a way which he could not fathom, though he accepted it, he also knew that Rachel was prepared to keep her relationship with him alive in justification of the same kind of continuity in her own life, despite her resentment of Steve, for example, and the awkwardness of her feeling for Vicky. Vicky, after all, had once been her closest friend, and friends of that kind tend not to lose each other no matter how many times and distances separate them. In fact, she was a little jealous of Vicky's happiness (Jim, on the other hand, found himself completely without any emotional response when he heard Rachel speak of it). As for Steve's claim of happiness with his second wife, she tended to mock it. It was a very light filigree of attachments but it was part of the frame that held him and Rachel together. Somehow it served its purpose a good deal better than most formal bonds.

II

Sally-Anne Harris, blonde. Medium height. Neat, attractive figure. Bright eyes of soft blue. Complexion fair. Small mouth with well-moulded lips. Firm chin. Strong but not pronounced jaw-line. Oval face, pretty. A remarkable smile. Twenties.

In this way Jim Nordon summarised Sally-Anne Harris for himself in the flip-up pocket-book he carried with him. She had been his third interviewee for the modest post of PA or administrative assistant when he had set about finding someone to replace Rhoda Jacobs. The pocket-book contained more than one such summary, including, incidentally, one of Mrs Rogers and several of those who had sat for portraits. He had made a habit of doing this on Stanley Worthington's advice, especially when taking a photograph did not seem appropriate. So Sally-Anne Harris had sat in front of him on the smart Italian plastic chair with her shapely legs crossed in an appetisingly demure pose and answered his questions in a formal interview conducted one afternoon in the unfamiliar surroundings of what had formerly been Rowney's room overlooking the Thames.

She claimed to be fully trained in using a computer, having already worked for various firms – a cosmetic manufacturer, a publisher, an oil company – and could supply satisfactory references, which she did. Why, then, was she applying for this very modestly paid job in this not very distinguished London borough? 'I got fed up with commerce. And the agency said there could be some "arrangement", isn't that right?' The emphasis placed on the word "arrangement" naturally caught his attention as did the claim to be 'fed up with commerce.' If the latter remark amused him, the mention of an "arrangement" made the whole matter seem suggestively indecent. 'I mean about the times of work, about the schedules.' She coloured awkwardly as this was added and he was almost equally embarrassed, because he had rather unwisely mentioned to a female voice over the phone at the agency something about it not being a formal nine-to-five job, though there was nothing explicit to this effect in the terms of the appointment. 'Yes, well, I'll have my laptop,' and he pointed to it on his desk, 'so that's where I'll be working, you see, and the kind of work I'll ask of you, as I explained to other interviewees, will be to do with checking data from files. Mostly, that is. And since all the data are accessible on our computer system, or practically all that matters, I'll have to trust you with some codes and passwords and things like that. I think that's what must have been meant when the agency talked about an "arrangement".'

'So it's quite confidential work.' She accompanied the remark with a charming smile. Unguardedly he smiled back. 'Yes,' he said, 'I suppose it will be.' Which was slightly too much of an admission for what should have been a formal interview. He realised he had unwittingly compromised himself. He would have to employ her if only to ensure the confidentiality would remain confidential.

For two weeks she helped him put Rowney's old room to rights, made coffee and faced up to the fact that the data accessible on the computer were far greater than either he or she had imagined. It gave him time, if not to start on his report, at least to learn more about her than the bare bones of her application. So she had been born in Guildford, where she still had a home address, had achieved respectable results at school but had not opted for university. Instead she had attended a computer course at a local college and had then gone travelling in Europe. She readily admitted that her

Spanish, like her French, was fluent but basically domestic. On coming home she decided on commerce, found work and a flat share in London. That was about all Jim Nordon learned about Sally-Anne Harris until he took her out to dinner one Friday evening.

It was then she asked, 'Why me?'

They had reached a degree of intimacy in their working habits to entitle her to ask. She sat opposite him with one eyebrow raised in query and he parried her by offering his glass of wine as a kind of rebuttal. She responded. Their glasses clinked.

'I wanted to paint you.'

'Oh, really.'

'It's a hobby. I paint portraits. In my spare time.'

She appeared interested, which surprised him. He had made it a rule never to mention his hobby to anyone at work, let alone invite sitters. He liked to jot down facial characteristics as a kind of visual mnemonic, that was all, but hers had attracted him because they were attractive. However, that was not the principal reason; there was also the issue of confidentiality.

'As I mentioned, we're going to have to work together for the next three months. I just wanted someone who would be co-operative and I could trust. And someone who didn't have to be "Miss Harris" all the time.'

'No, we agreed on Sally.'

'Yes. So you're Sally. And I'm Jim. We agreed, yes. So we're going to have to work together for the next three months, until September at the latest, which makes it slightly less than three months, trying to get this report together, as I've explained.' He had explained Charles Ball's plan, embellished with his own ideas, but what he had not explained was the degree to which she might become acquainted with all sorts of financial and other details of employment in the Borough offices, not to mention names and so on that could involve extremely private matters. This was where confidentiality came in and was partly the pretext for this dinner. He took in a deep breath. Through the busy background noise of the restaurant he asked:

'Tell me why you got fed up with commerce?'

'I got fed up with commerce because I got fed up with my last boss.'

'You found he was making advances?'

'He made no advances with me, though he tried. He just made a great many retreats.'

Behind her attractive appearance he could see there was a determined and wilful girl who could easily make a man retreat if she wished. He liked this. 'What made you suppose you wouldn't have to face the same sort of thing here in local government?'

'My father.'

'Why your father?'

'Quite simple.' She smiled. 'He used to work in local government. He left about ten years ago.'

'Where?'

'Surrey. At the Kingston offices. He hated his superior.'

This hardly seemed a good reason for her to choose local government work. Puzzled, he asked her why she had made the choice.

'Oh, he quite liked the work and he was good at it. He got a pension out of it. But he resented not getting the promotion he felt he deserved.'

Folklore of that kind had extraordinary powers of survival, Jim recognised. He grunted. 'So despite your father you chose local government?'

'No, I thought I'd try it.'

'Well, I'm glad you did.'

It was a bit unctuous and he over-quickly went on to explain, as if in answer to her first question, that he chose her, among other things, because she knew nothing about the staff or the procedures in the Borough administration. She would therefore not be known and new to it. She liked this. The conversation then touched briefly on her flat-mates, but quickly seemed to become an exchange of information that glanced very slightly on more intimate spots before veering away, kept in rapid motion by glasses of wine and the food. There was a gathering, increasing excitement between them, as of two people who discover many little bits of likeness and try to fit them together to make a recognisable, mutual pattern of interests. He found himself ready to tell her about his painting, realising with an access of real pleasure that he had not talked unaffectedly about his hobby with anyone until this moment, not even with Dave, who had at least shown a lively interest if little readiness to discuss detailed problems. With Stanley Worthington there was always the kind of formality of a teacher-pupil relationship despite their friendship. As for his interest in her, he knew already she was eight years his junior and that therefore sheer seniority came between them like a frosted glass inevitably likely to obscure his understanding of her background and upbringing, not to speak of her personality.

He would never of course have invited her out to dinner if he had not been attracted, and he supposed she wouldn't have accepted if she hadn't been flattered. In the course of the meal it became obvious that there was more than attraction and flattery in the charge of excitement that had gathered between them. Although she struck him as open and spontaneous in answering questions about her schooling and travels, she was reluctant to talk about her home and her parents and at no time did she mention a boyfriend. Naturally, he put no pressure on her. He was himself consumed by an equal reluctance to acknowledge his own fears. The greatest of them, as deep as a blue iceberg on a green Arctic sea against which all his hopes might founder, was the doubt about himself, about his ability to sustain a relationship beyond the sort of occasional, sexual meetings he had with Rachel. In any case, he suspected he had so much to hide from her that any kind of frankness would merely lead to embarrassment. The accumulation of such concealments, such little pebble-shaped fears, could gradually weigh people down. It gradually made them sink. He knew that. He could sense that kind of weight begin to draw him down into a green Arctic sea.

Then towards the end of the meal she suddenly asked:

'Do you paint every day?'

'Whenever I can.'

'Can I see some of them?'

At first it seemed a polite question. Although they were dining in a little restaurant barely a few minutes from Victoria Mansions, he had never intended to invite her back to his apartment. The question immediately needed to be fended off, he felt, until it occurred to him how stupid this might seem. Of course they might have coffee there and she agreed.

'I've given away a lot of them,' he had to admit. 'Or only charged very little, just the cost of materials.' He referred to the portraits he had done of other residents of Victoria Mansions..

'If you enjoy it, why don't you do it full-time?'

'I just don't think I'm good enough.'

'I'll be the judge of that,' she said rather self-importantly.

He asked her whether she had any hobbies or interests outside her work. It had always seemed inconceivable to him that people should live solely for their work. She paused before answering. In fact, she did not reply until they had left the restaurant and were walking beside shops. Lights blazed ineffectually in their windows, unable for the time being to outshine the sharp fine evening light and the clarity of a luminous blue sky mottled directly above their heads by small pearly clouds beginning to be tinged with pink. There was a faintly dried-out feel to the surrounding air.

'I've been worried recently about my mother. She's not been well.'

'Oh, I'm sorry.'

'It's what I thought the "arrangement" might be about, you see. About the times of work. The agency thought they might be flexible.'

'Flexible?' He frowned over the word in repeating it. 'I see.' But he didn't see. He merely realised she had probably kept this problem to herself throughout the meal as something far too important for light-hearted discussion.

'She has heart trouble. It isn't very serious at present, but it's worrying. At weekends, you see, I have to go home. I was wondering, if it got serious, whether there might be some arrangement about times of work.' She adjusted the long-strapped bag she had over her shoulder, as if the shrug of the gesture emphasised her problem. 'This evening I've got to go down to Guildford.'

He apologised for appearing so inconsiderate. 'Then shouldn't you get a train right away?'

'No, no. If I'm in Guildford by ten-thirty that's all that matters.'

His watch told him it was *FRI 19* and 7.45. The restaurant meal had been early. He asked whether there was any other help at home.

'There's my father. He's all right. He thinks he can't cope but he can really. They're both elderly. Mum was in her forties when she had me. I'm an only child.'

The bit of news explained, he thought, some of her wilfulness, even if it were not the wilfulness of a spoilt child. Indulged, perhaps; certainly protected and loved; and wanting now to return that love and caring when it was needed. The thought made him sense he was intruding too far into her privacy.

In the Edwardian lift in Victoria Mansions, which was exceedingly small, they were pressed up against each other.

There were mirrors on three sides of the cabin and they could study each other. To him the sight of his thinnish face and the distinct shadow of his chin and cheeks was an embarrassment. The downward flow of the light accentuated the hollows of his eyes and gave him a sinister appearance. On the other hand, her hair, just at eye-level, tickled his cheek. Her warm body excited him by its sudden gush of sweet perfume. In the glitter of the mirrors the softness of her complexion matched the shine of her eyes. Her prettiness dazzled him. Laughing, she looked round her.

'You certainly find what you look like in this lift! It shows you every little bit!'

'For some reason it seems to attract old ladies.'

She laughed again.

They creaked slowly up half-a-dozen floors, seeing empty landings and hearing through the lift's grinding progress the occasional faint noise of radio or television beyond closed doors. At the top he clangorously opened the gates and they literally squeezed themselves out of the cabin. The pressure of her slim body against his longer, fuller frame reminded him vividly of the way Megan had pressed herself against him. Smiling at the reminder, he showed her into his apartment.

'How long have you lived here?'

'It'll be five years in the autumn. Oh, no, more than that. Can I make you some coffee?'

'No, let me. You've taken me out to dinner, now the least I can do is make you some coffee.'

Her manner was so natural and undemanding that he directed her at once to the kitchenette. Friday was Mrs Rogers' day and he was pleased to see that everything was tidy. His fridge was filled; there were cartons of milk and a jar of instant coffee.

'Someone looks after you,' she remarked.

'I have a Mrs Rogers. She was in love with my lodger.'

The kettle boiled and coffee was made. He apologised because there were only mugs. They sat side by side on a small sofa that he had inherited with the apartment. His hand, if lowered, would touch her stockinged knee. She sipped her coffee and then put the mug back on the low table in front of them.

'You say she was in love?'

'I'm being facetious, sorry. She was devoted to him and loved to mother him.'

He explained about Dave, how he had been studying at University College, about the religious bit and the girlfriends. In a job reference it might have been rather tactless, but as a personal recommendation for a friend it was warm and appreciative.

'You two must've got on well.'

'We did. In our separate ways. We tolerated each other. Oh, I liked Dave very much. The place is rather empty without him.'

He poured her a brandy. She was already looking round the spacious room, hung with some of his pictures. Portraits of two elderly ladies hung on either side of a picture of his parents in the sitting-room at *Cotswold House*. He remembered Dave had complimented him on that. To him, looking at his own handiwork, there seemed to be more than a trace of harshness in the tonal effects that tended to make the complexions a shade too healthy and the eyes slightly too bright.

'Oh, I recognise them, they're your parents! You look like your father, you know.'

'So they tell me. I did that eighteen months ago. Now I've gone on to nudes.'

He was talking in a flip, idle way, like an imitation Noel Coward character. It was partly due to the glasses of wine, of course, but it was also due to the excitement caused by her interest.

'You mean, nude girls?'

'Nude girls, yes.'

'Why aren't there any here?'

'I keep them very decently out of sight in the spare bedroom.'

She gave him a mock-ironical, appraising look. 'Should I be on my guard now?'

'No. I've only had two models so far. I'm an absolute beginner.'

She picked up the large brandy glass in her slim fingers and turned the dark wine gently about in the wide bulbous bowl of the glass. Light from the window, even if faded and almost dusky, was caught in the turning glass and reflected palely back into her face. The whites of her eyes shone as she smiled.

'I'm beginning to wonder exactly why you invited me here, aren't I?'

'I'm not predatory. It's just that I tend to observe people, their shapes, their movements.' It was ridiculous being so candid. Perhaps it was the brandy speaking. He switched on a table lamp.

'You observed my movements?' she asked, blinking in the new light, apparently more startled by it than by his remark.

'Yes, I liked the way you walked. The movement of your skirt as you turned and went out of the office.' He checked himself. He was being far too suave. 'You have very confident smiles, you know,' he said.

She burst out laughing. '*My* confident smiles!'

'Yes.'

'You simply can't imagine how nervous I've been working for you.'

'Well, you don't have to be. I know I'm considered a bit of a recluse by some colleagues, but that's because I'm so keen on my hobby.'

'Show me them! Please!'

Her enthusiasm came as a slight shock, so that he was uncertain what she meant.

'My nudes?'

'Yes, your nudes!'

Her exclamation came with laughter, her head thrown back and her long blond hair shaken hastily out over her shoulders. He stood up as if the words were a command, explaining he had moved his easel from the main room into the spare room after Dave had left. They went out into the corridor and he flung open the bedroom door. A bare central light was switched on and shed a neutral glow over an untidy array of paint tubes, brushes, turps bottles and stacked supports of various kinds all spread out on a sheet covering the solitary bed. Hanging in disorder round the walls of the small room were pink- and dark-skinned nudes, all in rather casual poses, either crayon drawings or paintings, some in oils, some in acrylics. They were either on a chaise longue or sitting in chairs. Most of them were of the professional model, but there were several of the black girl, the art student. He had tried to draw or paint each pose as lyrically and warmly as possible, and he had succeeded in a general way, although there still remained the obvious suggestion in each study that an exercise had been performed, a technical difficulty faced and a problem of shape and colour identified, if not resolved. None of the studies had the assurance of touch that distinguished the portraits in the main room.

'Oh,' she cried, 'I think they're amazing! You mean you did all these?'

He nodded, looking at his own work as if it were not his at all. She began moving from one to another, gazing at each one, and idly his eyes followed the turn of her head, noting the curve of her shoulders and back as she looked upwards. He felt he could paint her with understanding and tenderness if she ever gave him the chance. Her arms, clothed in the summer dress with short sleeves, were shapely, sunburned a little and freckled, and he could feel the tip of his brush touch the surface of the support lightly to follow exactly their upward curving gesture as she reached up her hand with the large brandy glass to point to one of his latest studies:

'That's the best, I think.'

'Thank you.'

'She's a beautiful girl.' She pointed at the young art student. 'I can see now why…' Her pause stirred him to confession.

'Why I've put my nudes away in this room out of sight?'

'No, I don't mean that. No, I was meaning…' He did not know exactly what she was meaning and in any case she did not finish her sentence. She had turned and was looking at him. He found himself grinning with a silly embarrassment that mingled pride with guilt at having shown her so much.

'Do you think it's worth persevering with?'

'With your painting?'

'Yes.'

'Of course it is!'

He supposed he had really angled for her to say it. Apart from other residents of Victoria Mansions and Dave and his parents and Sam, his brother, he had never shown his paintings to anyone. Stanley Worthington and his special group did not count in this respect. He had always assumed his painting should be a private affair. It was not that criticism frightened him or that he felt particularly ashamed about his spare-time occupation. What most bothered him was a simple lack of self-confidence.

'I don't know.' He was in a confessional mood and became absorbed in an effort of self-explanation. 'I think I've got talent, but sometimes I wonder if there's any point in trying to persevere with it and improve it. I haven't yet got a proper style. That's what my teacher says.' The healthy, even lustrous tints of naked skin, the round sensuous thighs, the breasts with their pert little buds of nipples rebuked him. They told him that it wasn't talent, it was courage he needed. For instance, the young art student's pose (she had insisted on it) resembled Manet's *Olympia*, even to the ribbon round the neck, and he had tried to employ the same boldness and directness of expression. He was struck at that moment by the latent sexuality in the pose and the black girl's slightly glancing, inviting look. He wondered whether Sally had noticed it. She had.

'Of course you must. If I'd been that girl, I'd really have been flattered to have a painting like that done of me.'

She charmingly fluttered her fingers at it, as if acknowledging the sexual boldness of the pose and indicating at the same time she could never think of herself as having the same boldness.

He admitted it was just an exercise. 'You should have heard what she had to say about it.'

'Didn't she like it?'

He shook his head. 'She didn't think I'd been confident enough in my line. And it wasn't as good as the original. Perhaps when I'm a little more sure…'

'You're sure enough. You needn't worry about that.' She pointed to the more recent picture of the mature model that she had praised earlier. Then she went ahead of him back into the main room where the light from the table lamp vied with the street lighting visible in the window along with the pink sunset above the roofline of the opposite buildings.

'You don't have to be any more sure.' She swung round to face him and handed him the large brandy glass, now empty. He did not know by what right she could judge his work so positively, but he was happy in an ecstatic, utterly simple way. 'I must go, I'm afraid. I have to get to Waterloo and then to Guildford.'

'Of course.'

He held her large empty brandy glass in his two hands, as if it had become a gift, some prize or other that he'd received from her. They looked at each other. He was sure she had no idea at all how happy her praise had made him. It almost paralysed him. He searched his mind wildly for something appropriate to say and could find nothing. What is more, the protocol of relationships like this was always a mystery to him. Now, the bulbous glass extended stupidly between them, he found himself made embarrassed and ungainly by her warm shining eyes. Suddenly, as if recognising his awkwardness, she leaned up against him and kissed him lightly on the cheek.

'Goodnight. Thank you for the dinner and letting me see your paintings.'

He walked her down the flights of stairs to the ground floor rather than wait for the slow lift. By a lucky chance a taxi was passing. She jumped into it and sailed away into the iodine fluorescence of Kingsway.

III

It made her blush with annoyance and shame – her boldness, that is – and little flushes flowed over her in the flowing, swaying rush of the train journey to Guildford. 'Mr N,' as she confided to her diary later that evening, 'is now Jim' (underlined three times) 'but I can't call him that, which makes it very difficult really. Will it be the same as with J? Still, he's very nice. But I shouldn't have... Or should I?' She dashed such remarks down in her diary in a rapid handwriting that resembled the squiggles and curlicues of shorthand. It was partly a ruse to disguise confidences from her mother who used to glance in her diary from time to time (she knew that), no matter how carefully she concealed it. She never locked any of the drawers in her bedroom and she never wrote up her diary anywhere save at home in Guildford. The habit of keeping a diary had begun when she was twelve. She continued it now only when she returned home from her London flat-share. In any case, the question at the close of her jotting had been the real point and cause of the uneasy, shaky sense that she had gone too far perhaps, had given herself away, had cheapened herself or something of the sort.

From the station to her home was a fifteen-minute walk if she took the shortest route. For the last year she had always preferred to make a small detour down an alleyway between garden fences in order to avoid passing *Timbercombe*, the house on the corner of her own suburban avenue. Every visit home was surrounded by little moments of alarm at the thought that she might meet John Rowlandson of *Timbercombe*. She had been in love with him once. Most of her knowledge of sex had come from him – as if she ever confided that much to her diary, let alone admitted it out loud within the walls of *The Cherries*! (*The Cherries* – her home for five years – in an avenue full of houses with names like *Linton, Sunningdale, Bycroft, Woldingham, Southfield* and *Timbercombe, Timbercombe, Timbercombe*, the name booming and hammering in the ten o'clock dark and reminding her of all the impetuous things associated with it.) So she avoided that house, the one on the corner of her avenue, even in the ten o'clock dark, and walked along the narrow alleyway between fences of back gardens until it brought her out into an adjoining road lined with parked cars and with streetlamps at infrequent intervals and lit curtained windows in the front rooms of the houses.

She opened the front door quietly and let herself in.

'Your mother has gone to bed. We must be very quiet.'

Her father stooped towards her in the hallway, having just come downstairs. His hair was now quite white, she realised, as he stood directly underneath the glass-shaded lamp with its orange wavy stripes. They kissed each other and the instant her lips touched his cheek she felt as though she had been infected with some of his own embittered, defeated vindictiveness against the world.

'How is she?'

'As well as can be expected.'

He went slowly down the passage to the kitchen with that stooped back which suggested that it wasn't his job to welcome his daughter home or ask her where she'd been or why she hadn't come sooner. So it was going to be one of those weekends, she thought, taking off her coat. The smell of polish suggested why her mother had gone to bed early: she'd done too much, she never could tell when to stop in time.

'I'll make her a cup of tea.'

'Just made one. Just taken it up to her. I'm going to put what's left over in the machine.'

But she insisted on doing it herself, sending him off to sit in front of the telly that had been quietly making noises to itself in the front room. He grumbled about her insistence, but he went off all the same. She found there were barely more than a couple of plates, some cutlery and glassware left over unwashed from her parents' supper. She decided to do them herself without opening the dishwasher. It gave her time to think about 'Mr N' and for a brief moment she had one of her infrequent shocks of happiness. Such shocks seemed to burst round her out of the surrounding air, leaving her sure for at least one instant that she had a gift of happiness if only she could make that instant prolong itself. She held an ordinary glass tumbler in her hand, lifting it from the water, and stared at a light-yellow circular effect on the top surface of the draining board. A smudge of stain from dried coffee resembled the map of an island. Close beside it was another island-shaped smudge. She put down the glass tumbler and slowly drew a soapy finger from one stain to the other. A small, delicate and vanishing necklace of bubbles linked the two islands for a moment.

She reheated the water in the electric kettle, which had only recently boiled, and made herself a mug of coffee. It was a reminder that she had left her coffee unfinished in the apartment of Victoria Mansions. She sipped it between bouts of drying and putting things away. Her footsteps in the kitchen sounded sharp and very brisk, reminding her with a flush of pleasure how he had admired her legs and what his thoughts really must have been. Then the small amount of washing-up was done. She had to recognise she had done it partly at least in order to postpone the moment when she would have to go upstairs and explain it all to her mother.

Television noises, a creak from one of the steps in the stairs, the chunky feel of the wooden banisters and the pale mauve tones of the elaborate flowery wallpaper held out small grasping fingers to her as though waving to her for recognition or gesturing to her in desperate appeal like remnants from a Titanic disaster that was her own sense of personal desolation in returning home. She felt everything about this semi-detached home of hers had some clinging viscosity. It stuck to her and welcomed her return as if ready to glue itself to her more firmly. The mixture of light fragrances filling the air with rumours – no more – of polish and bath soap and dust and garden smells on this summer night made her tremble with the sort of irrational excitement and apprehension she had known as a child when she had climbed stairs (not here, but in the larger house where they'd lived before her father's retirement). Now she was excited and apprehensive for another reason: she did not know how her mother would react.

'Oh, my dear, how nice of you to come and see me! There wasn't any need.'

'Don't be silly,' she scolded fondly, 'of course there was.'

Her mother had that slight pink flush in her cheeks that was the signal she had done too much. There was no point in telling her what they both knew, so she drew up a bedside chair and kissed her on the cheek and held her hand in her own, feeling the boniness of it. The light on the bedside table gave the whole bedroom a misty, rosy softness and a feeling of locked-in comfort. Her mother always succeeded in giving her own parts of the house – this bedroom, her 'work room' (as she called it) downstairs and the kitchen – an air of soft, lived-in warmth, whereas the rest of the house had a kind of severe rectitude about its furnished ordinariness. She knew that this was exactly what she would want to create as the atmosphere in any home of her own, but she knew also that a man would resist it and perhaps become harder under its clinging influence as her father seemed to have done.

'Where have you been, my dear?'

'Oh, there was a lot of work. On Fridays, you know. Then I had something to eat with Mr Nordon. It's not all *that* late.'

Which was confirmed by the bedside clock showing half-past ten, but she knew her parents tended to expect her much earlier on Fridays. Her mother, though, smiled and patted the back of her hand, which was clasping her own. She felt like blushing and yet grew annoyed with herself, remarking sharply that she'd had a busy day and simultaneously knowing her mother could see right through her.

'I'm sure he's a nice man, your Mr Nordon,' was her mother's appraising, comforting, knowingly appreciative judgement.

They talked about how her mother was feeling, the plans for a holiday somewhere on the south coast, possibly Torquay, where they knew they could find a room with one of their relatives; or the fact that their long-standing home help was unwell and how difficult it had been to find a replacement. Then it was clear that her mother was tired. She kissed her goodnight. Leaving the bedroom, she looked back and felt her heart stabbed by an inch-long dagger of love and regret as she saw how old her mother looked with the bedside light shining softly on her grey hair and puckered, smiling face and the glistening appearance of her blue eyes. She closed the door and went downstairs.

Though she was quite ready to face the fact of her mother's heart condition, she was less ready to accept the submissive role of nurse and housekeeper. She increasingly recognised in herself something of her father's resentment. Nowadays it more than ever took the form of grumbling and bad temper. For her part, it took the form of wilfully resisting the need to play the part of loving only daughter to parents on a fixed income, although she recognised it was her duty. Her wilfulness was what most frightened her. It frightened her also that she tended to identify this wilfulness with her new feelings for 'Mr N' or Jim, as she ought to call him. She could feel herself wanting to transfer the protective, loving instincts of her nature to this sensitive man. He had so suddenly revealed himself to her and needed her so greatly and would respond to her love, she liked to imagine, with the unique delight and reverence of someone chosen especially for her, for her alone, forever and ever and ever.

Some hours later, with a sound of rain falling on the leaves of the apple tree in the back garden, she found herself awake and sitting up in bed and blinking her eyes at her father's face round the door, as he said in a whisper:

'It's your mother. I think you'd better come.'

****

On the following Monday morning Jim learned what had happened in Guildford and decided to apply for leave. After all, the annual conference of his professional association was due to take place in a seaside resort on the south coast. It would coincide with the final two weeks of annual leave to which he was entitled and it would give him an opportunity to consult with people from other organisations about the problems of cuts and redundancies and redeployment. Charles Ball grunted, talked about urgency and then agreed. He waved Jim away with the instruction to get in touch with Angus Phillips, the interdepartmental chief liaison officer.

'So it's leave you're after, is it? What on earth do you need leave for?'

The brogue and avuncular good humour were not always to Jim's taste, but he liked the Scotsman's trenchancy.

'It's my entitlement, you know.'

'Entitlement!' Angus's elaborate arpeggio of vowel sounds made the word sound obscene. 'You can't go around talking about entitlement! We're all here on sufferance, didn't you know that?'

'Please, Angus, a straight yes or no would do.'

'I have to check up. If you can be spared, you can be spared. As I was saying…' And he began checking by flipping through a card index '…as I was saying, you and I are here on sufferance. You can no more hide from me that you're a North Briton than I can hide from you I'm a Scot. In any case, you look like one, whereas I'm too old to look like anything at all, d'you know what I mean?'

'Please, Angus, just yes or no.'

'And what'll you be doing on holiday? Here, we are – oh, yes.'

'I'll be attending the annual conference of my association.'

'You'll be what? Ah, I see you're in Rowney's old room. That's the one with Italian chair, isn't it?'

'Yes, it is.'

Angus scratched his chin and studied Jim. 'You don't sit in that chair, do you?'

Jim denied sitting in that chair.

'I'll tell you, though,' said Angus, smiling, 'that what you need is an emotional safety-valve, not a conference. You have certain serious responsibilities, you know.' Which referred, no doubt, to what was already common knowledge of the indistinct kind that fuels gossip in offices. Jim began to object. 'No, no, I mean simply,' Angus insisted, 'you won't get your emotional safety-valve from attending a conference. Fighting a fish is a lot better.'

'I'm not going to fight a fish.'

'That's Sassenach's way of talking. I'm just telling you what you need, that's all. Attending a bloody conference is going to be a real busman's holiday, to my mind. You want to get the scent of the heather in your nostrils.'

Jim avoided a fishy story from Angus by thanking him. He aimed to get the scent of the south coast resort into his nostrils, that was all, along with the smell of the sea and fish and chips and the opportunity to do some painting. Of course, Angus was right. Jim knew only too well that what he needed as well as a holiday was an emotional safety-valve. It had been his thought all weekend. Having the apartment to himself, for some reason he had had no inspiration to paint and he had brooded. He had brooded on his failed marriage and on Rachel and then on Sally. He had come to the conclusion that it would be unfair to himself, let alone to her, to assume that her kiss had meant anything more than "Thank you".

If it did, he would simply be misleading both himself and her, because he mistrusted his emotions, recognising that he was in danger of reviving what had been the sudden, utterly convincing feeling of devotion he had felt for Vicky. He was not planning any closer relationship than the one he already had with Rachel, except that whenever he thought about Sally he felt a series of mild tremors of excitement accompanied by anxiety and uneasy anticipation.

Then the news from Guildford had decided him. She had emailed him to say that her mother had been unwell over the weekend but did not want to go into hospital, so she, Sally-Anne, was relying on the 'arrangement' to stay and look after her for a few days. He had responded by emailing her the news that he would shortly be taking two weeks' leave.

It was a postponement, no more than that, and he certainly did not wish to allow the 'arrangement' to become anything like a permanency between them. There was an additional concern that inserted itself into his life over lunch.

'Who's that girl you have now?' asked Dick Stephens from the accounts department as they sat at the same table in the refectory.

'She's away for the time being,' was Jim's evasive reply.

'You've got Rowney's old room, haven't you? It's the one with the Italian chair? Does your girl sit in it?'

'You're not the first person to ask me that today? What is it with Italian chairs?'

'Nothing really. It's just that Rowney used to say he liked to admire girls' legs when they were taking shorthand from him. Nowadays their legs are never visible when their working at computers. By the way, who the hell are Plath and Siegfreid?'

'Charles Ball suggested them,' Jim answered as casually as possible. The fact that word of this fictitious agency had reached the accounts department alarmed him. 'They're in New York, but they've got an office over here. The office is responsible for hiring people to study the possibilities of, er, changes in our arrangements.'

'Well, if it's Charles Ball, okay, say no more.' He took a mouthful of beef stew, chewed it and then said: 'The girls round here seem to get younger and younger, don't they?'

'Do they?'

'They're either too young or too old. My father used to sing a song with those words. "They're either too young or too old, they're either too something or too bold" – I can't remember.'

Jim laughed.

'My wife's thirty-five,' said Dick Stephens, 'and she doesn't look a day over twenty-five. Honest. I'm always amazed. And it's nothing to do with using some soap or other. What worries me is I'm going bald and beginning to look about ten years older than I really am, so one day someone'll be bound to mistake me for her father.'

Sally finally came back to work on the Thursday of that week. She looked pale but assured him her mother was better and even planning to have a holiday in Torquay with her father's sister, Auntie Mary. It would do them both good, she was sure. A smile lit up her eyes as she confessed her obvious relief at being relieved of the nursing duties for which the 'arrangement' had been the pretext. Although he shared an anticipated sense of relief at the thought of freeing himself from Charles Ball's designs for at least two weeks, the sight of her, notwithstanding her apologies for being away, revived all his earlier tremors of excitement. He knew the relationship was entering a crucial stage when the least hint of falsehood could be disastrous. He began speaking brusquely, as he tended to speak when displaying his efficiency at committee meetings, announcing that he had to attend a conference. He named the town, the hotel and the duration of the conference. 'Three whole days of conference business and seminars, just imagine.'

A bleakness of spirit came over him as he realised he had hit the wrong note and the mistake could be irreparable. The view of the Thames from his office window showed him barges being drawn up the pewter-grey river. Huge fluffy clouds simultaneously moved across the city's face like the many-times-magnified problems of life below them.

'I'm sorry, I make it sound officious and tiresome.'

What he did not say was the chance of painting. She looked at him in a way that was both appraising and reproachful, as if she knew he meant something else. He had inadvertently given the impression that their relationship was something that could be reduced to a series of snap decisions. The gaze of her blue eyes scorned such easy executive legerdemain.

'You mean you won't be painting?'

He grinned with embarrassment at his evasiveness. 'Probably not actual painting with oils. Oh, yes, I hope to do some sketching and watercolours. As soon as the conference is over.'

There was a momentary silence between them. Sitting in the Italian chair as she was, she lowered her head before saying:

'I owe you an apology, I know. I'm sorry I've been away so long. My mother's better, a lot better, but, you know, they're not well off now my father's retired and I feel sort of responsible for looking after them, do you know what I mean?'

'Yes, yes, of course.'

He had been looking fondly at her lowered head and the long, shining, evidently newly washed blonde hair as she spoke. Her bare freckled arms with their sheen of soft downy hair excited his readiness to be protective and understanding.

When she raised her eyes, they were moistly bright, with highlights in them as if she were wearing contact lenses, and in the timorous, slightly pleading look she gave him the eyes conveyed her refusal to be politely treated as if she were just another girl who worked for him. 'I just wanted you to know,' she said. 'And I'm glad you'll have a chance to paint. I meant it. You must paint.'

'It's nice of you to be so sure.'

'Oh, I am.'

She stood up and came round the desk and put a hand on his. The movement and the gesture frightened as much as comforted him. It seemed too theatrical, too like something seen on television or in an American movie, but her sudden overture was less of an embarrassment to him than the artlessness of it. She pressed his hand and at once turned away.

He rose awkwardly, because the wheels of his swivel desk chair didn't run backwards immediately, and took her gently by the shoulders. Her hair smelled of the shampoo and there was a light fragrance of powder from her cheek, though what he chiefly noticed was the soft upward rush of warmth from her whole body and the intriguing, delicate tickle of her hair against his chin. In that moment, standing close behind her, his hands on her shoulders, he could not fail to sense the expectation of her body towards him and know that it suddenly spoke of fondness more clearly than any words could convey. He stood there more than ever aware how audible were the normally beyond-doors sounds of other offices and feet in corridors and outside traffic, struck on the instant, as if the air had turned to glass around them, by the embarrassingly intense unnaturalness of what he was doing and the need somehow to break that constraining glass without causing the least degree of hurt and awkwardness. He was about to speak when she quickly came to his aid with a kind of jump, spun wound and beamed up at him.

'You must paint, you know, because you're good at it. If I were as good as that, I wouldn't be able to stop.' She spoke in what he felt was a sisterly, even presumptuous way, with a slight degree of the school-mistress's sternness in it. 'And what you're doing now isn't really what you ought to be doing, you know. You need someone to look after you properly.'

'And you're going to do that?'

He laughed as he asked the question. Their relationship seemed suddenly natural, unselfconscious, playful.

She made a face. 'No, I didn't really mean it that way.'

The phone on his desk chirruped. It was Stanley Worthington. He was reminded that at their last meeting Stanley had promised to give him the names of people he knew who belonged to the same professional association as Jim. They would very likely be at the conference. The phone call ended the conversation with Sally like the fall of a guillotine. The routine business of studying and accumulating the departmental data needed for Jim's report became her responsibility at that point and remained their mutual, official concern throughout that day and the following Friday. She worked in a small room next to his office. Jim was himself involved with a committee meeting until late that afternoon and did not see her before she left. Instead he found an envelope on his desk. He tore it open. The only words in bold capitals on the sheet of paper inside were:

'HAVE A NICE HOLIDAY'

Almost spontaneously he screwed the paper up and flung it into the metal basket by his desk. She had sensibly not signed it to avoid any chance of gossip but at the same time he found it too official. Maybe, he thought, that was right. He would have a nice holiday. They would not see each other for two weeks. Perhaps he would be able to harden himself to the possibility that their relationship would become the relatively simple one of employer and employee.

IV

'You come to me just like that, don't you?' Rachel said, not asking really so much as stating, and flicking her fingers as she spoke in a manner that he had often used when speaking to his brother Sam. 'I know, Jim dear, you're a busy man, but you take me for granted just a bit too much. One day I'll come to your Victoria Mansions and just plant myself there, bag and baggage. That may not please you at all.'

'Please,' he said and put his arms round her and drew her towards him. 'Whenever you like.'

'It's lucky for you I can't stand London. It's like going up to the third world these days.'

'My Victoria Mansions doesn't really count as London.'

'Oh, yes, they do! Stop hugging me too much. I feel you're going to squeeze all the breath out of me.'

But she spoke good-naturedly and did not try to push him away. He held her closely, loosening his pressure slightly but still holding her to him, because this closeness of body to body was the therapy he always sought from Rachel and which she always gave him so freely and without obligation. He did not trouble to ask her, and she certainly never asked him, whether they demanded of each other the emotional commitment that lovers were supposed to require of each other. He was deeply fond of Rachel and sure of her. She was not *inside* his life so much as always the haven *outside* him, the embrace that did not require to be given in return for some favour but simply as a reward for a mutual need. He was not to disturb her life, nor to ask of her more than the occasion of their intimacy offered, for it was an essential though unspoken part of the bargain on which their friendship was founded. So when she said she'd come to Victoria Mansions he was surprised.

'You've never done that, have you?'

'What?'

'Come to my Victoria Mansions.'

'No. And don't ask me why. Names, places, people, they all go together.'

'What's that mean?'

'It means, my dear, that for some reason or other best known to yourself you chose to live in a place named after the one person who…'

'All right,' he said over her shoulder, looking into the mirror above the fireplace, 'I know.' He gave a grunt or a laugh, it was a sound that could have been either. 'Have you heard from her?'

'Oh, about a month ago. That's why you really came, isn't it?'

'No. I came, as I said, to ask you if you'd like to join me on my holiday.'

That had been foolish of him. He had made the decision to see her on the spur of the moment. He had phoned, true, but he knew there had always been an understanding between them that they should never try to imitate the relationship of married people. A holiday together, even if arranged at such short notice, would have supposed a permanency in their relationship that might have looked too much like marriage. They were both outcasts from marriage who consciously sought to live alone on separate islands.

'And I said no.'

'That was the only reason. I always come to you at your command, but I don't count that as anything as trivial as a "reason". Because when I hold you I enjoy the warm and desirable firmness of your body…'

'Shut up! There's no need for anything like that!'

She gave him her bright imitation of shocked prudery, but she let him hold her and kiss her. In that momentary act of holding her he knew his own dishonesty and, with it, his shallowness. In the same moment their bodies recognised their familiar latent sexuality and pressed more tightly against each other.

'Right, enough said.'

'It wouldn't take very much, you can believe me.' She gently undressed herself from his embrace and crossed the room to the window. A vehicle came along the suburban street and made a loud exhaust noise just below them. Somewhere there sounded the musical-box chimes of an ice-cream van. Her room was on the second floor of a large Victorian house and though spacious it was darkened by trees lining the street. When she stood outlined in the rectangular frame of the window the outside light caused her brown curling hair to seem like dark frost patterns against the greenery. 'But you've grown out of marriage much more than I have. Vicky wasn't really for you, that's obvious, but you never understood her properly, did you? I think she had every right to find someone else. With Steve and me I know I was in the wrong. After a time I simply couldn't respect him. With you, my dear, I know I'd be happy in a formal way – I mean I'd have the material things that Steve couldn't give me because he was always so bloody poor – and I'd be happy as a woman. I'd be in control of the sexual side, that's really what I mean. But I wouldn't respect myself. I know I'd begin wanting something else. Oh, we've been over all this before. I just don't want to be made to feel dissatisfied. I want things to be as they are. They may not be ideal but they're not difficult, they're manageable. Let's leave things manageable, Jim dear.' She came back across the room.

'Of course.'

'Oh, you say that with such disappointment in your voice,' and to his surprise she approached and stroked his cheek with the palm of her hand but moved it away before he could seize it and stop her. Her stroking movement roused him sexually, like her professionally knowing, fondly insidious way of saying the words. 'I think you've got that special look, haven't you?'

'What special look?'

'There's someone else, isn't there?'

'I don't know what you mean.'

But he gave himself away by crimsoning as well as by making such a banal denial. She looked him straight in the face and he was unable to withstand the force of her scrutiny. He was obliged to turn his reddened face away from her.

'You know what I mean,' she said slowly. 'You don't have to hide anything from me. I suppose I know why you came here. I also know I'm not the only friend you have in the world.'

Her manner now irritated him because he'd never supposed she would be jealous, even though she had no real grounds for jealousy. But she added, dispelling all his suspicions in a way of which she alone was capable:

'I mean only that I think, my dear Jim, you don't yet know what I've already guessed. I mean you're probably in love and you don't know it.'

'This is ridiculous. I ought to know a thing like that if anyone's likely to, but I can assure you I don't think I'm in love.'

'Oh, that's like the civil servant talking! You *are* a civil servant, you know. An honest civil servant, the only civil servant I'm really fond of, but you *are* a civil servant and you're talking just like one.'

'Thanks for the testimonial.'

'But seriously.' She took his hands in her own. 'I mean what I said. You're probably in love. You deserve to be. Of all people I think you deserve to be.'

Her earnest and obvious sincerity embarrassed him. It made him feel not only self-conscious but also inadequate to the promise of happiness that she held out to him, regardless of his dishonesty, in the very clasping of her hands about his. He felt, moreover, that it had now become his duty to accept her Delphic prophecy.

'Please, please,' he said, freeing his hands and drawing her to him, 'if I'm going to love anyone, it'll be you. That's the most I can say for the time being.'

He felt her shake with a gentle laughter in his embrace and he could not tell whether it was a laughter of mockery or happiness. Except that they stood there, reflected by the mirror above the fireplace, in the afternoon's quietness, and held each other close.

Later he drove south. The afternoon was marked by occasional glimpses of sunshine flashing across the windscreen, followed by showers. It matched the uneasy, slightly anxious mood that accompanied his anticipation of the conference due to happen in a seaside resort he had never visited. When he stared out of the window of his hotel room at the dull, white-flecked, bluish waste of the sea, unmarked by a ship or a buoy, he thought the momentarily sunless, cloud-layered sky mirrored it too accurately. The sight oppressed him.

His room, though, was comfortable on the face of it, if unfamiliar, that was for sure. It had two beds and the accompanying furnishings of high-class accommodation, including a bathroom and shower. In a general way it was insulated from the sounds of the hotel and far enough above the traffic along the esplanade not to be too affected by it. In fact, the whole hotel strove to be as full of quality features as possible without being old-fashioned.

Rachel's words had been a shock. Much as he might have wished to ignore them, he knew they had penetrated deeply into him with a sword-like thrust. Their truth was reinforced by what Rachel herself represented to him, the very voluptuousness, the intercourse of his and hers, the nakedness to nakedness, the sex to sex, the completely intimate unsparing joy. It was love, or the truth of love in a carnal sense, but if he would be missing that love during this seaside visit, he knew that real love included a creative durability and shared richness that held inestimable promise for the future, for children, for family, for his own talent, with the grace of God. Still, here he was in his hotel bedroom and he was gazing out over the sea, letting his eyes browse on the enormously subtle variations of tint and tone that the foreground and distance of the marine vista offered him.

Below him, along the sea-front of the esplanade, crowds of people were already walking now the rain had stopped. They were walking under the plastic flags hanging from the lamps in bright clothes that he would convey with dabs of bright paint against the colourlessness of the afternoon, if he were to try to capture the scene in paint. So many were couples, the young who looked slim and innocent, the middle-aged who looked stout and satisfied, but it was quite possible the innocent-looking were as maddened by sex as the satisfied were glad to enjoy it without any struggle. He knew how much of a half-truth that was. It was only when you were a bachelor in your early thirties that you thought deeply about such a half-truth, as he did now and knew he was wasting his time. All he could understand properly was the hollowness of a marriage in which sexuality had perished. So he looked down at the people below him and wished them to be spared such knowledge.

He joined them out in the open, in the cooling but not chill atmosphere of the esplanade. Eastward, beyond the pier, the esplanade ended in a boating pool, bathing place and sea-wall at the foot of tall cliffs. Westward the esplanade stretched in a semi-circle round the bay, dotted with tall hotels and apartment buildings and one or two terraces left over from the nineteenth century. There was a long sea-front pierced at intervals by steps leading down to a sandy beach. Huts for deck chairs and the sale of items for the beach nestled under the wall of the sea-front. Much of the esplanade itself was given over to flowerbeds and gardens dotted with seats, along with a bandstand and amusements of various kinds. Then there was the main road along the esplanade full of sleek cars and multi-coloured buses.

Wherever he saw some point of interest, just a seagull perched on a wall, pebbles, for instance, scattered brightly on paving stones, raindrops still clinging to the underneath of wrought-iron railings like so many glass beads, the flags flapping overhead, he used the tiny camera on his smartphone to capture a picture. He never wanted to photograph the larger scene. Minutiae, that's what he wanted to record, the minutiae of being in one place at one time, because however much he might imagine he might paint this or that, he hadn't in fact brought any oil or acrylic or support. His aim had been to sketch while on holiday and remind himself of colour with the lightest dabs from his watercolour box. In any case, for the next few days of the coming week he had to be prepared to concentrate on conference matters.

So he walked idly along the front away from the music on the pier, sniffing the sea and hearing more clearly its beating softly on the distant sand. The white froth of waves ran along the beach as if an invisible zip were drawing them together. A few scattered children played on the sand, some were even out among the small waves. Farther out heads bobbed, young men and girls splashed about. Cries and shouts lifted above the soft wave noise like soprano voices rising above some deep choral surge. Life, he reflected, imitating art again.

He walked in a mood that was empty, though not unhappy, right along the esplanade. Then he turned back towards the centre of the town. Just as he was passing some shops the cloud layer parted and sunlight poured out with a golden clarity over buildings and people. Windows caught the sudden sunlight in intense dazzling flashes. The dust in the gutters sparkled. People's eyes had a lucid brightness. His mood changed instantly. He was prepared to enjoy himself. He bought whisky and peanuts and returned to the hotel.

Sitting in a rather stiffly upright armchair that felt like being in a tight bath, he watched the sea through his hotel window. The sun was still shining from the crevice in the western sky, though it was now low on the horizon and already beginning to fade. It gave the sea a gleam of clear varnish. A far ship shone white briefly. Sailing boats nearer shore were apparently static above shadows like momentarily glazed reflections on stilled waves. He sat mindlessly in his chair for several minutes, waiting for inspiration. When his thoughts reformed, he began wondering how he could live through ten days or so of this environment once the conference was over.

He was overwhelmed by a sense of the fatuousness of his life. How could he possibly imagine himself coming to this hotel for twenty or thirty years and sitting in a chair like this one? How could he believe that attendance at the conference of his professional association amounted to something for which he would prepare year after year? What did such authority as he had, such responsibility, such reputation or any other token of his professional life actually mean to him? Despite the sharp, enlivening taste of the whisky and the crunch of peanuts, he felt too tired and bored to find answers. He would easily drink himself into a state of temporary but artificial happiness that would be his future, as unoccupied by any other concern as the hotel room in which he was sitting. Looking round it, at the white luminosity of the dressing-table mirror, the unlit pendant lamp, the smart reproduction Constable on the pale-blue striped wallpaper, the hostile-looking armchairs, he thought it was a metaphor for his own present boredom. It also made him aware, like a scream beginning in the pit of his stomach, that he did not want this, not this bland, characterless void. All he really wanted was to paint. He felt, like the rising scream within him, that his other, his unofficial, his unprofessional life was pouring into the void of his present existence and filling it to the brim.

V

The conference centre was barely a block or so away from the hotel along the esplanade. He registered before midday the next day as was required and soon found himself in the company of several delegates he had met before. They formed an amiable group mostly consisting of married men and women who mentioned offhandedly that their spouses or partners were able to enjoy the freedom of the seaside resort while they had to do their duty and sit attentively listening to conference business. Of the two names mentioned by Stanley Worthington only one, Donald Holmes, was present, Jim discovered, but it turned out he worked in a neighbouring London Borough where financial cuts were high on the agenda. What is more, he knew Stanley through having met him as an advisor and judge at an art exhibition he had been organising the previous year. A meeting of minds and interests naturally helped Jim and Donald over several beers to have long and helpful discussions in the attractive new bar-room of the conference centre. A sort of fleeting friendship grew between them. Although Jim did not mention he was engaged in making a report, the problem of cuts, staff redundancies, departmental rearrangements and so on soon arose not only in their talks but also in the conference programme itself.

After the usual presidential speech welcoming delegates and the proclaiming by committee members of the healthy state of the association, there was a keynote speech by an eminent academic on aspects of the training required for posts in local government. The afternoon sessions were broken up into seminars on precisely the subjects with which Jim was concerned. The discussions often became heated. The discarding of jackets and ties due to the beginning of a modest heatwave seemed to loosen tongues. It was obvious that reports on redundancies were arousing similar concerns in a majority of local government offices throughout the country. Arguments over age-related plans, capping of governmental grants, financial ring-fencing, commercial and council confidentiality, inequality, favouritism, nepotism, taxpayers' revolts, even likely rioting, etc, etc, characterised the usually polite, well-mannered discussions of these debates. Jim had never experienced such strong language as was regularly used on this occasion.

The effect was to bring a much calmer, somewhat shame-faced atmosphere to the second day's business. A stiffly worded announcement from the president posted on the notice board beside the day's conference programme warned against such unmannerly behaviour. It also meant that many delegates absented themselves from the day's meetings. Partly due to the sudden warmth and the natural attractions of the seaside, groups of those whom Jim knew hired deck chairs and sat on the sand. Like Jim himself and, as it turned out, Donald Holmes, they took the opportunity to discuss issues raised by the previous day's seminars. It proved a very helpful lesson in greater understanding of certain principal features that Jim had to deal with in his report. He was so grateful to them that he bought them all drinks in the conference centre bar-room before lunch in the conference cafeteria.

The afternoon meetings were less contentious and better attended. Generally speaking anti- and pro-privatisation of local government services were debated at some length, especially refuse collection, its regularity and costs. Listening to the debates so tired Jim that, apart from taking copious notes, he could hardly stop himself from fits of yawning and was glad to retire to his hotel room once the sessions were over. He fell asleep almost immediately with a glass of whisky only half drunk on the table beside him and woke to find suppertime was almost over once he made his way down to the hotel restaurant. A cheese sandwich, however, and some coffee sufficed for his evening meal. He had amazed himself, he kept on thinking, by becoming so absorbed in routine conference business that for once he no longer had the nagging sense of futility surrounding his professional career.

The annual general meeting scheduled for the final day of the conference usually involved fairly automatic renewal of committee memberships, unless there were vacancies for some reason that led to votes, together with re-appointment of a president, the post being one of annual duration and supposed to be more honorary than authoritative. On this occasion voices were raised in protest at the notice placed the previous morning on the public notice board from the then president calling for more mannerly behaviour. Other voices supported the presidential action, expressed disgust at some of the language used in the debates and felt that guilty members should apologise. At this the newly appointed president used such authority he could muster to put an end to this fractious exchange of views by asserting that no speaker should raise any matter *ad hominem*. Happily this ruling was accepted. The conference concluded with mutual congratulations all round on achieving such a successful outcome.

Perhaps the fatuousness of the occasion confirmed Jim in the need to keep the business of the conference in mind. It prompted him to begin drafting his report. He had brought his laptop with him. He found the work of posing the pros and cons of likely savings in manpower, not to mention related departmental responsibilities and so on, acquired a kind of grandeur as the words filled the laptop screen. For three days or so his mornings were occupied with composing such blindingly obvious matters in the most rigorously official style, polite but deeply ambiguous, while afternoons were devoted to swimming and lounging in a deckchair as long as the weather permitted. By the end of the first week the weather stopped permitting it. Meanwhile he had tried more than once to get in touch with Sally, who had agreed to continue the work of accumulating data, but her smartphone had either been switched off or diverted to voice mail to which there had been no response. She had promised to let him know how she was doing and of course her silence puzzled and worried him. He decided he had had enough of this solitary holiday, even though it was not the first time in his bachelordom that he had gone on holiday by himself. The weather, offering light rain and prolonged cloudiness, more or less made up his mind for him. He would cut his losses and go back to Victoria Mansions.

Suddenly on the Friday morning the telephone on the bedside table rang. He had only recently returned from slipping out to make some purchases. With a slowness born of surprise he answered it after it had rung several times. It was a man's voice.

'A young lady came in asking for you, sir. It was about an hour ago and you were out. I'm very sorry it's taken so long to let you know, but the assistant day porter forgot to inform me and I've only just come across his note. In any case, sir, there was no message. She said she would call again tomorrow.'

He thanked the man.

'A young lady... no message... call again tomorrow.' Why no message? No identification meant that whoever it was either had the wrong address or it was some kind of trick. He held the receiver in his hand long enough to hear its soft low electric buzz mingle with distant traffic noises and music from the pier audible through the half-open window. No, it couldn't be Sally! That was the repetitiously echoing thought that seemed to go on bouncing back into his mind whenever he threw it out as irrelevant. And as the thought echoed, he

felt his mood change, he felt it made his heart quite light and buoyant, so that when he replaced the receiver and stood by the window looking out at the mirror of the sea it seemed to gleam with an inner polished brightness as if it were promising something.

****

She stood there in his hotel room in a pretty flowered summer dress, reds and pinks on white, carrying a white cardigan. Her long attractive legs were bare. Her bare arms were slightly more tanned than when he had last seen her and her complexion was bright with a soft dusting of reddish-brown hue from recent sunshine. He thought she looked amazingly healthy and fresh for someone who must have spent so much time staring at a computer screen. The tautness, though, around and below her shining blue eyes, giving them a faint grey halo in the brightness of her surrounding complexion, signalled an underlying strain. They contained an appeal as well as a pleasure in their brilliance. He read their message at once and held her closely to him, noting that this time there was no strain in the embrace as there had been when they had suddenly acknowledged their feelings for each other in his office.

'I'm very glad,' he whispered and kissed her on the cheek.

She gave a gasping laugh. 'Thank you. But I've got to make a confession.'

He didn't ask what it was. She freed herself from him and flung the long strap of her handbag off her shoulder onto one of the chairs.

'I should have rung you, I know, but I switched my phone off. I went home last weekend and Mum was better, much better, so I came into work and started doing what you asked me. Then my father phoned.' She gave several shakes of the head and gestured with both hands. 'He said they'd had words. It wasn't a real quarrel. It was something about not wanting to drive down to Torquay. It was much too hot, it wouldn't be good to have Mum sitting in a hot car for such a long journey or something like that. And could I come. He didn't know what to do about it, so could I come.' A short pause. 'So I went home. I left my work and went home. I'm sorry. I feel ashamed of myself. That's why I'm here. I wanted to apologise.'

He did not know exactly how to respond, but of the rival desires – whether to talk about her confession or simply overlook it – the second was the stronger. In any case, he had no wish to talk about office matters at that moment. 'Don't apologise,' he said. 'I'm just so glad you're here.'

She gave a gasping laugh. 'Then you don't mind?'

'No.'

She had rung the hotel that Sunday morning and said she would be coming. The full message could be decoded and amplified in due course, he knew that. After hearing the porter's words he had slept with greater depth and contentment than he had experienced in his Victoria Mansions apartment. Sea air, he thought, hardly daring to think that his subconscious could anticipate a happiness that all his conscious senses told him was impossible.

'I needed a holiday.' She spoke huskily and then cleared her throat. He had a fleeting sense that she thought the fact of her need a sufficient justification. 'I got so worn out, that's what really happened.'

Her apparent evasiveness did not surprise him. He kept on remembering what she had written in her note and assumed that she must have planned more than she now admitted. He asked where she was staying.

'In a small B&B place by the station. It was the first place I could find. I wasn't really planning to stay.' She drew the hair back from her face with the back of her fingers so that most of it, like a parted curtain, hung either side of her temples. Smiling, she avoided his direct look. 'If you hadn't been here, or if there'd been some problem, I was going to catch the first train back. I mean I really shouldn't be here at all. I should be looking after my Mum.'

She stood back from him when she said this and looked at him, blinking quickly, as if she expected him to be stern. Over-sensitively he felt on the instant that she considered him a substitute father. Equally, though, it was as if she were about to be stern with herself for being so impulsive and irresponsible. He asked about her parents.

'They've gone down to Torquay for a holiday. It'll be for several weeks. I imagine.'

Which was surely long enough for her not to feel responsible, he assumed and said so. She nodded and took his offer of a seat at that moment to sit down in one of the menacing armchairs that immediately surrendered its hostile appearance for one of put-upon dignity. The arms resembled suddenly the rather formal stateliness of the sides of a bath. He offered her a drink.

'Cheers.'

'Cheers.'

They sat in the armchairs facing each other. It was the first time they had been by themselves in a place that was strange to both of them and the strangeness of that fact momentarily tested the strength of their relationship. He had a feeling that the room was scrutinising them. He felt the inquisitive, mildly disapproving spaces of air and aroma fix their attention on them. Still, he could not help smiling with a boyish delight at the pleasure of having her sit in this bedroom, his bedroom, in one of these dreadful armchairs. Smiling, that is to say, at the curve of bosom and thigh beneath the summer dress, as if he were literally watching her naked in her bath.

'You've got a nice bedroom,' she remarked. 'Mine's very ordinary by comparison.'

'It's got two beds because I ordered late and this was their only room overlooking the esplanade. What did you tell your parents?'

'I told them I was going to act as your secretary. Because of the conference.'

He protested light-heartedly at this, saying he had never needed a secretary for the conference. 'I'm not an office holder. Maybe in a hundred years, if I'm unlucky. So what did they say?'

'Oh, Dad, he said of course, if you're a department head. I told him you were head of a department. He was impressed. And Mum'll be all right, even though she doesn't get on all that well with Auntie Mary. They're used to each other, that's the main thing. The house they've got there is quite large.'

On the face of it the holiday arrangement seemed satisfactory. He shook his head, smiling with a pleasure that stretched the muscles of his face and made him feel slightly breathless. 'I can't really believe you're here. It seems incredible. I'd tried to get in touch with you, you know, but couldn't. And I was busy with so much business stuff – there's this bloody awful plan to disperse some of the departments, that's one thing, and of course there's the report on reorganisation, which I've been working on. Anyhow,' he added, taking a deep breath, 'I'm glad you're here. You planned it, though, didn't you?'

'Planned? Oh!' she was disconcerted. But there were still things that she knew he did not understand. 'You don't mind, do you? I mean *really*?'

'Of course I don't mind. I'm glad, really glad.'

He bent forward and touched her wrist. As a gesture it was too avuncular, too elderly, even silly, and he thought of Rachel – what if she had been here? But the aim of the gesture – to reassure, to say 'I love you for it' though wordlessly – did reduce the strangeness that was in danger of mounting round them like so much silt. Then their smiles met. His gesture became unnecessary. If the air had been inflammable, it would have caught fire from the momentary warmth in their eyes.

'Lunch?'

'I'd love some.'

They found a small restaurant called Roberto's. There were the usual empty bottles of Chianti and a few nautical motifs in the décor. In a far corner a young man strummed pseudo flamenco music on a guitar. For a Sunday lunchtime in a south-east resort the place was unusually lively, but not overcrowded. The flamenco music, however inappropriate for an Italian restaurant, created an air of such ephemerally sensuous romance with all its husky twanging that it whisked them into an almost frantic need to confess. At least, that was his reaction to it. In an effort to fend off the shivers of alarm at the possibility that she might have found him here with Rachel, as well as the shivers of delight that her closeness caused him, he talked rather busily.

'I was beginning to worry about myself – what I'd do with this so-called holiday, I mean, how I'd spend year after year attending my association conference in different hotels, the same old thing year after year – and then suddenly you appear out of nowhere. Or almost out of nowhere. I've got to get used to it, you know.'

She was watching him, smiling her blue-eyed luminous smile, content, red-lipped, blinking a little with pleasure and uncertainty. And he looked back at her, feeling vaguely for one of the few times in his life that he was with someone who required him to be uncompromisingly natural, the *natural* Jim Nordon, and wondering equally vaguely whether he could ever match the ideal state of naturalness her bright gaze demanded of him.

'I've sort of grown used to the self-indulgence of bachelorhood,' he announced rather abruptly, as if it were a justifiable confession. 'So I'm not used to a relationship. Have you told anyone about us?'

'I'm not a fool, you know, Jim,' she answered with a surprising flash of annoyance. 'That's one of the first rules. Don't tell *them*, the others. Not if it's serious.'

Not if it's serious!

He was touched more deeply than he could have imagined by that admission. That she should have said the one word 'serious' with such ferocity, along with such naturalness, amazed and humbled him. For several moments they were becalmed in a mutual silence. He couldn't summon up enough inspiration to express exactly what he felt, and she was evidently embarrassed by having been so unguarded. The moments of calm were filled with the in-rush of noise from surrounding tables and the twanging music. Then the first course was brought and the tension faded.

'Do you know this place?' he asked. 'I don't mean this restaurant, I mean this seaside resort.'

'No, not really. I think my school once came here on a trip. We went bathing. That's all I can remember.'

Since she had mentioned it, he asked her about her school. She told him she had lived all her life in Guildford and she had gone to a local school there. There had been nothing special about her school career, except she had been quite good at swimming and had won a cup for being the best swimmer of her year. She passed all the necessary exams and then had done a two-year IT and secretarial course.

'By that time I was nineteen. I wanted to get away, so I went to France and then Spain as I told you and took those jobs.' She told it all briefly and cogently. To him it was all so full of complex feminine experience that he knew he would probably never know what made her look at life so steadily and strong-mindedly, or why, since she looked at life so unflinchingly, she should have made *this* choice and not *that* choice.

'I'm still not sure of myself,' she admitted finally, giving the impression that she was speaking partly to herself.

'About your life, you mean?'

'Oh, about life, about anything. The girls I share the flat with have both such interesting jobs. One them is always flying off with her boss to the States. The other's always meeting film stars and celebrities and people.'

'Well, in Department Z10 you're not likely to find that kind of excitement, I agree.'

She raised her glass to her lips, sipped and put it down. 'I think,' she said deliberately and slowly, 'Department Z10's been quite good fun. In the last two weeks I've thought quite a lot about Department Z10.'

'When you've been at home, you mean?'

'When I've been at home. Your home's in Manchester, isn't it?'

'Yes. My home *was* in Manchester. Or not far from it. My parents still live there.'

He didn't ask why she should ask, although he recognised she was curious. She drank some more wine.

'It's your turn, you know, she said. 'I've told you about myself. Tell me about...' She gave a dainty wave of the hand that suggested he should tell her about all the personal things that he had never told anyone else. Her eyes were very bright as she spoke. 'Tell me about your wife. What was she like?'

The pseudo flamenco music had stopped. The young guitarist was talking to someone at the bar. Waves of pleasant conversation from other tables circulated round them and induced a mellow atmosphere of confessional intimacy. He felt it didn't matter what he said or how he said it, the substance would be transmitted with the utter frankness of someone confessing the deepest, most secret, things of his life.

'Her name was Vicky, short for Victoria. She was pretty. She had brown hair and brown eyes. Her figure was neat. She kept herself very trim. Why am I telling you all this?'

'Go on.'

'She was a school teacher. I think she had a real vocation for teaching. Perhaps in the end she preferred her teaching to her marriage. I know the fact that we were both working put a strain on our marriage from the very start and eventually that strain became too great. For the first six months, though, it was a good relationship – a really good relationship in every way. I'll always be grateful to Vicky for that.'

Though he was helped by the inoculating effect of the wine, he found it hard to confess the most intimate parts of the story of his failed marriage. He had thought about it all so often, but he had told them only to his brother Sam, and what he had told had never been a total confession of the sexual problems that finally undermined their relationship. No doubt it had foundered chiefly on his and Vicky's mutual failure to tell everything, on a lack of true frankness. Looking up into Sally's bright eyes, he felt himself hypnotised into a naked candour that would express far more of the truth than he had ever confessed before.

'One day she came across the picture of a girl I'd known when I was a student. I suppose I should have thrown it away. She asked me something like 'How well did I know her?' and I blushed because, well, I'd known her very well – oh, that sounds silly, we'd been lovers, that's what I mean.' He looked across at Sally to see how she reacted to this. She was smiling in a composed way and all she did was nod her head slightly. 'She and I had had a passionate physical relationship. It would never have led to marriage, but it was good. Well, what happened – and this was the absurdly stupid part of the relationship between Vicky and me – was that she suddenly became jealous and resentful, quite understandingly, I admit, because I had given the impression that I had enjoyed *that* sex much more than sex with her. She accused me of not being truthful. True, I hadn't been completely truthful. I hadn't told her everything about Megan – that was the girl's name. Vicky was justified in reacting as she did, I suppose, but I blame her for the way she did it. It meant that our marriage practically came to an end as a sexual relationship at that point. After that we gradually drifted our different ways – Vicky more and more towards all her school activities and I, well, I started to paint, but most of all I spent longer and longer at the office. That's one of the reasons I've been put in charge of Z10. My career succeeded where my marriage failed. And, well, she found someone else. In the last two years of our marriage we were polite to each other, but we just couldn't stand each other. We were both glad when it was over.' He paused before adding: 'My painting saved me.'

Had he been truthful now, he would have mentioned Rachel. She, after all, filled his life with all that Vicky refused to give him, whose body, pressing nakedly to his in their lovemaking, had a gently engulfing sensuality that he would carry round with him for days afterwards like a subtly imprinted sensation of kisses on his skin. He said nothing about her now, because he was suddenly overwhelmed by shame at having said so much. He simply finished his glass of wine and then, his hand shaking slightly, poured fresh glasses for both of them.

'What's she doing now?'

'Who? Vicky? She married again. They moved to Bristol. They've got two children.'

'Do you ever see her?'

'No.'

The single, absolute negative of that word summed up all that his marriage now meant for him. He hoped the subject would be buried for ever.

****

'Sunday,' she murmured.

The sun immured them in its heat. The flush of its warmth over them came and went gently like the sound of waves farther down the sand and among the rocks. All that came to them above the to-and-fro of this sound was the distant medley of voices from elsewhere on the beach, usually high-pitched bleeps of sound and cries arising from the continuous murmur of the seaside. It was years, he realised, since he had been able to turn his head on a towel on a sandy beach and see a girl beside him in nothing but her swimsuit. She was lying on her front with her head turned towards him and she was studying him, the whites of her eyes shining a little from the bright sun reflecting into them off the whiteness of the sand. He lay in a similar position and studied her. Their eyes spoke to each other fondly. The young, fresh look of her skin glowing a little from the sun protection she insisted they both wore, the firm but delicate curves of her shoulders and arms, the line of her back like some beautiful sensual promontory against a deep blue sky – these were all things he wanted to treasure and love and never let out of his keeping. He could not explain to her, save by appearing soppy, how magical was the happiness that her presence created in his heart. Her eyes, blinking against the fierce surrounding light, glittered back at him reciprocal messages that he could not fully decode but seemed to acknowledge her own happiness. She moved her hand up the towel towards him and he took it and clasped it.

Later they bathed. He stayed among the shallower waves with the responsibility for keeping an eye on their things. She could swim much more strongly than he could and swam away from him out to a buoy moored apparently on the horizon. The sensuously refreshing effect of the sea water, even if cold as he stood and watched her, seemed both to cleanse and inspire. Distance puzzled him. The rise and fall of the sea and the dazzle of the sunlight on the water at one moment lifted her, at another obliterated. Almost as continuously in a coming and going fashion he found his ears were filled with pop music from a radio perched on the rocks behind him. A family with small children had claimed that area while the two of them were sunbathing. He watched and listened simultaneously. Slowly Sally appeared to grow nearer. Then, a little to his surprise, he suddenly saw her rise up some distance from him and begin walking towards him. She glistened like a mermaid. She had her arms raised in waving, lifting her breasts, and her walking was slow and elegant, with an easy swaying of the hips as she stepped through the waves with a motion like climbing stairs very slowly. Closer to him, she drew off her bathing cap so that her hair, which she spread out with a shake of the head, flowed down in streaks over her face and shoulders. In her slimness and neatness she looked so perfect that he wanted to paint her at that arrested moment, coming from the sea, glowing wet, the sun directly above, and smiling.

A small child, one of the children on the family on the rocks, perhaps attracted by her as much as he was, ran splashing into the waves towards her. He was closer to the child than she was and when the child fell forward into the water he rushed at once and picked her up. The movement was so swift that the child didn't have time to start crying. She looked directly into his face with the first wrinklings of tears already affecting her eyes and stopped. For a moment he thought she would scream to be put down. Instead she surveyed his face and eyes in a curiously intent way as she sat in the crook of his arm. A look of reassurance slowly replaced the wish to cry and impulsively she flung her small arms round his neck and hugged him. Then he put her down. She ran off contentedly towards her family.

'You're good with children,' Sally remarked. 'You ought to have children of your own.'

She leaned against him as she spoke and put an arm round his waist. Their two bodies, though no more truly alert to each other than any skin to wet skin, flowed softly up against each other as if the shallow waves were bobbing them together. He turned and kissed her on the lips as her smiling face was tilted towards him. She pressed against him more strongly, almost with the impulsiveness of the little girl hugging him, and kissed him back while the waves swirled round them just below the level of their knees. He felt her body reach towards his spontaneously. The kiss created a singing note in his limbs as if he were a tuning fork, ringing its purity throughout his body.

****

To her the sunshine was a natural element. She could hardly have enough of it. It was often difficult for him to persuade her to leave the beach even though an evening breeze might have sprung up that was already driving the majority of bathers back to the protection of the esplanade and their hotels. All she needed to do was slip back into her blouse, tight faded jeans and sandals, carrying her swimsuit and beach gown in a large bag. Seen through his sunglasses, her tan gradually changed from a light mahogany tint to one resembling ebony. The sand oozing between her toes would excite him with its bland whiteness on her brown, and the dried clusters of sand grains on her suntanned skin when she sat up from lying on the large towel were a continuing irritant to his desire for her. But at night, after a meal in his hotel, she never stayed, nor did she let him stay at her B&B. Only once did she invite him to her bedroom and then only to smell the scent from some roses he had given her.

Far more important than his feelings for her, which were often shamefully lustful, was the much surer knowledge that they were friends. There were times when they enjoyed a mutual silence. It fuelled their confidence. When she told him about her home, or he discussed his past, each of them seemed to find touchstones of common experience that made familiarity easy. But all of these were incidental items. What made them sure of each other was something she put into words better than he could.

'I've got a trust in you, Jim, that I've never had in anyone else.'

He couldn't take advantage of that much trust. Her parents she liked, but she found them terribly conservative and couldn't trust them to understand her like he did. So she said. Each day he watched her scribble a postcard to them in Torquay.

Are on the beach today again. Lovely weather. Yesterday we went to see the new James Bond. This is a picture of the grotto up on the cliff at the end of the esplanade. Keep well. All my love. Sally-Anne.

Towards the end of the week the weather changed. Thunderheads built up in the west and by the Thursday night, just before they left the beach for the last time, there were flashes on the black horizon. The air had become very still. She came back to his hotel bedroom to have a shower. As the water was running and he listened to her singing, the heavy thundery rain began outside. He opened the large drawing pad he had bought especially for this visit and so far hadn't used. He had not brought any paints except for his watercolour box, but a wide selection of pencils was all he needed. He sat waiting for her in nothing but underpants. She came out of the bathroom busily drying her long hair with a towel and wearing his dressing-gown. When she saw how he had prepared things, she stood with her arms raised holding the towel and her mouth open.

'I want to draw you,' he said.

'How?'

'On the bed.'

'Will it take long?'

'Just lie on the bed.'

'With?'

'Without.'

'You mean?'

'Naked,' he said.

'Do you want to turn me into another nude for your gallery?' There was an attractive ferocity in the way she spoke. It delighted him, but it matched the authority with which he gave his instruction.

'Yes. Naked.'

After a moment's hesitation, in a swift but rather proud movement, she let the dressing-gown slip from her and laid the towel on the bed's counterpane. The flash of white skin where there was no suntan charmed him. Her body had no marks. Naked she looked less vulnerable, more complete as a person, and this was not due as much to nakedness as to a natural composure and feminine assurance. Her swimmer's neatness and strength showed in the firm contours, the smooth compact shoulders, the line of the arms and the wide but gently rounded curves of the hips. It was as if her naked body was as much in its element in the warm thundery air of his bedroom as it had been in the sea only an hour earlier.

'Lie in any way that's comfortable for you.' he instructed.

She gave him a slightly ironic grin and lay back with one knee raised and her head resting back on the pillow. He switched on the bedside light to give an increase of illumination because the exterior light was so poor and likely to be variable. As a result the whole of her right side was illuminated, her right shoulder, arm and bosom and the curving length of her body down to the raised knee that projected into the foreground of his picture. It was not a pose he had tried before, but as soon as his pencil tip first touched the virgin white sheet of drawing paper he felt a fresh, light vigour enter his movements. To his surprise and good fortune – he would never dare ascribe such success to his skill – he managed to achieve a likeness at once. It was one of those occasions when a picture tends to draw itself, though he knew well enough the danger of such an excess of confidence. Her face and figure quite simply began to come alive. Feeling by intuition that he could get the shading of her body right, he drew the bolder shapes of her figure quite strongly and developed the principal deeper facets of her features and hair. He regretted that there was no colour and knew that to do her full justice he would have to do a painting, but as soon as he was certain of this he realised he was growing tired and stopped. Practice had told him that he could work on through this initial tiredness for a short while. Now, seeing her eyes closed and a noticeable relaxation of her pose, he knew he had done all he could. He didn't want to do the least thing to spoil the fresh effects his drawing had achieved.

'Is that all?' she suddenly asked from the bed.

'Yes.'

'Can I see?'

He held up his picture for her to see. The instant she saw it she started exclaiming.

'Oh, it is me! Oh, Jim darling, I think that's clever! Oh, you mustn't stop! You've got to be the artist you want to be!'

It was a shock for him to find his naked model so excited by his drawing of her. Jim Nordon, the painter, had been utterly absorbed by his work. Nonetheless, he was deeply surprised at that instant to find himself reverting to another personality. With other eyes, those that had seen her chiefly through sunglasses, he looked at her naked body as she stood unselfconsciously in front of his drawing and admired it.

Instantly he put down the drawing pad and took her in his arms. For the first time since he'd begun the drawing he noticed the continuous downward race of the rain outside. She let him hold her and run a hand down the curve of her back. Her arms went round him. Her body was warm, warmer, he thought, than his, and so softly sensual and gentle in its pressure against his, with a warm soapy fragrance rising from it. Although she made a small indefinite protesting noise, as if he had taken her by surprise, unresistingly she let herself be lowered back onto the bed. He stripped and lay naked facing her, feeling her yield completely to his stroking movements, as though they literally suborned and enslaved. His fingers were greedy for all her physical beauty and she seemed urgently to demand his touch. All shyness quickly turned into an exultant confidence. He pulled on a sheath. She opened her legs and his sex entered her with a first smooth gliding motion.

The initial eager lubricous thrusts merged into a rhythmic sweetness, into rising gliding delight. They moved together in an increasingly fierce bed-dance, in which the rhythmic creaking of the bed seemed nothing by comparison with the noise of the rain. Everything was governed by the quickening flow of their sexual pleasure. Her sex and his were in harmony, continually fusing in pure sharp riveting joy. They were creating a sexual completeness spreading from leap to surge to rapture. They thrust against each other, she willingly succumbing to the rising ferocity of his movements until, yielding and giving simultaneously, in an explosion of energy, the ecstasy flowed wildly through both and she joined with his own ecstatic crescendo that made him quiver and gasp and laugh in spasms. It was magnificent and idiotic. He withdrew from her gasping and laughing, his ears full of the noise of teeming rain.

VI

Just as if the noisy waterfall of rain had penetrated their lives, they were caught in a literal torrent of love towards each other. In the last few days of their holiday, every moment seemed to acquire an intensity of feeling that made their relationship into a delightful craving. He loved her with a kind of savagery. He felt driven towards her body's passionate feminine strength. She, in turn, with an almost equal ferocity, took him and let all her own suddenly released sensuality encompass him and carry his surge and match him. She became freed from all the constraints that had seemed to enclose her life previously. He recognised this freedom and respected and cherished it.

After the storm the weather of course changed. There was light rain and the beach was deserted. People sat about in cafes and restaurants along the esplanade, the brightly coloured goods sold for the beach, the Disney animals and multicoloured propellers on sticks, the gaudy beach balls all flapped and jiggled sadly outside the beach stalls, the traffic made a swishing noise and the pier music sounded melancholy in its strident emphasis on love. People promenaded up and down the sea front in wet-looking garments. Paradoxically, though, this kind of weather always filled him with a private happiness. It was like the weather of his boyhood. A large part of his recollection of the southern Manchester suburbs was filled with the gentle hush of rainfall and the grey marine tinge that the eastward flowing cloud from the Atlantic brought with it. Now, when they went out for a walk along the esplanade, the light rain beat in his face like a soft spray and he felt he could literally smell the faint odour of coal dust that had always been present in the Manchester rain of his boyhood.

She pined for the hot days and the beach. Though he loved the brightness of her eyes fringed by wet lashes as she smiled towards him through the wetness, he knew it held no real private magic for her. If the colder rainy weather invigorated him, it made her fretful and a little irritable. Once they went out in his car. They drove along the coast for a while with the sea to their left. It looked a sullen layered grey with fringes of white where the waves were breaking and she suddenly demanded he stop. When he reasonably pointed out he couldn't stop on a main road, she grew sulky.

'It's like living in a box!' she cried out. 'I've got nothing against your car or the road or anything, except it reminds me the whole time...'

'Of what?'

'Of Sunday outings. Of being driven about by my father. Of holidays in boxes. Perhaps you never had holidays in boxes.'

'I know what you mean. Only the holidays seemed a lot bigger than boxes when I had them.'

'Rainy holidays. One after another. Then, finally, my parents got the message. We went to Spain.'

'And you lived in a box in Spain?'

'And we lived in a box in Spain. And we flew there in a box with wings, and we drove about in a box with windows.'

'But there was one big difference?'

'Yes, of course there was! You could take the lid off and let the sun in! That was nice. It was a bit like being in a box, though, with a big sun in it.'

'All right, I'll stop. Driving a car is a male supremacist occupation.'

'Why do you say something like that?'

'I don't know. I just thought of it. In any case, there's a car park over there.'

He drew off the road to a headland where other cars were parked. Below them were rocks and the sea and a path down to a beach. She jumped out of the car and flung up her arms in joy. Facing the distant sea, she cried out: 'I love you, I love you!'

'We could go to Spain now,' he said. 'If you wanted to.'

'Just drive off now, you mean, and find an airport somewhere and fly there?'

'Yes.'

'No, I don't want to. This is all right. It's English and cosy. I'd be jealous in Spain. Jealous of the senoritas. I don't have to explain, do I?'

No, she didn't have to explain. If she looked at a man of her own age in a restaurant or walking along the esplanade – and there were plenty of places where young men eyed her and then him and gave the impression of totting up their chances – he had tended to have a sharp spurt of jealous feeling. In the fine rain, after they had got out of the car, he recognised that maybe the whole point of love was to be jealous of the loved one. It was enough: he put his arm round her waist. Together they set off down the slope to the beach. Hardly anyone else was about. They were happy in sight of the sea and the approaching roar of the waves.

Most people had stayed in their cars, it seemed. He kept on wondering about jealousy. Like the soft beat of the on-shore wind on their faces, that splashed her long hair in streaks about her eyes and mouth, jealousy itself seemed to billow from the grey sea as if it were coming from their pasts and seeking to be recognised and admitted. He felt tempted at that moment to tell her about Rachel. The wind and the sea noise might well blow it all away and leave his conscience free. Instead, he found she was confessing before he had the chance.

'There was someone else, Jim dear,' she said. 'Before you. I should have told you.'

'You don't have to,' he murmured, the jealousy inside him louder than the wind and the sea. No fine rain could appease it.

'He was called John. I thought we were going to be married. He's been the only one, though. You've got to believe that. When you talked about the girl you knew as a student...'

He made a gesture, a movement of the hand towards the waves, as though he were disposing of the recollection of Megan, but an uncertainty in his throat made him say nothing for fear of his own dishonesty.

'It was with John. I thought, you see, he was serious.' She paused, trying to control the splashing of her hair. 'But he'd gone off to Canada. I don't know why. I never heard from him. So it was over, completely over.'

'Thank you. You needn't have, you know.'

'I wanted to.'

'I'm glad you did,'

The jealousy evaporated. Her admission created a softening and sweetness between them that was like the touch of the fine rain. He kissed her lightly on the cheek and she turned and offered her mouth and their lips came together in a moist tingling pressure that exposed their love to each other louder than all the waves.

Their holiday drew to a close shortly after. On the Saturday, their last day, sun poured onto the town from dawn onwards. They bathed early, while the tide was far out and the water seemed to be shallow for miles. As he swam slowly in the chilly water, insufficiently warmed as yet by the sun for it to lose that cavernous, icy exhilarant feel of the deeper ocean, he saw the town bright with flashes of sunlight from windows and a burnished grey-green of far hills seeming utterly remote, as distant as a lifetime away and unattainable in its crystal brilliance. A breath-catching, aching sensation of the moment's fugitive happiness swept over him like a shiver from the severe pure coldness of the sea. It stayed with him and recurred at moments throughout the day. Lying together on the sand, the sun holding them both in the hour-glass of its heat so that time made no movement for them, he gazed lovingly at her face and noted with delight the way her fine blonde hair curled about her ear and neck, offering an even finer fan-like shadow to her cheek and the white towel on which she was lying. Children's cries, sea-sounds, gulls, the little irrupting frou-frou of music carried on the breeze, the tinier rustle of clothing or the page of a book moved sharply by some darting eddy of air, and the occasional fly lighting on the skin or buzzing near the face – these were the only separable incidents in the continuum of the heat, save for the sudden aching sensation that flowed over him and made him conscious of losing some infinitely precious thing that he could not identify. Until he knew exactly what it was. Yes, he knew exactly.

He told himself without uttering a word: *You must paint her*! The drawing would not be enough. *I must paint her*! *I must paint her!* he repeated.

****

She would go back to *The Cherries* first. Her readiness to be his nude model was conditional upon that. So for several nights after being in the office he was alone in his apartment in Victoria Mansions. He studied the pictures he had taken, both those related to the pose and others he had taken of her on the beach and at points on their strolls round the town. When she returned, she willingly lay in the same position as she had adopted for his drawing, though now it was in the second bedroom where he had set up his easel and canvas at the foot of the bed. There would be a difference in the pose as in the circumstance, he knew that, but what he did not recognise immediately was how different would be his approach. The old familiar 'apartment' with its virtually permanent, if latent, aroma of turps and oil created for him an environment so different from the dull atmosphere of his office overlooking the Thames that he himself changed, or his personality in some odd way became enlivened, enriched, authoritative as though the painting, the performance of creating on the white canvas, changed him. With the squeezing out of the first coil of paint onto his palette, that special aroma took possession of him and he found a fresh, light vigour entered his brushwork. He had fixed a bedside light so that the whole of her right side became illuminated as in the drawing. It was important for him to get that particular yellowy electric glaze to her skin as nearly as possible without dominating the natural skin tones. He painted with absorption, delighting in the success with which he captured by various means the variations of tint and shade in the colouring.

She had found *The Cherries* as she had left it, just as he had found the Borough offices the same. Although he had been busy with his report, there had been meetings to attend and issues to see to, so that 'work' had been endured for the greater part of the day. He had waited for her return to have these evening sessions of painting, although she always resumed her earlier habit of going back to her shared flat each night despite his quite daring suggestion that she could stay in the apartment if she wished.

'When you painted the others,' she asked rather naughtily, 'did you make love to them as well?'

He went on painting for a while before he answered. 'No, of course not. The relationship had to be formal and completely professional.'

'So if you make love to your model, it's better for you, is that right? I mean you're likely to make a better painting?'

'If I love my model, as of course I do, I would naturally hope... yes, hope...'

'What?'

'Hope to do better.'

These were questions that had been raised more than once with Stanley Worthington. Mostly, and quite justifiably, they had been dismissed as pointless and irrelevant. There were no rules. Was there even any truth to didacticism in art? Did he, or could he, try to achieve a certain infection of the viewer with the original emotion that he as a painter had experienced? And if that experience were love? He had to acknowledge that the true effectiveness of visual art depended to a great extent on the rather naïve Tolstoyan idea of artistic contagion, but he was never sure exactly what that meant.

'I try to express the love I feel, yes. I try to bring tenderness and lyricism and clarity to the way I use paint. Tell me that I'm now sounding pompous.'

'Jim Nordon, you're sounding pompous!' she cried and jumped off the bed. She joined him in surveying what he had done. Her mouth lengthened into an appraising and gradually approving smile. 'Jim darling, it makes me feel… well, I know it's me and I should be flattered. But because it's me, you know, I feel a bit ashamed. When people see it, they'll know at once you've painted me naked.'

'You don't like it?'

'Oh, I think it's good! Like the drawing! I know you've only just started. There's an obvious likeness, though. You've got my look.'

'So if I finish it, will you have it?'

'Oh, no! You must keep it! Where would I put it? I couldn't take it home! Keep it here with the others!'

He considered the painting again. Even though it was in its early stages, he felt he had started right. On the other hand, he had never before been faced with this personal problem of not knowing why he was doing it. He covered it over and collected up his palette and brushes with the intention of cleaning them. As he turned to use the basin, he inadvertently glanced at her and couldn't help noticing how vulnerable she appeared both in her nakedness and in the look she gave him.

'Jim,' she asked, 'you are serious, aren't you?'

'I am.'

'How serious?'

She began quickly dressing. It unnerved him to be asked such a direct question. He knew the answer or thought he did.

'As serious as I can be.' Was he lying to himself? He had already sorted out a number of possibilities – sharing the apartment in Victoria Mansions, marriage, life as a painter, having to move – none of which he had taken seriously. At that moment they liquefied into an irrational swill of phobias and doubts. 'As serious as I can be,' he repeated, not looking directly at her.

She wrestled with her dress as she put it on and he lifted the cover and looked again at the painting. There she was looking at him from the dark background of the bed, with the light shining on her right side and on her left the thin halo of lighter tints that merged with and was scarcely inseparable from the looming far blankness of the bedroom wall. The innocence, vulnerability and trust in his portrayal struck him forcefully. He could not bring himself to face the painting and turned instead to the window.

'I love you,' he said.

'Say it to me,' she said behind him.

He turned round and looked in her face. She was looking at him so eagerly, he almost winced from the thrust of her gaze.

'How should I love you?' he asked. 'I should love you royally. I should love you obediently and with honour. I should love you selflessly, steadfastly, graciously. I should love you with all my heart. I should love you more than I can ever love anyone.'

Her expression became one of simple amazement. She rushed to him and held him. He naturally put down the palette and brushes as he felt her give a shudder in his arms.

'What is it?' He saw tears in her eyes.

'Oh, I've been so silly,' she said. 'I've been silly, terribly, unforgivably silly.'

VII

They had remained discreetly apart during working hours. Faced by the severity of Charles Ball's eyes sloped towards him over the rim of reading spectacles, Jim found himself reverting to type. He had trained himself over the years to close his mind to everything except the task at hand. The preparation of the report involved studying files, checking back on policy decisions, calculating literal savings in one instance, forecasting possible areas of difficulty in other instances and then looking at the broader implications of what soon appeared to be not simply a process of retrenchment as a fundamental change. He was absorbed by the task. Each evening, reflecting on his day's work, he felt appalled at the ease with which he had reverted to type and let his job take precedence.

Precedence, that is to say, over his relations with Sally. He could almost hear the sound of Dave's boisterous, taunting laughter. Often enough, of course, Dave had kidded him about his abstention from sex, but quickly enough sex now became a staple of his life. He had grown used to the small egoisms and indulgences of bachelorhood during Dave's absence in vacation time. They included the arrangement with Rachel of course, discreetly as private as possible, certainly not a subject to be discussed with Dave. No, now that Sally shared his bed he found himself facing a different problem. Too much of the relationship felt like marriage, but he enjoyed it as she did, except that he found himself having to suppress little spurts of annoyance at her untidiness. 'It's a reaction against Mum's mania for tidiness,' she explained, charming away his fussy little objections. She had moved into the apartment within a matter of days after the modelling had started, having had a disagreement with her principal flat-mate over her contribution to rental and utility costs. He soon accepted her light-hearted, untidy ways and was secretly more bothered by the morality of their shared life than the practical side of it.

'Of course we're living in sin!' she exclaimed once almost with delight. 'My father'd tell you that at once. He knows all about what's right and wrong. Except , you know, I'm not a fool, Jim dear.'

He knew that over sex her apparent lack of care – or untidiness – was no more than a front. She had told him that because she had had some trouble with period pains she was taking the pill on doctor's advice. More to the point in his opinion was the fact that she was someone who liked taking risks. Her impulsiveness towards him was a symptom of her impulsive reaction towards many things. There was also the quite convenient fact that her parents remained on holiday – they planned to be away the whole of July – and Sally balanced her father's sternness with her mother's quoted advice that 'You must get to know the person you're going to marry.'

Jim accepted the advice, knowing he had better reasons for accepting it than she had, since her own self-confidence secretly astonished him. She talked quite frankly about the need to live together, to test each other, *to be sure*, as if she were reading his thoughts. It was also on her insistence that he paid his regular weekly visits to Stanley Worthington's special art class and discussed with Stanley the possibility of setting up as an artist, a portraitist, on his own. Her confidence in him tended to reveal to him more starkly than ever his own lack of self-confidence. If he renewed his faith in his ability to love someone, as he did the more he knew Sally, he still found it hard to think of his painting as more than a therapy. For that reason he put aside his work on the portrait of her in the nude. In a cowardly way he preferred for the time being to do what he had to do, in fulfilment of Charles Ball's Machiavellian designs. Though he discussed the possibility of change, he knew in the depth of his heart that the basic insecurity remained, just as he could hardly let himself believe completely in the permanence of the happiness that Sally's presence always gave him.

Perhaps he drank a little more than he should have done. The summer weather came with heat most days and the apartment tended to bake under the sun's day-long cooking. On their return from the offices on the embankment, the first essential thing was a drink. As for Sally, she made it clear she was staying only so long as her parents were on holiday. After that she would have to find somewhere else. Why? Because… Because she did not know how well her mother was. Because she had been getting rather worrying phone calls from Torquay. And if, *if*, well, her mother needed looking after, she'd have to go to *The Cherries*, she really would, she owed it to them.

'I owe it to Mum,' she explained, as if that was all she needed to say. 'I really do.'

Okay, so for that time away, she admitted, she would not enjoy the sex that he offered, the loving intimacy, the way he made her come, the sheer splendour of that frankness, that excitement. Then, on a Friday evening toward the end of July, when he was lying naked beside her, the doorbell rang. He knew it was unwise to make love so early in the evening. In any case, he felt slightly drunk. She did nothing but lie beside him and make a face. He pulled on casual trousers, a shirt and bathrobe. The gong-like tinkle was repeated by the time he was in the hallway.

'Oh, Jim, I can see I've disturbed you. Were you about to take a bath?'

'As a matter of fact I was.'

Mrs Dora Pratts-Morris, who stood in the doorway of his apartment dressed in a formal summer garment that had flowers on it and straps over bare shoulders, gave an understanding smile.

'I won't keep you a moment. If I may just have a word with you?'

She had a lien on Jim's time and attention because she had been one of his sitters, an occupant of another flat in the same building and an admirer of his work. On her insistence, he had painted her in an evening dress. She had been an excellent sitter and hers had been one of his best portraits. They had become good friends.

'Well, you know, I…'

'If it's not convenient, I can call by later this evening, after you've had a bath.'

'No, I, er… I can postpone the bath. I was only taking one because it's so hot.'

'Oh, it *is* hot, isn't it? I've been out in the Square most of the afternoon in one of those deck chairs.'

Jim was naturally worried about Sally's presence, but he knew that fact was unlikely to be concealed for long from other occupants. 'I have someone staying with me,' he said, showing Dora Pratts-Morris into the main room. 'And Mrs Rogers, as you know, is on holiday. For this reason, well…'

'Oh, I know how it is. I often have people parking themselves on me in the summer. All kinds of relatives come up from the country in the summer and think I run a sort of rest home for hay fever sufferers or victims of backache from too much strawberry picking. Why they should imagine London is an oasis of peace and quiet in the summer, I can't think. So I know exactly what you mean when you say you have someone staying with you.'

Having launched herself into this monologue, she had reached the main room and with a little squeal accepted the whisky on rocks that Jim poured for her and for himself.

'So nice, thank you so much. I really mustn't stay long. What I wanted to ask you was a favour.' She took the glass of whisky, held it towards him in gratitude and sipped. 'Yes, a favour. I'll pay, mind. Can you, do you think, do another portrait of me? It's not really for me but for my brother in California. He was so envious of the one you did before – he came over here on a short visit a fortnight ago but you were away and I've been away since, so... I was saying, he was envious of the one you did before, the one I've got down in my flat, and he asked me to get you to do another, so he could have it in his home in California. He lives in – oh, what's it called? Pacific...Pacific something. Pacific Pallisades, something like that. It overlooks the ocean. It's a lovely place. So that's why I wanted to catch you this evening, if I could.'

Dora Pratts-Morris was a widow. Her father had left her a good deal of money, which was supplemented by her own private income from investments and the ownership of family mineral rights in the Far West. Her face was broad, fresh-skinned, classic in its features, with the defiantly informal look that ladies of the eighteenth-century English landed gentry seemed to possess as a natural defence against sophistication. She liked Jim because he was talented and prepared to make his portrait of her flatter that essentially youthful 'county' look. But she was also fond of him with that rejuvenating gladness which aunts may feel towards young nephews. They may not meet often but when they do they usually succeed in showing delighted mutual interest in each other's activities – for an hour or so, perhaps, or an evening or a weekend, never much longer. And the wise aunt never seeks to prolong the pleasure, nor does she ever reveal how really deep is her pleasure in rediscovering her youthfulness in his company.

'I don't know whether I'll be able to do another painting all that soon,' he said.

'There isn't any hurry, there really isn't any hurry. In the autumn some time, when it isn't so hot and there aren't the temptations to be out of doors so often. That would be all right. I simply wanted to let him know you would be willing. He's such a busy person. He's off to somewhere in South America on business tomorrow, so his email said, and not sure when he'd be back. If it could be a kind of Christmas present, that would be perfect.'

There were distinct noises from a bedroom. Sally had dropped something and had then banged a drawer. Dora Pratts-Morris knew the layout of the apartment sufficiently well to recognise that the sounds could only come from his bedroom.

'Are you doing another one?' she asked.

He was not quite sure what she meant. For all he knew she had probably discovered long ago that he had been painting nudes. He suspected, though, she did not know anything about Sally.

'Another one?'

'I was wondering whether you might perhaps have another sitter... How stupid of me! I had quite forgotten you said you had a friend staying with you.'

She was utterly unconvincing, but shrewd enough to realise she couldn't fool him. In literally a few seconds while the ice clinked in both their glasses and both drank to fill the silence, he knew she had begun to suspect that this was no 'friend', no 'sitter'.

'I've not been painting portraits recently, you know.'

'Oh.'

'No, I'm painting nudes.'

'Nudes. I see.'

She raised her eyebrows and moved her head slightly in a give-away of surprise that she tried to turn into a look of understanding and admiration of the difficulties of such painting.

'Yes, the female nude. I started by copying from reproductions, but now I find that I have to have real models.

I can't get the real natural skin tones unless I have a living model.'

He hurriedly drank most of his whisky and felt the ice tumble from the bottom of his glass against his lips.

'I suppose you prefer to have young models?'

He should have known her well enough to expect her to ask such a question, but he was taken by surprise. He showed it in an awkward: 'Will you have another?'

'No, I've still got plenty, thank you.'

He tipped more whisky into his glass. 'Yes, I, er... Naturally I prefer young models, but I imagine that a well-preserved lady like yourself, Dora...'

'Really, really, no, I wasn't meaning...'

'You'd prefer the old jewels and tiara, I'd imagine. I could do you in an off-the-shoulder evening dress if you like. You've got good shoulders, you know.'

'Really, Jim, my dear man, I shouldn't dream...' There was hidden laughter in her rebuke. 'No, I'd want one like the one you've already done. The sort of thing that can be hung on a perfectly respectable wall in a perfectly respectable home in Southern California. They're still very conservative people out there, you know.'

'Difficult, that.'

'Oh dear.'

He reflected a moment. Sweat was breaking out strongly on his forehead and round his neck. A pleasant, but not strong, blurring sensation was seeping through his awareness of reality and making him feel hot and bold.

'You see, Dora dear, I think my painting has entered a new phase. I've been thinking quite seriously of giving up my job and becoming a painter, doing portraits full time. It's rather as if I've become honest, do you know what I mean? I've begun to move from the face and clothes to the real naked person beneath all the trappings. It's like the animals in *Animal Farm*, they had to be naked, no ribbons or decorations, do you know what I mean? No ribbons. My ribbons are my job, but I'd like to cast them off, make my own revolution like the animals. It's a new thing for me and it's exciting. For instance, I might have to insist in doing you with bare shoulders. If you're not prepared to reveal any more.'

'Jim, my dear man, of course I'm not prepared!'

'A pity, that.'

'You've changed, I can see that. But if you're having a revolution like the animals…'

'No, not a real revolution, no, no, but I may be changing…'

'Yes, you're changing,' she agreed.

'You're probably right,' he agreed in turn.

'You're much more urbane,' she said. She gave the "urbane" an emphasis so resonant of daring and masculine suavity that the poor word, overladen with such heavy meaning, sounded quite flat and shy of itself. 'Pardon my mentioning it,' she added quickly, 'I think you're letting your drink get the better of you. Ever so slightly the better. So you don't think you'll be able to do another. Oh!'

At that moment Sally sashayed into the room in a sarong-type garment that she'd recently bought from an eastern import store. She looked fresh, for her suntan hadn't faded, and her hair, brushed out into sparkling tresses, fell in a light cascade down to her shoulders. He jumped to his feet.

'This is Sally-Anne. Mrs Pratts-Morris. Dora. Dora lives in this building and I did a portrait of her about a year ago.'

'How very nice to meet you,' said Sally in an over-polite voice that ever so slightly parodied itself.

'I'm delighted,' said Dora Pratts-Morris.

'Sally is modelling for me,' said Jim in a hurry.

'Oh, are you?'

'I wouldn't say I'm modelling exactly.'

'No, I shouldn't say that. She's not modelling exactly.'

'I think,' said Sally in elaboration of what Jim was saying, 'I'm more a helpmate, a friend…'

'Yes, I think that's better, much better... A whisky?'

'I will,' said Sally. 'Hot, isn't it? Thank you.'

'Oh, awfully hot,' said Dora. 'How I envy you being able to wear a sarong! I'm afraid I just wouldn't look right in a sarong.'

'It's nice to get into something that's almost the same as having nothing on at all.'

'How right! I know exactly what you mean.'

There was a repetition of the gong-like sound at the end of the hallway. The two women looked at Jim who was standing more or less between them.

'I think I'd better go and see what that is,' he said.

Dora Pratts-Morris was on the point of explaining that she felt she ought to be going because she was sure... But what she was sure about, Jim didn't wait to hear and he hurried into the hallway out of earshot.

'Jim, how are you?'

'Sam!'

'Yes, it is me. I am.'

This was a rhyming joke that instantly evoked for Jim a smell of soap and joint bath-times in the south Manchester bathroom of their home. His first impression of his brother, whom he hadn't seen since just after Christmas, was one of sheer age. Sam's thin, long, patient face had grown considerably more lined and the perspiration beading his forehead where his hair had receded suggested so much strenuous expenditure of effort, leaving such a greyish tinge to his cheeks, that Jim wondered for a moment whether he might have something seriously wrong with him.

'You're looking well...'

'I'm not looking well,' said Sam.

'No, I meant...'

'I'm exhausted by climbing up all the stairs. I couldn't get your lift to work.'

'It's capricious, I'm afraid.'

'That's about the only privilege age had left to it. Am I going to be invited in?'

'Yes, yes, of course. You're not all that old, Sam, are you?'

He reflected momentarily that he and Sam were hardly likely to share the same bath with any pleasure now. Sam had a bony look about him.

'I'm exhausted by heat and your stairs. That's the only reason I may be showing my age a bit. I can hear you've got some people...'

'Yes, I have. Can I ask whether you've come for any special reason?'

'I've come because our mother's not heard from you for about two months. No one's heard from you, in fact. And I had to come and see someone down at Lincoln's Inn Fields.'

Sam had their mother's curiosity, their father's role-playing mannerisms and his own sweet-and-sour, warm-hearted, put-upon view of things. He never really resented being used by others, but he liked to give a spurious effect of quasi-independence and thus ensure he wasn't completely taken for granted. But if there was ever any overstepping of the mark in a moral sense – that is, if what was asked of him perhaps exploited or humiliated – Sam had refused, stubbornly refused, with rock-like firmness. He was his brother's slave out of fondness and not by right. Jim naturally respected this instinct for moral integrity in his brother. Sam understood more surely than anyone could adequately define what 'privacy of the individual' meant.

'Sam,' said Jim, 'I think I ought to tell you. I've got a girl with me.'

'Without benefit of the law, you mean? It's about time.'

'Yes, I mean that.'

'There's no need to look so contrite. What our mother would like to know is, just as I'd like to know – when will the law be allowed to play its part? You can legalise relationships, you know.'

'Of course I know that.'

Jim led his bother into the main room where he found Dora and Sally standing on either side of the Edwardian *art nouveau* fireplace. They had obviously been exchanging intimate details between them and held fresh glasses of whisky. He introduced his brother.

'I never knew,' said Dora. 'What a dark horse the dear man's turned out to be. Are you really his brother?'

'Sam, that's me. Sam, I am.'

'That's how you normally introduce yourself – Sam I am?'

'Yes. It's a joke we had as boys.'

'You know, this evening's become so full of revelations!' Dora exclaimed.

'How do you do? I'm Sally,' said Sally and shook hands with Sam. 'Not Sally I am, but just Sally.' Jim had told her about his brother but could not remember exactly what. Sam wouldn't release the handshake at once and Sally, faintly colouring from the curious look she received, smiled, saying:

'Jim told me you'd do anything he asked. Is that right?'

'That may have been true back in the time when we were both boys together, but now I take my time about doing things. Any road, he's not calling the tune now.'

The 'any road' seemed to Jim an unnecessary northernism on Sam's part. The homeliness of Sam's whole attitude towards Sally seemed to be taking far too many things for granted, and he protested.

'No, no, I wasn't hinting anything at all. I just meant it's my wife who calls the tune in our family and that's how it seems to work in most families, in my experience. No, I won't have any whisky, if you don't mind. I'd rather have a beer.'

Jim had to go into the kitchen to get a can of beer from the fridge. While he was there, loud laughter came from both the ladies at something Sam had said. Then there was more laughter. There was only one can of beer in the fridge. Jim unzipped it and poured the frothy blond liquid into a glass. Just as the head of the froth promised to trickle over the brim, he heard shuffling footsteps in the hallway and Sally came in.

'I'm not going to be left alone in there while the two of them tell dirty jokes.'

'They're not telling dirty jokes!'

'I think they think they're dirty.'

'I didn't know Sam knew any.'

'Jim?'

'Yes?'

'You haven't told anyone, have you? I know you hadn't told Mrs Pratts-Morris.'

'I'm not sure what exactly I hadn't told her?'

She smiled and sighed and leaned back against the such modest wall space as there was in the kitchen in a movement that inelegantly made her stomach stick out, filling out the sarong as if she were pregnant. The garment accentuated the youthful, girlish suppleness of her figure in a sexily quite explicit way.

'I think I'll have to tell my parents,' she said.

'Why not? Why not? We needn't have any secrets.'

'But what am I going to tell them?'

She had turned her eyes sideways to look at him and he noticed how brilliant the whites looked against the darker colouring of her complexion.

'Tell them we're going to get married.'

She didn't react to this remark. He knew how glib it sounded. They had talked about marriage more than once before. He had tried to be as objective as possible. Then, as now, and at any other time, he supposed, there was only one marriage that he had tried to talk about objectively – his own, which he thought he had already interred for ever.

'You're just kidding, you know that,' she said in soft voice.

After a burst of laughter from Dora, they heard Sam say:

'Did you hear the one about the two astronauts? Well, there were these two astronauts...'

'I'm not kidding,' he said.

She turned her eyes back towards him again.

'Do you know something? I got put off young men of my own age because John – you remember I told you about John – he couldn't stand up to my father.'

'So I've got to stand up to your father?'

'I think you ought to meet them.'

'Of course I ought to. And I will tell them I want to marry you.'

Sam had finished, it seemed. There was another sharp trill of laughter. Then there was silence. Jim and Sally knew they had to stop lurking in the kitchen.

****

'To stand up to her father.'

He wondered what she meant by this. It was unreal to think that a father could have the lawful power to prevent his daughter marrying when she was over eighteen. There might be circumstances, but clearly they were unlikely to apply in this case, or so he assumed. Of course, the father could wield some kind of emotional authority over his only daughter and for an only daughter the pressure exerted by family loyalties, especially her love for her mother, would be strong, as he knew it was in Sally's case, much stronger than his mother's influence over him, for instance.

Any such explanation always met the simple response in his scrutiny of it: Why bother to stand up to anyone? You're free. And immediately he would be bound to admit that he wasn't as free as he imagined. Are you free to get married, Jim Nordon? he would ask himself. Will you take Miss Sally-Anne Harris to be your lawful wife? Are you prepared for that much responsibility? He couldn't be sure. At once his mother's emotional sway, the fear of repeating what had happened with Vicky and the habit of bachelorhood forced him to acknowledge that he wasn't free. In addition, if he couldn't trust himself to do what he most wanted, which was to be an artist full time, devoted to painting portraits, how could he trust himself to make any responsible decision? Secretly, largely out of cowardice, he was bound to admit, he had always assumed there was a certain inevitability about life-changing decisions. They were either made for you or you became involved in them and they left you no choice.

Her parents returned from their holiday at the end of July. The first he learned about it, in a direct sense, was when the phone rang one evening (Sally was in the bath) and a girl's voice asked rather hesitantly whether there was someone there called Miss Harris. It was the first time anyone had phoned for her since she had moved in because he had assumed she always used her smartphone for personal calls.

'There is,' he said.

'Your phone number got put on a pad by this phone, that's why I'm ringing. She's called Sally-Anne, isn't she?'

'Yes.'

'Perhaps you'd give her a message.'

'Yes.'

'Her father rang up here a few minutes ago. He said they're back from their holiday and he wanted to know where she was. I had to tell him she wasn't here. And I didn't know where she was.' The girl's voice paused. 'Are you sure she's there?'

'Yes, she's here. Is that the message?'

'Yes. Except he also said something about not wanting to disturb her mother. Do you want me to tell her father, if he rings back, that she's there?'

'No.'

'I see.'

'Thanks very much for letting me know.'

'You *are* Jim, aren't you?'

'Yes. I suppose my name's there?'

'Yes. And there's a heart with an arrow through it. And some blood.'

'Will you do something.'

'What?'

'Destroy it!'

The girl laughed and put down the receiver. He tapped on the bathroom door where Capital Radio was loudly advertising Japanese cars. He received no response so he pushed open the door and the music blare of a new pop song replaced the advertiser's cajoling voice. He told Sally what he had learned.

She was sitting on a stool, naked, with legs crossed and paring her nails, making little sharp to-and-fro movements. Her back was half-turned towards him in the doorway. He could not fail to notice the curving lines, almost painted, where the pinkness of unsunned skin met the coppery health of her suntan. She moved herself a little towards him without uncrossing her legs, simply by turning on the stool. Shaking back her hair, she stretched out an arm to end the radio noise and looked faintly puzzled.

'Did she say who she was?'

'No.'

'Maybe it's a new girl they've got to replace me. I did leave your name, true. But I don't remember drawing a bleeding heart.'

'That's what she said.'

She sighed rather dramatically. 'You know what?'

'What?'

'Once he finds I'm not there he'll start going round there and asking questions and whoever that girl is won't find her life worth living until she tells him your telephone number and eventually comes here and demands to know what your intentions are. So that's just for starters.'

'Oh, but he can't!'

'You don't know my father! Oh, yes, he can!' She waved the little nail file about in the air. 'He actually got on to the police and the local hospital once when I was late getting back from John's. He's worse than the Mafia. He practically makes boyfriends pay him protection money.'

He resented being classed as a boyfriend and said so.

'Oh. Jim, I don't mean you! I was joking. Hand me a towel and give me a kiss.'

She pouted her lips out to him and he kissed their heart-shaped cluster. The scent of powder from her body drenched him.

'So you want me to stand up to him?' he said.

'You'll stand up to him all right, I know that.' She stood up and wrapped the towel efficiently round her right up to the armpits. 'Mum rang me to say they'd be coming back either today or tomorrow. She used her own smartphone, but he hasn't got one. They're too new-fangled for him. So that's why he used the landline and rang the only number he could find. But that girl, she didn't tell him this number, did she?'

'No, I told her to destroy it.'

'Let's hope she does! But Mum knows I'm staying with you, though she doesn't know your phone number. Anyhow...,' she flung the nail file into the small cupboard above the basin. It was full of her things – soaps, bubble bath stuff, hand cream, toothpaste, talc, a *ladyshave* – and he had to scrabble each morning amongst all of them to find his shaver. She closed the cupboard door on the inner disarray and for an instant his own face shone mistily back at him in the steamed-over mirror on the door-front. 'Anyhow, I know what I must do. I must arrange for them to meet you. We'll go down to *The Cherries* for lunch one day. How does that suit you?'

He followed her into the bedroom.

'I'd be delighted to meet your parents. Of course I would. But on a weekend.'

She said nothing. Instead she sat down in front of the dressing-table, stared straight into the mirror and began vigorously brushing her hair.

'You know that,' he insisted.

'I know how polite you can be, Jim dear. Of course I do. What more do I know?'

'What do you mean?'

She restarted her vigorous brushing. 'Who do I tell them you are?'

'I thought they knew.'

'You're my boss. Yes, they know that. What else are you?'

'Can I be your fiancé?'

'Are you? Really?'

'Yes, I am.'

'So that's what I'll tell them? Jim Nordon, my fiancé. Okay?'

She stopped brushing and raised her eyes to his as they were reflected in the mirror.

'Yes, of course.'

The acknowledgement made him feel cold. She said nothing, simply started her vigorous brushing again. Her eyes weren't raised to his in the mirror and he looked down at her slim back, tightly and smoothly wrapped in the towel. Her body had a firm, well-defined look, particularly when it was naked or covered by nothing more than a sarong or a bikini. It had a natural young dignity, a feminine wholeness and neatness, that made her look sure, in a defiant way, of her independence and demonstrably certain of her rights.

'Is he going to talk about doing the honourable thing by you?' he asked. 'Is that what I should expect?'

'Dad doesn't talk like that.'

'How's he talk then?'

'He'll probably call you "young man" – it's a sort of upstaging way he's got. Then he'll probably tell you straight out you'd better marry me or he'll fetch his gun down.'

'Has he a gun to fetch down?'

'Yes, I think he has.' She flung the brush down among the mass of face creams, antiperspirants, deodorants, hair sprays and so on that littered the dressing-table. 'Do I get dressed now or go to bed? What's the time?'

They went to bed. The next day she rang her parents. It was arranged that they would go down to Guildford the following Sunday for lunch. Before that she invoked the 'arrangement' that permitted her to skip office work if her mother was unwell. She returned to *The Cherries* for half the following week before coming home to Victoria Mansions in time to act as Jim's guide for the lunch visit.

Her absence was permitted and understandable. He knew she had to smooth over such worries and annoyances that *The Cherries* might have before their arrival. None of that could be done satisfactorily unless she was there in person. 'I *must* be there,' she had pointed out in justification of the 'arrangement' and absence from work. To calm her father's anxieties and likely hostility was her natural priority, but she was more worried by her mother's apparent enthusiasm at meeting the 'famous' Mr Nordon, about whom she had heard so much, all of which, as Sally suspected, merely concealed her readiness to suffer her own heart problem as quietly as possible.

Jim accepted these needs. Since he was reaching the end of his report, he felt the equally pressing need to consult with Donald Holmes, for instance, on certain issues they had discussed at the conference. At the same time he was surprised to learn from Stanley Worthington that his art centre was keen to recruit someone with administrative experience to organise art matters after a previous appointee in the job had suddenly resigned. At the same time, of course, Sally's absence became more and more noticeable in the apartment. He could not call out to her or hear her laugh. He cooked himself ready meals and drank a bit too much whisky and studied the unfinished nude still fixed on the easel. Words exchanged over the phone tended to reinforce him in the conviction that the nude painting would never be as good as his drawing, so as he listened to her softly spoken indictment of her father's fussiness and her mother's refusal to talk about her weak heart he came to the final conclusions that he ought to scrap the painting completely. Which he did.

It became August. London was full of tourists. It was a dry-as-dust subject of conversation in the staff canteen, as dry and dusty as the London pavements and parks. The water features in Russell Square were one of the few instances of freshness in the dry-as-dust metropolis. Pigeons took refuge in the water's silvery spray, preening themselves and hopping about, only to swoop away as dogs chased them. Rising prices, weekend demos, sex scandals, poor harvests of this or that, statistics on the world's undernourished, the Israel-Palestine on-going confrontation along with unrest in the Middle East were a summer lightning on the skyline of Jim Nordon's consciousness. He assimilated such facts as he could believe but felt no wiser. His feelings for Sally and their growing complexity were in the foreground of his world. They had all the massive, imponderable grandeur of encroaching thunder clouds.

The Sunday was hot, part of a bank-holiday weekend, and the A3 to Guildford was therefore crowded. He liked to drive fast whenever he could and was always frustrated by the processional dignity of holiday traffic. He had wanted to be punctual since Sally had said her father could fuss like mad over unpunctuality, but a traffic snarl-up at the first Guildford junction off the A3 meant a delay of twenty minutes. It gave a nicely honed edge to his temper. Guided by Sally, he found *The Cherries* without difficulty and parked beside it.

A neat, between-wars, semi-detached house, it had artificial black Tudor-style woodwork that laced together whitewashed pebbledash with brickwork at ground level. The windows had diamond-shaped leaded lights. In the upper sections of the bay window at the front there were even little stained glass inserts of leaves and roses. The front garden was dominated by two trees ('flowering cherries' as Sally pointed out rather proudly, hence the name), an ornamental brick front wall and a circular rose bed surrounded by a small front lawn. A tarred curving path led to the front door and a similarly tarred driveway ran along the side of the house to a car parked in front of a garage at the back.

Suddenly, looking at Sally seated beside him the moment he parked, her head turned to show him the house, he felt a recurrence of his own childhood and adolescence, not to mention his marriage, the same similar, though not identical, semi-detached shapes linked to one another with the inexorability of paired, bonded individuals, male-female, sex to sex. You could imagine from the outside the rough shapes and relationships of the rooms in all the houses, the roughly familiar, encrusted smells in each room, the roughly similar noises of footsteps on stairs, of doors being closed., people talking downstairs, the myriad secret muffled furtive noises from bedrooms, of noises made strange and eerie in sickness or when rain fell against windows or leaves were scattered like noisy mice along the street. Then there were the times in adolescence when it seemed the house ached with the furtive secrets of your sexuality and you were maddened by the compulsion to masturbate and you would manufacture fantasy after fantasy about the girl down the street in a house like your own, that you'd never been inside but could easily invade, and she'd wonder at your laden organ and then smile and yield.

'Come on,' Sally said, 'we'd better go in. I've told you I've got a plan about this visit.'

She was wearing a smart summer dress he had bought for her in an Oxford Street boutique. It gave her a suave and lissom appearance that was reinforced by high heels. A total effect of near-Ascot perfection was achieved that she slightly overplayed by assuming the nonchalance of an 'old' girl returning for a prize-giving ceremony. Naughtily he noticed but did not mention that the pleats of the skirt were crushed about her bottom from so much sitting in the car.

'My dear,' exclaimed a grey-haired lady in a short-sleeved flower-print dress, putting her arms round Sally and kissing her the moment the front door was opened, 'I'm so glad you've got here. I was beginning to get worried. You said midday but it's now close to half past.'

'It was the traffic.'

'Yes, I thought it must be.'

'This is Jim. My mother. And Mum dear, can this be put in the fridge.' She handed over a bottle-shaped carrier bag.

'Yes, I'll do that. You shouldn't, you know. How nice to meet you, Jim.'

He kissed her on powdered cheeks. She gave a little laugh of embarrassment. Despite her slightly suntanned complexion, Sally's mother had the puffy, drawn look of someone in poor health. The worried and vulnerable gaze that she directed at Jim told him at once how right Sally had been to worry on her mother's behalf. But there was another feeling beneath the vulnerability, one of inquiry ready in the instant to burst through the tightly disciplined politeness of her greeting.

'We've been so anxious to meet you. May I call you Jim? Yes, well I'm Eleanor. Sally has been saying so much about you, you see. Oh, yes, and I'll put this in the fridge in a moment.' She held up the bottle-shaped carrier-bag. 'For one thing, staying at your place in London, we've heard about you being a painter.' Then she contradicted herself. 'Or perhaps I've got it wrong. You *want* to be a painter, that's it, isn't it?'

'Mother, we can talk about it all later,' Sally said,

'Yes, yes, of course we can. Oh, please come in. So silly of me to keep you both here without inviting you in.' She gave another little laugh of embarrassment. 'Your father's in the garden. Does Jim know, er, that your father doesn't like it when people…'

Sally kissed her mother and hugged her protectively.

'Mum doesn't like it,' she explained to Jim, 'that's what she really means, when people talk about her health to Dad.'

'No, I wouldn't, of course,' said Jim, overcome by momentary nervousness at the complexities of etiquette in the Harris household.

'He'll probably mention it himself, then it'll be all right,' said Eleanor, smiling as if that likelihood solved everything. 'Do come inside. Isn't it hot today?'

'It's very hot,' Jim agreed.

'The car was stifling in the traffic jam,' Sally was saying as they entered the porch.

'Oh dear, you were in a traffic jam,' her mother said.

'Yes, that's why we're late.'

'We're having drinks in the garden,' her mother said. 'It's nice to be able to enjoy the garden, I think.'

'Very nice,' Jim agreed.

The hallway with its polished linoleum and gong on a carved table and pictures tapping lightly against the wall in a through breeze was cool and, despite the fact that windows and doors were open, contained as if stoppered in a bottle the raincoaty, faintly pungent, dust-rich, polish-waxy smell of such places. They went down a passage beside the stairs and into the dining-room with French windows opening onto a small stone terrace. Steps from the terrace led to a lawn, some rockery, an artificial fibre-glass pool in which an electric fountain jetted up a pencil of water and apple trees, offering pleasant shade, where an almost bald man in shirt sleeves and spectacles was sitting in a garden chair and rose when he saw them coming.

'Glad to see you,' Herbert Harris said, extending a hand, smiling only to the extent of the extended hand, as if little beyond his reach was deserving of his smile. 'You're late, you know.'

They explained about the traffic.

'Traffic! Traffic! I keep on saying to Eleanor, there are far too many cars about these days. So, anyhow, you're here. What'll you have to drink?' He waved his hand round an array of sherry, white wine, cider and gin. 'And I'll tell you one thing, which is to my mind among the most ironic things that's ever happened to this country. I suppose you'll have a sherry, Sally-Anne.'

'I'd like a gin.'

'I think it'll be a sherry.'

'I'd like a gin, please.'

He pursed his lips. 'As I was saying, the most ironic thing that's ever happened to this country is that its most eminent seat of learning. What'll you have?' He had turned to Jim.

'Cider, please.'

'It's dry, you won't mind, will you?'

'No. I like dry cider.'

'The other stuff's muck. I quite agree with you.'

'Dad,' said Sally, 'my gin. Please.'

He passed her the gin bottle and a bottle of tonic. 'Its most eminent seat of learning.'

'Herbert dear,' said Eleanor.

'What, my dear?'

'You haven't poured Mr Nordon's cider.'

'All right, I know that.'

'I just didn't want you to get carried away with one of your stories before everyone's been given a drink, that's all.'

'Right. I will give everyone a drink. Your cider, young man. Sherry for you, my dear. Sally-Anne has... Are we all set now?'

'Yes, dear, thank you very much.'

'I just wanted to say, in that case, that one of the most ironic things that's ever happened to this country... You know... dammit...'

'What, my dear?'

'It's gone clean out of my mind, clean out of my mind... That's one of the things that happen to me since my retirement. I simply...'

'Oh, you'll probably remember it later, my dear. It's always like that, I find. I remember a thing, then it suddenly slips my mind, and the next thing is I've just left the shop or wherever I've been when I suddenly remember it and give a little shout: Cream Cheese! Or Parmesan! Parmesan!'

'I find I simply can't remember names. Since I've retired I simply can't remember names properly.'

'Luckily it's never really serious. I've never really been troubled by it, you know.'

They seated themselves.

'Mum,' Sally said, 'do tell Jim about the holiday.'

'Well, we had a very nice holiday. It was warm practically the whole time. I'm not very fond of Torquay, but I quite like it. Mary, that's Herbert's sister, has a large-ish house, so there was no problem in that way, but she's always so busy with her little activities, her charity work and things like that, which means you've got to fend for yourself a lot, you know, but I didn't mind that. She'd leave some cold meat for us and I'd boil up potatoes and some vegetables and that sort of thing. There was a nice woman who came in to do all the dusting and some of the washing-up. We did go down to the sea quite often, but it was nice sitting out in the garden. It was nice, Herbert, wasn't it?'

'We had a quiet time, that was the main thing. I slept well. I think we both slept well, didn't we?'

'Oh, yes, I found it a very good place for sleeping. I don't know how Mary always manages to keep so active. I'd sit down after lunch, you know, and fall asleep. I'd want to go to bed early, that sort of thing.'

'There was a chap at work. I think he was in charge of ways and means. He was a war veteran. He'd been in Singapore, I think it was. He used to…'

'My eyelids used to feel as if they had heavy weights on them. And then you'd wake up, sudden as anything.'

'He used to fall asleep in mid-sentence. It was some kind of illness – malarial, I believe. Do you have that kind of thing nowadays, young man?'

'No, I don't think…'

'A chap like that'd be before your time probably.'

'We didn't go out on outings very much. We didn't really feel like it. Donald, that's Mary's husband, was of course at work. He's a lawyer.'

'No, we stayed in the garden mostly.'

'You've still got your healthy colour, Sally-Anne dear, haven't you?' said Eleanor.

'Mum dear, I've only been up in London a couple of days in Jim's apartment. I couldn't lose it in a couple of days.' She looked sideways at Jim, smiled a quick, covert smile, unsnapped her small handbag and drew out a little mirror. 'I've managed to keep it, Mum, you're quite right. And so has Jim.'

'You're both looking so well,' Eleanor agreed. 'That seaside holiday must have done both of you a world of good.'

'Yes, it did.' Sally put away the mirror. 'It was good for both of us.'

She said it almost dismissively. Jim recognised that the conversation was edging into a more confessional mode when embarrassment might be unavoidable. He knew how she had hoped to avoid being drawn back into the cloying past she associated with *The Cherries*. There was a momentary silence.

'More cider, young man?' Herbert Harris asked.

'No, thank you.'

'Sally-Anne dear, let's you and I go and get the lunch ready and leave Dad and Mr Nordon…'

'Jim, please, Mum.'

'Jim, then.'

'You two go and get lunch,' said Herbert Harris.

'It's only some cold meats and some salad, I'm afraid. I thought on a hot day it'd be better to have a cold lunch.'

'That'll be fine,' said Jim.

Herbert Harris poured himself another glass of sherry. Sally and her mother went across the lawn and into the house through the French windows.

'Where are you from?'

Jim told him.'

'I don't know that part at all. But I thought I caught a touch of the accent in your voice. One of my best friends came from Manchester. He's dead now.'

'Have you lived here long?'

'I bought this house when I resigned. We used to have a bigger one. The problem was that a man called Sanderson – I can remember that name well enough – got in my way. He wouldn't say yes and he wouldn't say no. When I asked him straight out: "Are you going to support my promotion or aren't you?" he'd never say. Bloody awful man. That's why I never got on as well as I deserved. So I resigned.'

Jim thought at first he could categorise Herbert Harris quite easily: an unimaginative, resentful, old-fashioned man even when young, who would do his job well enough provided the boundaries were fixed and the effort more or less agreed and wouldn't like changing his plans come hell and high water. Practically the only features of his face that reminded Jim of Sally were the blue eyes, though his were like opal-quartz, waxy, not brilliant and youthful like Sally's. His chin, for example, was strong like hers but not as prominent, given to resentment and challenge, while hers was always confident and resolute, as though ready to meet whatever the world offered. Jim knew, though, that you didn't categorise people like Herbert Harris as easily as all that. They very often possessed a capacity for understanding majority taste and opinion that someone like Jim couldn't always be sure of. To Jim the unimaginativeness of the type rankled simply because it tended to place expediency before the need for change.

'Sally-Anne tells me you've got on very well. You're in charge of a department, aren't you?'

'I am.'

'You're young to be that,' Herbert Harris observed. He sipped his sherry. A silence fell between them filled with the splashings of the pencil of water in the little pool, some children playing two gardens away, a radio or television in a nearby house and someone calling 'Ralph! Ralph!' out of an upstairs window, followed by 'What?' and 'Oh, you're down there!' A car passed along the street on the other side of the house. 'I suppose they're promoting much earlier these days.'

'No, they reorganised the departments two years ago.' He preferred not to mention that Z10 was fictitious.

'I got out, you know. Decided I couldn't stand it.'

Jim was more puzzled than surprised by this remark. Sally had never told him that her father had resigned, which was presumably what he meant. He could not be sure how to react and compromised with an indefinite noise suggesting half interest, half amazement.

'There comes a time when you've got to get out. It takes courage, of course.' Herbert Harris drew his lips tightly together. 'So when I was sixty I joined a local club. I used to make furniture – amateur, following designs, that sort of thing – and so I made furniture. I was good at it. I spent two and a half years there. Of course early retirement meant I forfeited a fuller pension, which makes life difficult now. But I don't regret making the change, don't regret it at all.'

For no very clear reason Jim felt inadequate in the presence of this statement. It emboldened him to be much more emphatic in what he had to say. 'I'm glad you have no regrets because I've been thinking…'

Before he could finish Herbert Harris had grunted and asked, brusquely and rather rudely:

'What are your intentions, young man?'

HELL! Jim thought. 'My intentions?'

'Your intentions towards my daughter?'

'She hasn't told you?'

'She may have told Eleanor, but I have no idea.'

'I intend,' Jim said clearly and boldly, 'to be your son-in-law. She may not have told you but I am telling you now. I am her fiancé. Is that clear enough?'

Herbert Harris pouted. He looked down at the table and the line of bottles. 'Thank you. That's all I wanted to know.'

'I apologise for not seeking your approval beforehand, as I presume I should have done.'

'I imagine Sally-Anne made the decision. She's like that.'

'Yes,' said Jim, feeling bound to concede that much. 'And she says she has a plan for this visit.'

'You'll get married, of course. But if she's decided for you…' Herbert Harris dispelled the likely accompanying issues that Jim anticipated from him – the costs, the whereabouts of the marriage, the possible date – and launched instead into a mixture of reminiscence and complaint. 'I remember my own father-in-law to be, Eleanor's father, saying the same thing before we were married. He was in the army. Always made a habit of rapping out his remarks. I think it was because he once said that to me: "You'll get married," meaning I'd be marrying Eleanor because she was determined on it, and we'd only known each other a couple of weeks, mind you, when he said it. He knew what she was like, just as I knew Eleanor was after me. She's always been like that. God knows why she wanted me – I was forty-five at the time. But once her mind's made up about people, well, she's… she's…' Perhaps the hesitancy, so obviously due to Herbert Harris's concern for his wife, gave rise to a more compassionate train of thought. 'The trouble is she's not been well.'

Jim nodded in sympathy. It was hard for him to keep on meeting the stern gaze from Herbert Harris, who appeared to drive home his words with a steady boring brilliance of the eyes.

'She doesn't like talking about it, but she was very unwell just before we went down to Torquay. Then she apparently got over it. But she's not looking well. Sally-Anne's been an angel, of course. Heart trouble. I suppose she'll have told you?'

'Yes.'

'It comes and goes, that's the trouble. And Sally-Anne wore herself out, I'm not exaggerating. She's very fond of her mother, she dotes on Eleanor.' There was a brief pause. Then he added, in explanation of something or other: 'When you get old, you know, it's the sort of thing that happens. For one thing, if someone doesn't tell you what's the matter, you begin to get really worried. Eleanor doesn't tell me how unwell she is, Sally-Anne doesn't let us know where she's living. And no one told me you were going to be my son-in-law.'

The resentment was back. Jim tried to avert it by apologising, but before he could muster the appropriate words Sally appeared in the French windows and called to him. The coincidence of the call and his own inarticulacy made him offer a very abrupt apology and set off on his way across the lawn.

'Lunch'll be ready in a moment,' she said. 'Mum always gets in a panic now when she has visitors and I've got to help her by giving moral support, but I wanted to tell you something. Let's just go up to my room. Do you mind?'

No, he made clear he didn't mind. She ran up the stairs ahead of him without looking back. He followed her, already aware that, once she was back home, she could exert her authority without fear of contradiction. The hurried way she flung open the door at the head of the stairs and rushed ahead of him into the bedroom was a demonstration of this. She closed the door as soon as he entered.

'Look,' she began whispering, 'I feel silly bringing you up here like this. What I wanted to tell you is…' He saw she had a handkerchief at the ready, but the sight of the room, as tidy as a museum, inhibited her from confessing anything. For him it seemed so completely unlike her. The pink quilt on the bed, the ornaments and framed photographs on the mantelpiece, the photographs of school groups on the walls, a poster of a pop group, a large picture of a pop star, a record player and a pile of cassettes, a few books and, on top of a chest-of-drawers, a line of dolls graded according to height. The room had a clean, unlived-in smell. It seemed to date to Sally when she was ten years younger.

'It's so tidy,' he said, 'I can hardly imagine you've ever lived in it.'

'Oh, that's Mum. She wants to keep it looking like a teenager's room. She keeps all sort of things wrapped up.' This enigmatic statement and the ensuing pause led him to look more closely at her. He saw she was on the point of tears. She dabbed her eyes. 'I can't see my silly old room without feeling a bit weepy. Don't be surprised, please. I get like this when I see how Mum keeps it. How have you got on with Dad?'

He explained that he had told him about being a prospective son-in-law.

'Oh,' she cried in a shriller whisper, 'that's Mum again! I told her you were my fiancé. But he may have forgotten. He's like that.'

'You never told me he made furniture.'

'Didn't I? Sorry, I should've done. Yes, he made a chair for himself. It's down in the sitting-room. The garage is still his man-cave, I think. He doesn't do much work of that kind nowadays.' She turned away from him, as if what her parents did or failed to do, no longer mattered very much.

In that instant he caught sight of her figure in the splendid near-Ascot outfit reflected in a long free-standing mirror, an object in a gilded frame that stood by the chest-of-drawers. He was reminded very strongly of the first time he had seen her naked in the hotel bedroom. She faced him with the same proud look despite the shine of tears in her eyes.

'Do you know,' she said, 'I'm so weepy now I think I might be... It's what I wanted to tell you...'

The incomplete sentence caused a little explosion of shock in the air of the room. Its implication was clear to him at once. He knew he should have guessed. So, his rapid thinking went, that was why she was so keen for him to meet her parents, that was why she wanted to initiate him, that was why she was whispering.

'You mean?'

As soon as he spoke he knew how foolish it must sound. He knew exactly what she meant.

'I don't know, I don't know, she said.

He held her closely as her shoulders heaved a little and she wept.

VIII

'Are you pregnant?'

He asked the question quietly and as confidentially as possible. They were driving back to London along the A3.

'I don't know. I didn't mention it back there because you know how it is, it would have caused a fuss and I've missed periods before. I thought it would be safe taking the pill.'

What she did not say, but he knew she implied, was that being pregnant would somehow seem a bit like blackmail and could even divide them through the very complication it brought to their lives. He glanced round at her. She was drawing back her hair from her face with the back of her wrist in a familiar way. He had grown used to thinking it as a signal she was unsure of herself or irritated.

'I can understand why you didn't want to mention it to your parents. But I'm happy, I mean that. I love you all the more... Yes, all the more...'

The lights of a car ahead crimsoned. There was some obstruction and they slowed. She blew him a kiss, but her reluctance to talk about it was a silent comment on their whole day at *The Cherries*. They'd not been able to talk about it in her bedroom because her mother had called them down to lunch. Afterwards the afternoon had been spent sitting in the garden. Her father had talked about his career and then had come the little crisis that brought a sudden, intense strain to the whole visit.

'What's that? Painting, you said? What kind?'

Her father barked out the questions. Sally had blushed a bright red. Jim would never have dreamt of mentioning he had painted her in the nude, but her blushing made the subject seem indecent in a way that the setting of the small suburban garden accentuated quite nakedly as if it were full of pointing fingers. There was a dreadful pause in which no one knew what to say. It was one of those moments that imposed hypocrisy on truth and made candour seem an embarrassment.

'What kind?'

'Portraits mostly.'

'Oh.'

Jim spoke of his painting with a defiant sharpness that challenged Herbert Harris to ask more. He had wisely refrained. The conversation drifted by fits and starts until they had left after tea and supper. A glass of champagne had been drunk to celebrate their engagement, but there had been no chance to ask Sally what she meant and now her reluctance to say anything more worried him. He knew he should feel happy and proud for both of them at her pregnancy.

Instead, he knew there was something else. It was *The Cherries*, her father, her mother's poor health and his own night-time homeward journeys by car in his boyhood. His thoughts peered into that quarter century of memory like the car's lights shining into the oncoming cat's eyes and dark of the A3 and the antennae of approaching car lights on the other carriageway. He thought he saw the silhouetted shapes of his father's and his mother's heads in front, lit by the dashboard glow, while his brother and he sat in the back. Everything then, on those Sunday evenings, felt simultaneously chilly and exciting, mysteriously dark and gloomily predictable. Everything seemed suspended in anticipation of the arrival home and the next day's school when there'd be no sand left between his toes and the smells of the school would replace the fresh, free smells of the seaside pools in which he and Sam had played.

The visit to *The Cherries* had made him look more deeply into himself than he had looked for years and all he found there was a number of questions. Was he really a painter? Or was he merely trying to challenge the concealments and deceits of Subtopian England? Was he merely pretending to escape from everything *The Cherries* meant to him – the security, respectability, supposed decency? And if Sally were pregnant, how much longer could he go on pretending that his apartment in Victoria Mansions was a viable bolt-hole from the twenty-first century?

In any case, it was due to be pulled down. The likelihood of pregnancy demanded that he must not just think about moving but devote himself to actively seeking a new home as well as a new career. *The Cherries*, of course, meant to him the home similar to his own, his home in *Cotswold House*. It was fenced-in, compressed, impregnable in its assertion of its self-justifying and self-regarding truth. That truth demanded conformity and he had conformed. He had conformed to his mother's wishes, had conformed to the demands of his career, but in his marriage that conformity had come unstuck. In the ungluing he had found himself denied the creativity latent in himself. Whenever he looked in the shaving mirror he saw a Frankenstein's monster, someone he had created of himself that sought to be loved, sought to be creative, but could never truly find that love, never truly find the accompanying creativity. That was the worst knowledge because it implied that he might never be able to respond to Sally's love. No other splinter of atomised logic was a more poisoned ice crystal in his heart than that. Suddenly, though, she started speaking.

'You think sometimes a thing's going to be all right and you're not bothered by it at all, and then suddenly someone says something, or you see the look on someone's face, and suddenly everything's going to be a disaster, you know that for sure. Other times you think nothing could be worse than what's going to happen – and with my parents you can be sure of that, they're absolutely predictable, don't you ever try talking politics with them, I warn you, that's one thing – but today, which could easily have been a disaster, just avoided it, I think. If you can actually *talk* to my father instead of becoming a punch-bag for his opinions, that means a lot. It means we'll soon enjoy ordinary conversations with them. Probably.'

She let the noise of the engine wash away that last word. They were once again going fast into the Sunday darkness. He guessed what she very likely wanted to say and hesitated about saying. It concerned her mother's health. By the end of the visit Eleanor Harris had begun to look tired and frail and they had left as much on her account as because the conversation had almost dribbled to a stop after they had drunk the *Veuve Clicquot*. Her devotion to her mother had been demonstrated once again. It reinforced the fact, as he understood it, that if her mother fell ill, she would go back to *The Cherries* either to look after her or to run the house for her father. There were two pressures on them for the immediate future, he thought: the pressure for him to finish the report and her readiness to look after her parents. There were no other immediate choices.

'You did like them, didn't you?' she asked.

'I liked them. I liked your mother very much. Your father did all the things you said he'd do and I do feel a bit like a punch-bag. But the champagne was a brilliant idea. They know now we're engaged.'

'I said I'd planned something. I thought that would do it. Dad was impressed by the *Veuve Clicquot*, wasn't he? He always wants to be the boss when they have visitors and can never stop talking. In a conversation he's about as helpful as planning blight.'

He laughed. 'That sums him up pretty well.'

'Now you know what I've had to put up with. The last thing I wanted was to talk about pregnancy. That'll have to wait.'

'Sally-Anne, I love you,' he said.

Suddenly she seized hold of his arm and held it tightly.

'Jim darling, thank you. Thank you for trying to be part of the family. Thank you for making it such a nice day.'

****

For the time being she did not know for sure whether she was pregnant and he did not know whether he should leave his job. So he nervously drafted and redrafted and she obediently typed one version after another of his report. Now and then, glancing up from his desk, he would look out at the rainy, wintry-looking Thames – it had turned into a typically English August – and tell himself:

'*Jim Nordon, you're a bloody coward. Give up the* job *now. Do what you really want to do.*'

What did he really want to do? He really wanted to paint. And he wanted to marry Sally. Could he afford to give up his job and support Sally and a baby? As for his painting, how long would it take for him to earn any money from painting portraits?

Coward!

'*Yes*,' he told himself, looking at the rain-streaked pleasure boats making creamy bow-waves on the featureless grey river water, '*you're a coward. You must persuade yourself there is life somewhere else. You don't have to recuperate any longer from the twenty-first century. Give up on Victoria Mansions before they give up on you.*'

In the evenings he painted her. Sally wore her favourite outfit for the painting. It had a smart velvet jacket and a full ankle-length wine-coloured skirt. He knew as soon as he started it that it would be the happiest portrait he had ever done. He photographed her from different angles, so that she did not have to keep a special pose for the actual portrait; but he referred back to these pictures to ensure an accurate representation of her features and the intentness of her look. She was smiling as she leaned slightly forward in a wooden armchair, her lips parted a little as if she were about to laugh and her hands holding the chair's arms as though she were going to rise and come towards him. He lavished as much skill as possible on the brushwork to capture her alertness and vitality along with the variations of colour and shade in the hang and folds of what she was wearing. A great deal of detail was necessary to accompany and fill out the vividness of the pose. Before it could be finished, one early Friday evening, he was suddenly confronted by the true meaning of his cowardice. The ding-dong bell rang at the apartment's front door and Sally went to open it.

'Jim,' she called, 'it's someone for you.'

****

He was looking straight into the light hazel eyes of Rachel Wallace. She stood in the doorway of the apartment with a small wheeled travelling case beside her and a long-strapped handbag over one shoulder. Her eyebrows were raised slightly and the delicate rays of lines about her eyes were contracted with the beginnings of what looked like an amused or embarrassed smile when she saw him. All he could see at the first inclusive glance was the firm womanly shapeliness of her figure under the blue cotton suit.

'Jim dear, I'm very sorry. I can see I should have phoned you.'

'Rachel, you're the last person...'

She began speaking quickly. 'I've been staying with my sister in Birmingham. I'd just got to Euston and the stupidest thing, you know, I found I'd left all my money, my cheque book, my credit cards, I'd left them all behind. I was desperate. I can't think why I'd done such a stupid thing. My sister'd driven me to the station and I had to rush to get the train, but it wasn't that, no, it was just my own stupidity. Then I had… well, I suppose it wasn't the most brilliant of thoughts… but I remembered you lived in Victoria Mansions in Southampton Row and that it wasn't very far from Euston. And your name was there down below, in that special brass frame with the floral motif. The Apartment. I took the dreadful old lift up here.'

He was glad to let her talk. She kept on looking beyond him, almost over his shoulder, obviously studying Sally. He knew from the way she wore her light summer suit that she expected him to be aware of her body. It seemed to him it was all he could be aware of, the words floating over him like so many dead leaves that blew in with her. There was a physical conspiracy between her body and his. It seemed that, standing there in the hallway, no matter what words they spoke their bodies were already pressing towards each other, exchanging their own passionate messages. So strong was this physical communication between them that he tried to distract Sally's attention.

'Rachel, my dear, you'll want some money, won't you?'

Then Sally herself interrupted him. 'Please, do come in,' she said.

'Of course, of course,' he said, 'yes, do come in.' In annoyance at his own confusion he broke into introductions. 'I'd like to introduce you. This is Rachel – Rachel Wallace. Rachel, this is…'

'It's Sally-Anne Harris.' She extended her hand with determination and for a moment disconcerted Rachel by actually taking her suitcase from her while seeming to offer to shake hands. 'Come in. You must be tired after walking so far,'

'Well, I am, yes.' Looking faintly overwhelmed, Rachel stepped into the hallway, avoiding Jim's eyes.

'I'm sure you two'll want to have a talk.' Sally ran her eyes across Jim's face as she spoke. Her fierce blue gaze told him all he had suspected. Then she hesitated and glanced back. He saw the vulnerable look. It was too much for him. He deliberately looked away. He knew it was treason. It filled the air between them like a stench. 'Excuse me. I must tidy myself,' she added and slipped away into the main bedroom.

'Have I come at a wrong time?' Rachel asked.

'No, I've just been painting. It's a portrait of Sally-Anne. In the early stages.' He asked if she would like a glass of wine.

'That would be nice.'

He led her into the sitting-room.

'How spacious,' she was saying. 'I would never have thought an apartment as high up as this would have so much space.'

'It is spacious. Do have a seat. I used to paint in here. Then my lodger left.'

'Oh. Dave someone, wasn't it? I remember you saying.'

He poured her a glass of wine and they said 'Cheers.' He kept straining to hear sounds from Sally, but she made none of her usual noises. Rachel sat down and crossed her legs in a sexual pose that gave every impression of splendid unselfconsciousness. Her skirt had ridden up slightly to show the dark sensuous cusp where the two lower edges of her thighs met.

'Are they your pictures?'

'Yes.'

'Very good, Jim dear. Very good indeed. I get the impression of being watched. They are just a bit severe, aren't they? Perhaps they don't entirely approve.'

She spoke a fraction too loudly. He thought she must want Sally to hear, as though she were trying to assert her prior right to Jim's attention by this means. He tried to steer her to another subject.

'You're looking well,' he said. 'Have you been on holiday?'

'Not really. I gave up my old job because I'd found a new one that was better paid, but it doesn't start for a month. So I've been fancy free. Do you mind if I smoke?' He offered her a thick glass ashtray from the *art nouveau* mantelpiece and struck a match for her. Inhaling, she went on, as she took the cigarette from her mouth and he noticed for the first time that she was wearing lipstick: 'As a matter of fact I went to Bristol.'

'I thought you said you'd come from Birmingham.'

He was trying to get her to talk a little more softly. The look of anxiety that passed across his face as she mentioned Bristol did not escape her notice.

'How much does the girl know, the one who's called Sally-Anne? How much?'

He was tacitly grateful to her for acknowledging without fuss that Sally was not just an artist's model. 'I've told her.'

'You've told her about Vicky, you mean?'

'Yes. Please, my dear, do keep your voice down.'

Rachel blew smoke about, then with a fluid wrist movement dispersed its cobwebs from her face. 'Sorry, I didn't realise. It's talking in those fast noisy trains. You've got to shout to be heard. Or at least that's how it was in my carriage. I did come from Birmingham actually, but I'd been to Bristol first.' She was now talking in a kind of stage whisper and leaning a little sideways, almost blowing the words towards him even though he was sitting beside her on the sofa. 'Vicky's been very unwell. They had a bad quarrel. I went down to be with her for a fortnight. Things are patched up now, but she was in a terrible state, all weepy and hysterical and drinking a lot when I first got there.'

'Vicky never used to drink.'

'No, I know she didn't. The quarrel or whatever it was, it really knocked her out. So I had to spend a lot of time listening to her talking about all the problems they had and drinking a lot to keep up with her. The children are lovely.

All right, Jim, I won't go on about it. I can see you don't want to hear.'

He was relieved. 'And then you went to Birmingham?'

'Yes, I went and stayed with my sister. That was a hell of a lot quieter. Boring, in fact.' She finished her wine and held out her glass. 'Do you mind? Talking of Vicky's drinking makes me thirsty. You look well, Jim. Suntanned, leaner.'

'Thank you.' He was worried by Sally's absence and annoyed at his own awkwardness. Here they were being so formal to each other, he and Rachel, as if they hardly knew each other. He handed back her glass refilled with white wine. She smiled up at him.

'You're happy, aren't you?'

He responded with a smile of genuine, overt pleasure that took possession of his face like a seizure.

'You know I am.'

'I'm pleased for you. And a bit jealous.'

'You don't have to be jealous at all.'

'I wouldn't be human if I weren't, would I?'

He shrugged his shoulders. 'I know you'll like Sally.'

She waved a hand at him. Long emotional explanations appealed to neither of them. 'Of course, I'll like her. If I get the chance.' She sipped the wine, looking up at him brightly. 'We're old friends, and old friends' friends are old friends' friends. I think that's worth saying.'

He tried to disregard the cynical tone in her voice. 'Do you mind if I go and find out what's happened to her?'

'Please.' Rachel gave a regal hand wave.

He despised himself for being so callous towards her. But he was thinking all the time about Sally. Supposing she might be in the kitchen, he glanced towards it in the hallway and then saw that his bedroom door was closed. He opened it gently. Sally was sitting in front of the dressing-table. Immediately, from the position of her spine and arms, bent forward, so that she was leaning on the glass top, her elbows among the disarray of her cosmetics, he recognised a stubbornness and hostility in her pose. He stood in the doorway, feeling challenged by her.

'Aren't you going to join us?'

She did not even turn to look at him. Slowly he closed the door. He knew by the stiffening of her figure that his words and manner were insensitive and inept.

'I'm so sorry.'

'Don't be sorry,' she said rigidly, sternly. 'It sounds so pathetic. No, I'm not going to join you. I'd be completely out of place, you know that.'

He was tongue-tied by shame and the sheer complexity of the many things she might insinuate. It was one of those moments when there seemed to be no chance of rescue or retrieval.

'I don't know who she is, but I could tell at once she was someone you didn't want me to know about. I don't remember you ever saying,' and her voice rose, as if the very thinness of her meaning had to be given a louder tone to support it, 'you knew anyone called Rachel.'

'There are lots of people I might not have mentioned to you.'

'You know I don't mean that.' She had her father's sharpness as she spoke. 'Rachel is someone else and you know that.'

He knew she was right. It was as if he had been caught all over again with the photo of Megan in his hand. In a stupid way over which he had no control he could feel the colour begin to rise in his cheeks.

'In any case,' she said, 'I've been thinking. I used my phone just now to find out how things were at home. I'd been thinking about Mum. From her voice I could tell she wasn't feeling too marvellous. And so…' She shook her long hair and gave a sigh. 'And so I think I ought to go home. I can get a bus down to Waterloo.'

He crossed to her and placed his hands on her shoulders. She held herself stiffly beneath his touch, less in resentment, it seemed, than to seem unappeased. Their eyes met in the mirror. She returned his look, her eyes blinking rapidly.

'Now tell me who she is?'

He lifted his hands from her shoulders. The upward tilt of her eyes reflected in the mirror held him more firmly in their gaze than if they had been looking at him directly. The warmth of her body expressed to him quite clearly the secret heat of her feelings. He knew he could hide nothing.

'We were lovers.'

'For how long?'

'Since Vicky and I got divorced. Rachel was one of her friends.'

She folded her arms. He saw by the set of her mouth and the way she deliberately looked away from him how much she mistrusted him.

'Why didn't you tell me?'

'I don't know. I hadn't really thought about it. If you don't want to believe me, don't believe me. Rachel and I are… are…'

He gave a flick of the fingers. It was a stupid, dismissive gesture that simply acknowledged his foolishness. He would never have wanted to dismiss his relationship with Rachel like that. When he had rehearsed the words he would use to tell Sally about her, he had always found grander, finer things to say than such telexed nonentities culminating in a flick of the fingers.

'Jim darling,' she said, swinging round on the stool and shaking her head, 'you're a bloody fool! You should've told me! Now I don't know how many other Rachels there may be. And perhaps I'm just another of them.'

'No, there aren't any others. And you're not, you know that. I mean it.'

'Oh, don't be so bloody contrite, so bloody... Now I'm swearing and I hate swearing.' She paused, fiddled with her hair, drew her lips tightly together. 'I think the best thing is if I go. I need to be calm.'

'Sally darling, for heaven's sake!'

'I have to go and look after my Mum.'

That caught him. He could hardly stop her and yet with Rachel in the other room he could hardly insist that she stayed. She began collecting things together and putting them in an overnight case lying open on the bed already full of things from the bathroom.

'Hand me my nightie, please. And my slippers are on the other side of the bed.'

'There isn't any need for you to go now, is there?'

'Jim darling, I think perhaps...'

It was obvious to him what she would say. His dishonesty had breached the trust that had been built day by day between them. It would take time, not words, to repair the damage. He watched her quickly throw item after item into the case and then click it shut.

'Sally darling,' he started saying.

He murmured something about driving her to Waterloo, but as soon as he mentioned it he knew that he could just as well be offering to drive Rachel home to Orpington. Whatever he might say tended always to implicate Rachel and re-open the whole question of his reasons for hiding Rachel from her.

'I'll phone you,' she said. 'Bye, Jim darling.'

'Is there nothing I can do?' He spoke spontaneously.

'No.' She shook her head, smiled and kissed him. He tried to hold her but she slipped away from him and went out into the hallway.

'Sally darling, for heaven's sake,' he managed to say, feeling assailed by a desperate sense of loss at the thought of her leaving, 'you can't just...'

She blew him a kiss from the front door at the end of the hall and stepped out onto the landing. Practically as soon as the front door closed he heard the gate of the lift crash shut. She had gone.

He hesitated for one moment, wondering whether to run down the stairs after her or go back to Rachel. Rachel had of course heard their voices and the closing of the front door. She came out of the sitting-room into the narrow hallway.

'Sally's just gone home,' he explained.

'I hope it's not on account of... I mean...'

'It's her mother.'

But she could see, just as his voice told her, that the sudden departure had everything to do with her. Yet she did what he knew she wanted him to do and what in any case their bodies demanded of each other. She held out a hand to him and he took advantage of her gesture to reach towards her and fold his arm round her as it had done so many times in the intervening years since his marriage ended and Sally came into his life. This time it was different. They embraced each other in familiarity and relief, but also with a kind of premonitory recognition that they were celebrating the end of their relationship.

It came over him with almost paralysing force that Rachel's unexpected arrival meant something conclusive. No matter what they might say to each other, they did not need each other as they had done before. Or perhaps, if he was completely truthful with himself and her, he would have to admit that he could not turn to her again as he had done. It was not simply that Sally had come into his life. More important, he had hardly given a thought to Rachel in the last few weeks. Sally had supplanted her completely. She knew this quite as well as he did. In holding Rachel so close for these several instants in the narrow hallway, he was telling her how precious she had been to him and what pleasure they had shared together, but he was also admitting that it was all in the past. The present suggested a much greater finality. It was as if they inhabited a totally finite moment that simply had the words THE END stamped on it.

'You know, Jim dear, you mustn't pretend.' She took her arms away from him and he released her also.

'No, I know I mustn't. Sally's gone because I never told her about you and me. I think I hardly need to tell you that.'

There was one of those awkward moments that are more deadly to a relationship than the most brutal sarcasm. Rachel turned back into the sitting-room.

'I think it's time I went.'

She did not say it was time for her to leave for good. He offered to drive her to Orpington. After some hesitancy and rather stiffly she agreed. The wheeled suitcase plus the two of them just managed to be inserted into the elderly lift. Almost wordlessly both observed themselves in the mirrors as they shook their way down floor after floor. Once on the ground floor, in the lobby of Victoria Mansions, she asked him what he was going to do. Meanwhile they walked to where his car was parked just off Queen Square.

'I'm finishing a report. The final draft's to be presented to my boss in a week or so.'

'Mr Ball, isn't it?'

'Yes, of course, I told you. Charles Ball. He'll shortly have to read it. And then I think I'll do what you've done.'

'You mean you'll change your job? Oh, Jim dear, that's risky.'

'I think I'm going to risk it.'

'What'll you do? Commercial art, something like that?'

'I will paint portraits.' He never thought he would say it so confidentially. 'Yes,' he said and repeated the sentence. He added, less as an explanation, rather to bolster his self-confidence: 'If I resign, which would be a wise thing to do if I become known as author of the report, my resignation could be made to look like redundancy.' At which point he knew he was beginning to sound as if he was talking to himself. With a terrible renewal of the sense of finality that he had felt while holding Rachel in his arms, he realised that he was very likely never going to see her or talk to her again.

'You'll have to be lucky,' she remarked as if her luck had just run out.

'I will.'

'I hope you are, I really do. Your painting's good, but...'

She could go on saying 'but', he knew, ''but this... but that...' and she would be perfectly justified in doing so. They took their seats in the car and he drove. A few limp words were exchanged. They were of course being very polite to each other. When they reached her street, they had more or less exhausted pleasantries and had fallen silent. He saw there were tears in her eyes. Without looking at him, she slipped out of the car, retrieved her wheeled suitcase from the back seat and literally ran away from him. Before he could climb out of the car himself, he saw her pull the wheeled suitcase bouncily over paving stones and give him a final wave. Then she disappeared up the steps into her house. A desolation descended on him as he drove back. Idiotically, stupid tears of his own poured down his cheeks. He had hurt Rachel unbearably and he had hurt Sally. He recognised the cost of his dishonesty.

When he returned to Victoria Mansions he flopped into an armchair without bothering to turn on any lights and was instantly asleep. Some time later he awoke, perhaps startled by the sound of a vehicle braking with a squeal, either from Queen Square or Old Gloucester Street, then he saw the patch of night sky, more grey than black, and uprising street lighting providing an artificial sense of dawn and felt for the first time the awful silence of Sally's absence, even the absence of her breathing, beginning to fill the apartment. That was when the first pang struck him. He stood up. Her voice and movements and footsteps were on the edge of the silence, about to enter and have an existence, but precluded, unheard, void. Nothing could change the fact of her absence or diminish the possibility that in so casually waving her goodbye he had perhaps waved her out of his life, as he had waved Rachel.

A series of old late-night sounds returned to inhabit the apartment. It was after ten o'clock, time for the elderly residents of Victoria Mansions to be going to bed. He thought then as much of Rachel as of Sally. He had thought that he was surer of Rachel than of any other person in the world, could share more completely with her, and yet he knew they would probably never have been able to stay together. The effort of the day-to-day and the routine of it would slowly have eroded their relationship. But with Sally it had been all the intimacies and understandings of marriage. They had grown slowly together, enclosed within the relationship, and he had supposed that they would eventually bloom and prosper in the natural way of marriage itself. Now that she was gone he realised how foolish it had been to suppose anything of the kind. He could phone her at *The Cherries*, of course, but it was anger as much as regret that made him resist the impulse.

He was angry with himself for not telling her about Rachel. More stupidly, he was angered by what he had thought would be her reaction. Most of all, he was angry with his present life, with his work, with the report, with his painting and the apartment, this bolt-hole from the twenty-first century. At moments of emotional crisis he had tended, equally stupidly, to hate his surroundings, as he had hated the semi-detached house in Harrow. He paced now from sitting-room to bedroom to bathroom, from the smoke-stained smell of one, to the unfinished portrait in another and the supper things unwashed in the kitchen. The bleakness was in both himself and the apartment, a bleakness composed of the apartment's silence and his anger and hurt and hatred. And he felt exhausted by such a clashing of emotions and dropped on to his bed and again fell asleep, waking up in the early morning with a determination to get away. He would try to start again; he would go back home. In his pocket, though, neat in its little nest of deep blue artificial silk in its smart box, was the engagement ring he had been on the point of giving Sally once he had completed the picture.

IX

Traffic was light as he drove northwards in the early morning. It was easy to maintain a steady seventy on the motorway and zoom quietly past one lumbering high-sided vehicle after another. The swoop of motorway through cuttings, under concrete bridges, out along straight lengths of wide roadway under layered cloud or up stretches of upland ridged with trees and pylons and brick houses startled into upright poses beneath tilting hats of roofs offered a kind of movie show of continually on-coming glimpses, but always silent and only gradually emerging more brilliantly as daylight grew stronger. The farther he drove northwards the thicker grew the cloud. After an hour or so it began to rain the smacking summer rain of the Midlands like small fistfuls of water being flung against the windscreen. He had to reduce speed and soon decided it wasn't worth it. He knew he needed coffee and a rest. The motorway service area turned out to be full of busloads of people wearing religious badges on their way southwards to a rally in London. It took him fifteen minutes in a slow queue to reach the coffee and the cashier.

The couple who sat opposite him looked startled at his yawn. It was his first of the morning. By this time, though, he thought his mother would very likely be sitting up in bed with a newly made cup of Teasmade tea. The newspaper would not be delivered for another hour. That world of his childhood, the house itself so quiet at such an early-morning time you could hear the grandfather clock in the hall ticking away, audible from the farthest bedroom, and beyond the bedroom curtains the opposite hillside perhaps looking a dull grey-blue in the rain and the long steady hushing murmur of rainfall merging with the house's quiet and reducing the little steely drumming of the tick-tock to a smoother, blander softness. This all built up around him through the noise of the motorway cafeteria and was as real in his imagining as the thick-lipped rim of the coffee cup and the taste of the doughnut he had just eaten or the almost noiseless to and fro movement of vehicles along the motorway below the cafeteria window. He began to feel he was living on two planes of reality. It was a feeling he had had sometimes before but never as strongly as now.

Then he felt waves of alarm sweep over him. What he was doing, when he considered the events of the last twenty-four hours, was an admission that he had lost the two most important relationships in his life. All he could think of doing was to go backwards. He could not explain any of this to his parents, at least not now. He could hope they would be willing to accept his return home as an act of contrition for his failure to keep in touch. This would be his hope for his mother, though as soon as she heard he was intending to abandon his 'good job' for something as insecure and unreal as the life of a painter she would be openly censorious and dismissive. So he was alarmed at the very craziness of what he was doing, at the lack of foresight he was showing in driving this far without having thought of proper reasons for his behaviour, at the folly of imagining that he would solve anything by returning home so abruptly. There remained only a sort of conviction that this was the only way to make his future clearer to himself.

When he saw himself again reflected in the mirror of the gents loo, he noticed that the tan had almost gone, perhaps drained away by the bleak fluorescence of the lighting, and the skin of his face had tautened with tiredness. He had the grey preoccupied look of someone under strain, though at that very moment he felt no strain at all. He felt tired, no more, and with the tiredness came a certain numbing even of the alarm signals to himself. The coffee, far from rousing him, had the exact opposite effect. He recognised only the symptoms of drowsiness, to such an extent that when he reseated himself in front of the steering wheel he pressed the release lever and let the back headrest gradually recede until he was almost supine. By fits and starts the drowsiness quickly became a sleep through which he heard vaguely the sounds of doors slamming and car engines starting up nearby. Otherwise, like a very soft hypnotic voice, the only continual sound that penetrated momentarily to his consciousness was the patter of rain on the car's bodywork and windows.

He must have slept for more than an hour, waking suddenly from a dream in which he distinctly heard Sally laughing. He could not tell why she laughed. The recollection reminded him of the picture and her eager look as she rose towards him. His mood had undergone a change, he realised. He could be angry at himself, for sure, and be justified, but it was a futile emotion to take home. No, he had a much more certain reason: his father's health, the talk of an operation, what Sam had told him. Why he hadn't thought of that earlier he did not know. Knowing it now, he felt furiously confident in what he was doing. Except there was another reason, more personal and powerful, that he hardly dared admit to himself. It was called *The Steep*, public parkland no distance from his home *Cotswold House*, where as a boy he had always gone on a sort of pilgrimage to seek himself, to test himself in God's eyes, to find what was intended; a holy place, a haven of such utter peace he imagined it inhabited by angels. In a controlled fury of conviction he drove back on to the motorway and into the lightly flicking rain and the spume rising in the wake of heavy vehicles.

****

The rows of houses were exactly as he remembered them. First came the railway bridge that adjoined the score or so of shops and the Baptist church on the corner, the once opulent thirties-style cinema converted to a DIY store and the grocer's now greatly enlarged and turned into a chain-store supermarket. Then there were more shops. Then there was the place where he had seen a dead dog, newly run over by a car. The place where he had fallen off his bicycle. The place where Evans the window cleaner had lived. The garage (now refronted, he noticed, and renamed) where the family car had always been serviced – a forecourt lined with second-hand cars, plastic prices on their windscreens and red plastic flags fluttering above them. The tall houses behind trees and long front gardens where the two Stephens boys had lived. All the houses of pre-1914 vintage with the cars parked outside because they had no garages, the little rows of palings, the tiled paths to front doors. Then where the buses stopped at the end of their route out of Altrincham and all the houses were more recent, a trifle prim, less anxiously pressed against each other but no less anxiously self-concerned, with garages beside them and low brick walls fronting the pavement. Neat, yes, and a bit serious-faced, even slightly frowning, but each of them exuding a melancholy confidence as the road rose fairly steeply, the space opposite them a golf course and beyond that the area of public parkland called *The Steep*. Then came a big old Victorian red-brick mansion half concealed by a high brick wall and more houses until, set back from the road, were the wrought iron gates of *Cotswold House*.

Two things surprised him on seeing it. The name itself, fixed as he always remembered it on a piece of wood in unevenly spaced chrome letters, had now been carved professionally into a piece of wood screwed on to the iron-work. The second thing was that the house had been newly repainted. The gleaming smartness of it was startlingly emphasised at that moment by a flash of sunlight that set the windows sparkling and made all the after-rain foliage of the shrubbery in the front garden shine as if sprayed with high-gloss paint.

Then came the first actual problem. Despite the stiffness from driving, he felt reluctant to leave his car. Even when he had climbed out and stood on the gravel outside the front gate, he wondered whether he should park there. If his parents were out, it would be in the way, or if their car were still in the garage, his would have to be moved. Whether to park or not to park there assumed an awful existential significance, a Shakespearean 'To be or not to be'. The question was answered by a shout:

'Are you the chap with the wood?'

It sounded like his father's voice, a bit crisp, though not querulous or hostile. As he looked wildly round him to identify it, he saw his father in the neighbouring garden, looking over the hedge.

'No, it's me, Jim.'

'Jim! So it is! I didn't know you were arriving today, your mother never said anything,' all of which spoken in a tone mixing surprise with alarm at the possibility that such an unexplained arrival meant trouble but accompanied by his hurried steps along the paved pathway the other side of the hedge and the click as he unlatched the neighbouring iron gate, 'and you're looking very well, my dear chap. I'm here because the Jenkinses are away and I go in when I can to see if everything's all right. So what brings you unexpectedly back here?'

A dozen or so years of managerial authority in a local insurance office gave a certain actor's professionalism to his father's affability. Jim had always noticed the role-playing in his father's treatment of life, the faint but perceptible adjustments of tone and manner, not to mention body-attitude that he used in responding to social differences among his clients. The behaviour had the near-genuine look of a good reproduction. It evidently showed concern without being inquisitive, interest without implying commitment and was sufficiently distanced to allow for a quick change of mood.

His father was tall, though not quite Jim's height. He had a lean, vaguely tanned face, with few small lines in it save for several deep lines, almost furrows, on his temples, below his eyes and round his mouth. They were lines suggesting experience rather than anything careworn. This was partly another symptom of his father's role-playing, for it catered to his private vision of himself as a doer, a hard-bitten out-of-doors type, no matter how greatly at odds this was with his generally desk-bound job. Especially at weekends, particularly when gardening, he gave this role credibility by wearing a sporting tweed cap with a pronounced peak. This he now raised in a gesture which could have been politeness but quickly changed to a scratching of his forehead, before he replaced the cap and looked Jim straight in the eyes. His father's eyes were the most striking and attractive feature of his face. They were remarkably innocent in their faintly appealing, injured hazel moistness. They were the eyes of someone who pleaded with life not to test him too keenly and yet watched the world cannily and with calm assessment. They hardly ever brightened when he laughed and they never lost their innocence when his generally immobile expression suggested shrewdness and hardness.

'You see, I thought you were the chap bringing some firewood. He fills up the boot of his car at weekends and brings it down from up there,' pointing to *The Steep*, not grey-blue now but a vivid summer green of woodland and bracken in the midday sunlight. His eyes pointed sharply into Jim's face. 'Are you up here to do with your work?'

'No, I came to see how you were. There was talk of an operation. Sam told me. And I've been so busy with drafting a rather important report, I haven't been in touch as I should have been.'

His father's eyes responded with a perceptible misting of disbelief. 'Well, it's good of you, my dear chap. You must have been driving all night. How long can you stay?'

'Till tomorrow afternoon. I can find myself a room in Altrincham. I've brought some overnight stuff.'

'What nonsense!' His father rapped him on the arm. 'You'll stay in your old room. I don't suppose you really want to... No, well, we'll talk about things a little later.'

To Jim what his father was about to say suggested either that Jim's own problems, the *real* problems, would be discussed a little later, or that his own, his father's problems and the impending operation would be discussed. For one moment his father withdrew his eyes and looked rather distractedly round him. Jim knew what had never occurred to him as a cogent matter in the past couple of months was any real concern over the likely exploratory operation. On the instant, pretexts and excuses fell neatly into place.

'I've been anxious,' he lied.

'I'm going in on Tuesday. It's just tests to start with. Come on into the house.'

'You're sure it's not serious?'

'I can't be sure of that. When doctors get their hands on you, who can be sure of that?' His voice was strong, slightly defiant. He pointed to the front garden. 'They're going to widen the road next year, they say, so I'm going to leave that front part alone. Come on into the house.'

Jim followed his father down the gravel driveway. He could not fail to notice how elderly he looked. It was almost as great a shock as realising how forgetful he had been. Not to have thought once about his father's health! To have let it slip his mind completely! The sheer egotistical selfishness of it stunned him.

'Look who's arrived!' his father called into the kitchen through the open back door. 'Jim's arrived! Jim's arrived!'

His father had a way of shouting his messages. It was obvious that someone, most probably his mother, was upstairs using a vacuum cleaner. The noise reached the kitchen down the stairs. His father marched through the kitchen, which was filled with the smell of baking, and shouted again at the foot of the stairs:

'Jim's here! Jim's here! Can you hear me?'

Jim recognised this was familiar behaviour. They all shouted at each other in their family, he remembered, and it rather weirdly reminded him that one difference between his own marriage and his parents' was that he and Vicky had never shouted at each other. She had not been the shouting type. If she was angry, she lowered her voice to a stage whisper. It had been one of her most menacing weapons.

'What was that?' came his mother's voice through the declining whine of the vacuum cleaner and her head peered over the banisters at the top of the stairs. 'Who's here?'

'Jim, my dear. Look!'

'But you never said...'

She was considerably shorter than his father and at first glance seemed older. The grey hair, covered by a head scarf, and the pouchy cheeks in a round face perhaps exaggerated this look of age. Really it was her manner, inclined to be fussy, even finicky, that bore the hallmark of elderly behaviour. The way she came down the stairs without hurrying, as if declaring that she had been working her fingers to the bone and deserved a rest, imparted even to her smile a degree of truculence that was not, happily, matched by the warmth of her pale blue eyes.

'So you came, Jim dear. I thought you would.'

They kissed each other on the cheek. He knew in the stiffness of her body that she was grateful though she resented having to say so. With his mother it was always his body that reacted to her moods. She had a way of communicating what she felt or intended by simply being physically present to him.

He had never learned to master this power of hers. It tended to disarm him.

'I think you've been on holiday, haven't you? You're looking well.'

'So are you.'

'No, I'm not looking all that well. But I can't complain. You're only as old as you feel, I always say. We've been wondering, you know, if you knew…'

'About father going into hospital, you mean?'

'Yes.'

'Sam told me it would be soon. That's why I decided early this morning to come up here.'

She looked at him, pursing her lips very effectively, and using her body language to dispute what he said. 'Sam has kept in touch. He's been very thoughtful.'

Jim overlooked the rebuke in this. 'I know I should have been in touch, but the drafting of a report about possible staff cuts and cuts in this, that or the other has been keeping me busy for months. Still, I know I should have done better. Well, there it is.' He shrugged.

His mother unwrapped the scarf from her hair and shook it. 'We'll have some coffee. Lunch will be a bit late.'

They sat down round the kitchen table, spread with a brightly coloured cloth. His father smoothed the palm of his hand over the cloth, looked at Jim with eyes innocently soliciting sympathy and suddenly spoke about retirement. 'I'll be sixty next year, you know, and there's this new pension scheme for early retirement. Your mother and I were thinking it might be worthwhile.'

Jim was reminded of the feeling he usually had on returning home, that he was expected to participate in discussions that had been going on already for weeks or months and to which whatever he contributed would very likely be treated as no more than a child's unhelpful interference in an adult conversation.

His mother was not be deterred from the previous topic. 'It all depends on the tests, the hospital tests, and there's no knowing what they show.'

'I thought it was going to be an operation,' said Jim.

'No, no, just tests. They changed their minds, so Dr McGregor told us.' His mother spooned instant coffee into mugs and then poured on water. 'White or black?'

'White for me, please.'

'They couldn't make up their minds, that's what I think. These so-called experts never can. And they'll never tell you, even if they really know something. I don't trust them, not one inch.'

She spoke as Jim had heard her speak at meetings of the local Townswomen Guild. It was when she spoke like that that her lips grew thin in the pursed irritability of their ensuing silence.

'They're just doing what they're trained to do,' said his father, 'and they do it as best they can. I feel all right in myself, you know. It's those x-rays. Down here,' pressing his hand to his stomach and shaking his head in bewilderment, 'when the pain starts, it's like a needle being driven right into me, do you know what I mean? If they can get rid of that, well, I don't mind what they do.'

'How long has this being going on?'

'Since last February. I was lifting up the desk in the office – I can't remember why, something had rolled under it – and that's when it started.'

He described how the pain had come and gone, worsened and lessened, and finally, about last May, their doctor had decided further investigation was needed. Certain tests had been made and now more were needed. Jim did not ask what was suspected, fearing he would be told the worst, but it pleased him that his father spoke of it all with the mixture of professional earnestness and practical good humour that he would have shown in selling life insurance to a prospective customer. Both he and his mother were silent when his father had finished speaking.

Jim sipped his coffee from a blue and white striped mug, while his mother, her elbows placed on the table, slowly dry-washed her hands. The sole sounds were the slow ticking of the grandfather clock audible from the hall and the noises of meat roasting in the oven.

'We had the outside of the house painted,' said his mother, as deliberately changing the subject as she might have put up an umbrella at the onset of rain. 'You may have noticed.'

'It looks very smart.'

'It cost a lot of money.'

'The inflation these days is said to be so good, but I don't think it is,' said his father. 'We'll never be right again as we were.'

'And what about you, dear? What about your work?' His mother was being polite, though she had guessed (as he knew she had guessed) that Jim had not returned home solely on account of his father's health. 'All the cuts you mentioned, are they going to affect you?'

She looked at him with such politely innocent inquiry in her pale blue eyes he was grateful for her inability to act a part convincingly. He wondered when she would broach the question of his future, for he had assumed she had heard something from Sam, if only a different and garbled version of his relationship with Sally.

'Very probably.'

'Seriously, you mean?' asked his father.

'Yes, seriously.'

'You mean you'll get the sack?'

'Very probably.'

'I thought you'd said the job was secure.'

'It probably won't be the moment my report leaks out. I've suggested ways of reducing staff and amalgamating departments and dispersing them to less expensive sites.

That's what my life's been about in recent weeks. And now I've had enough.' His voice acquired an edge of anger. 'I think I'm going to do something else.'

'What?'

'What I've always wanted to do.'

'You mean, become a painter full-time?'

He grunted a rather irritable agreement. It shamed him that he was having to admit to it in such a curt and irritable way.

'It's your decision of course.'

'Let's say I've always wanted to become a painter.'

'Sam said,' said his mother, 'he'd met a girl in your flat. A very attractive girl. It would be nice if you were to get married again, Jim dear.'

There it was, straight off! He knew the parental reasoning, or at least his mother's: he, Jim Nordon, would be foolish to marry if he threw up his good job! The petulance of his own thinking came as a shock. In annoyance, feeling the colour rising in his cheeks, he stared at the tile work at the back of the sink unit. A petulance of an earlier age, of his adolescence and all it evoked for him, infected him with its presence in this kitchen like a spirit of place.

'I want to get married again,' he found himself saying. 'In fact, that's one of the reasons I've come here. To tell you that Sally and I are sort of engaged. I know that sounds silly, but the reason I couldn't let you know earlier was because she had to go home to look after her mother, who's not well. She has a heart problem.'

'Sally? Is that the girl's name?'

'Sally-Anne is her full name.'

'It would be lovely,' said his mother. 'But I'm sorry to hear about her mother. That must be very worrying.'

'It is. So we haven't announced anything.'

There was so much he did not want to tell, dared not tell. He blinked, looked down at his cooling coffee and the back of his right hand that was lying on the table cloth, and took in a long, steadying breath. His father unexpectedly came to his aid by saying a bit retrospectively:

'Her parents, I hope, are better than last time. What a hole-in-the-corner affair that reception was!'

'Oh, that was because Victoria's father was ill,' his mother protested. 'Don't you remember? He had one of those hip operations. It was the only time he could have it, so he had to go into hospital. It wasn't anyone's fault really.'

'It was a bloody hole-in-the-corner affair, the poorest reception I've ever been to. I'm not surprised you and Victoria split up after a start like that.'

'Please,' hushed his mother. 'We agreed we'd never talk about it.'

Jim felt completely indifferent to the mention of Vicky, always referred to politely by her full name. He recalled how she had stood in this kitchen – the only time she had come to *Cotswold House* – and deliberately dropped her cigarette on the floor and squashed it with the heel of her shoe. He'd mentioned it to her afterwards and all she had said in her usual soft voice was: 'I couldn't find an ashtray so I dropped it on the floor.'

'So how long will you be staying?' asked his mother, evidently glad that the most pressing topic had at least been broached.

'Just tonight, if I may,' he answered with a suitable diffidence, and when his father mentioned that he had talked of staying in Altrincham his mother chimed in with protests about that being nonsense, his room being always ready for him, he must know that, and so on. They finished their coffee and he walked out to his car to fetch his small travelling case.

There was very little in the way of true conversation possible between him and his parents, Jim realised. He took no pleasure in acknowledging to himself that he was partly to blame. He could find nothing spontaneous to say about

Sally and the problem of her mother, nor at all costs did he wish to mention the possibility of pregnancy. His parents' lives had developed fairly traditional routines that resented novelty or any kind of disturbance. They were reasonably warm and responsive to each other, or they had reached some rough-and-ready working compromise in the decades of their marriage that allowed for exchanges of opinion on a reasonably civilised level. There were no real intimacies, though, no talk of personal matters. Sam and he had long ago agreed on the reality of the generation gap and the barrier to discussion of personal problems.

His room had changed since he had last slept in it. An extra bed had been added. It was now quite cluttered with furniture. 'Sam and Debbie came with the girls at Easter and we put an extra bed in here for them,' his mother explained. Otherwise it contained everything familiar from his boyhood. Apart from a table and a bookcase, a couple of chairs and a wall cupboard, the one piece of furniture that most dominated his memory, as it still dominated the room, was a very large wardrobe in very dark stained wood with a long mirror fixed to the door. His small boy's awe of it had gradually yielded to an adolescent narcissistic delight in the mirror's witness to his strength and manhood. The spots on his face had been squeezed and burst open before it, the hairs on his chin and chest inspected in it, and there also he had studied with shameful excitement the filling shape of his penis.

Opening the wardrobe, he found only two things in the dark, moth-balled interior. One was an old box of watercolour paints resting on top of dog-eared and curling sheets of his old paintings. When he took them to the window and looked at them, he suddenly realised his teenage enthusiasm for painting. The art room at school, the sitting-room downstairs, exterior views of *Cotswold House* and a series of pen-and-ink landscape sketches were some of the subjects that emerged as he flipped through the sheets. There were no faces, no people in his world at that time, he thought, and it struck him that he had been far more preoccupied by perspective and geometry at that age than by the challenging relationships of planes and curves involved in portraying human features. *I was arrogant, that's what I was. Arrogant because I had imagined there were always rational solutions to human problems. And arrogant because I had enjoyed the power of winning, or at least being able to do something sufficiently well to win some of the time.*

The second thing was his bag of golf clubs. He hadn't used them for years. The last time he had played he had unexpectedly encountered Vicky, had seen her with her colleague, the man by whom she now had two children, and then and there, as he prepared to putt at the sixth hole while they were teeing up for the fourth, he had been overwhelmed by a paralysing fury at the blatancy of the cuckoldry. Whether or not they had seen him, he neither knew nor cared. He stood utterly still for several seconds, then he walked out of his game, returned to the club-house pale with fury, threw his clubs into the boot of his car and drove home to the Harrow house. Later he rang up his partner and apologised. But he had never played again. The clubs had been part of his luggage on some trip to *Cotswold House* in the intervening years, he couldn't remember exactly when, and they had been left in the wardrobe ever since, dried earth still attaching to one of them.

Over lunch he asked his father whether he'd like to play golf. 'It'd do me good, do us both good,' said his father despite his mother's protests. Hitting a golf ball wasn't likely to strain him too much, he was sure. They drove to the local club and played three holes before it began to rain again. It was no good. Jim was out of practice and tired. For some reason or other he constantly found his eyes straying to the distant green blur of *The Steep.* He felt a growing need to make a pilgrimage to that holy place, simultaneously apologising to his father for beginning to feel the effects of his drive from London. They both recognised the need for a drink in the club-house bar. In the course of it he found himself confessing something he'd never mentioned to his father before:

'Every time I've come back up here, I get the feeling it's never been the place for me. I don't hate it, I just want to get away from it. Is it suburbia? Have you ever felt you wanted to get away from suburbia just because it's suburbia?'

The silly question elicited a laugh and a slight shrug.

'I've never been really ambitious. I could just about afford to buy the house, so that's why we've stayed. You're hurt, you're still smarting, my dear chap. You were always the sensitive one, weren't you? That marriage, it wasn't right. Of course I know your mother has her own ideas. She's never wanted life to offer itself to her but always asked something of it, always anticipating and hoping for this and that. If you want to give up your good job and try your luck as a painter, I say good on you. I'm not like that, though. I'm like Sam, we just accept. Or I should say Sam's like me. It's because deep down we're lazy. We prefer expediency. And neither of us is very gifted.'

Jim felt annoyed at hearing this from his father, although he had to admit there was some truth in the self-disparagement. He also felt a wave of humility and concern rising in him for his father's health and evident fragility. He regretted he had made him play even three holes.

'What nonsense!' his father exclaimed. 'I enjoyed it, I really did!'

That night in bed, listening to his parents downstairs though unable to hear exactly what was being said, he recognised it was by no means the first time his adult self had seen his home for the unimportant, confined place it was, but it was the first time he had been properly aware of its mortal weakness, his father's anxiety over his health, for instance, and the impotence of his mother's attitudes. What he recognised also, as features in the legend that might sustain his recollection of the place for the rest of his life, were the comforting noises of television from below along with his parents' voices in some brief exchange, or the squeaking and cracking of pipes as water was run for a bath, or the virtually unending tick-tock of the grandfather clock in the hall. They would be the familiar, old-world remnants of the myth of his boyhood and adolescence as he fell asleep.

****

The Steep was a large area of public parkland visible through his bedroom window. If it had been blue-grey in the rain of the previous afternoon, it was now a gloomy viridian speckled with highlights of chrome green and yellow in the morning sunlight. It wore the bracken on its steep slopes like a gleaming new-washed wool of green. The small copses of trees, mostly conifers and silver birches, that stood out in this woolly greenery looked like tall people standing in embarrassed stillness before the arrival of royalty. *The Steep* had dominated his boyhood, he realised now as he looked at it, more than *Cotswold House* or his parents or his school. It had been the place he had always gone to be alone. Yes, he had begun to think of it as somehow holy, where prayers rose to divine hearing more perfectly in its silence than anywhere else and therefore a place to which one went as on a pilgrimage, with intent rather than as a casual visitor. Like his apartment in Victoria Mansions, it had assumed the place that was his real home, the place of his most private worries and hopes.

Over his breakfast his mother, still in her dressing-gown, scolded him for having taken his father to play golf.

'It was too much for him. I knew it would be. Now he'll have to spend the whole morning in bed. The job's getting too much for him. He'll have to retire soon.'

Though the words were a litany composed of rebukes and anxieties, Jim could tell she was less concerned about his father than about him. She kept on looking at him with the sort of dramatic reproachfulness that she had used when she felt he had let her down as a boy.

'Mother, will you please stop looking at me like that.'

'I am sure I don't know how you think I am looking at you. A cat may look at a king.'

'Yes, but the king is never sure what the cat sees.'

'Very well.' She thrust her chin forward. 'The cat sees someone who's going to throw away his chances, that's what the cat sees.'

'What chances?'

'You know what I mean.'

He knew from the way she looked at him and challenged him with the forward stoop of her shoulders over the breakfast table that they need hardly use words. They could read each other. Or at least she could read him. He ate some cornflakes noisily.

'If I decide to give up what I'm doing and paint portraits instead, or simply take my paintings round from door to door, then I'll be taking a chance, not throwing it away.'

'It's your own life,' she said, shrugging. 'A girl's not going to want to marry you if you...'

'Please, mother!'

His annoyance showed sufficiently for her to stop. That was the one difference between her treatment of him now and what he could have expected from her ten years ago. She busied herself making toast that he was too annoyed with her to say he wouldn't eat.

'So, my dear, how long are you staying?'

'Until this afternoon. I ought to be back in the office tomorrow.'

'So it's a short visit, isn't it?'

'Well, I wanted to see how Dad was.'

She picked toast gingerly out of a pop-up toaster that had evidently stopped working and waggled fingers in the air.

'Oh, this silly thing!' Putting toast on his plate, she said: 'You didn't come home just on his account, did you?'

'Not completely, of course. I wanted to see you.'

She placed both arms on the table in a loosely folded position and looked at him solemnly. 'You know that isn't it really, is it? You really wanted to tell us something else. That's what I think.'

Her motherly concern for him was so inept in its embarrassment, and yet so close to the truth, that he suddenly felt like saying rudely: 'Tell me then!' but didn't. Her blue eyes scrutinised him in a way that begged for a love he felt quite unable to show her.

'No, mother, I can see it was a mistake. I shouldn't have come back. I should have gone to a psychiatrist, but since I didn't have a psychiatrist to go to, I thought the next best thing is to go home, see how my father is, retrace my steps, try to find out where it all began. When the floor of your world just disappears, what exactly do you do?'

She reached out a hand and touched him. In almost automatic reaction he felt like withdrawing from her touch at once, but he forced himself to keep his hand still beneath hers.

'I know what you mean, my dear,' she said softly. 'You must do it your way.'

'Right.'

So I'll do it my way, he thought, trying to smile at his mother.

'You're old enough to know what's best for you. I am sorry about what happened between you and Victoria, but it can't be helped. Just don't take too long making up your mind, that's all.'

He was admonished more by the oblique reference to his age and supposed maturity than by any of his mother's direct scolding. So long as he stayed here at *Cotswold House* he would be bound to feel waves of reproach splashing out of her towards him. Their relationship would always be slightly awkward. Just as awkward as the touch of her hand resting on his and the replica of true affection it suggested.

'I'm going to walk up *The Steep*,' he announced.

It was brusquely said. His mother accepted it with a faint smile.

'Very well, my dear. You'll be back for lunch, won't you?'

He would be back for lunch, he said, hating the fact that each had to resort to such coldness simply because it was easier than trying to be kind. *Cotswold House* meant to him the pretence in his relations with his mother, the uneasy estrangement of their mutual feelings. If either the one or the other had been able to discover some abracadabra that would really unlock their feelings – her love for him that he resisted, his fondness for her that she seemed to disbelieve with every movement of her body – then they would instantly discover the language and gesture to express all that was pent up. No abracadabra was available that Sunday morning.

The Steep had usually been deserted on Sundays. This morning he was surprised to find a great many people making the trek up the field from the stream and across the wide stretch of grassland below the reservoir. It was only above the reservoir that the hill became steep, where the land rose sharply and the tall bracken clustered together with the density of a practically uniform green ice, the topmost fronds sticking almost motionlessly on to blue sky like elaborate Christmas decorations. The trek of Sunday visitors crossing the grassland below soon disappeared when he looked down from the bracken-surrounded path leading up *The Steep* itself. He thought vaguely how times had changed. Ten years ago he would probably have been alone on the steep path and the only sound apart from birds and insects would have been a distant summoning of bells from the blurred sprawl of distant suburbs. Now he could feel people all round him, even if he only saw the occasional head above the icy bracken and heard the occasional voice. People seemed close at hand, perhaps watching and crouching like the bracken itself. Yet when he actually confronted people coming down the same cleft of a path through the broken fronds it was usually a reason for greetings and some laughter and calls of 'Lovely morning, isn't it!'

The Steep had at its topmost point a disused quarry and a picnic area. From this site the whole of the south-eastern suburbs of Manchester and outlying areas could be seen, mostly a chequered blur of buildings and greenery but with some focal points such as churches, high-rise blocks and the airport. On this particular morning a haze was already beginning to obscure the distance. Almost motionless small clouds shed wispy strips of shade over what looked like a river bed of nearer suburbs. Apart from a very slight breeze, there was hardly any suggestion of movement save for the stately motion of people in the channels of the bracken slopes and children and younger adults playing games in the open space of the quarry. The shouts of their playing echoed in a heat-dulled soft booming over the entire area.

Once the quarry had been reached Jim strolled on into further scrubby, less frequented woodland. It was easier to walk here among trees and little bracken. The shouts almost passed from earshot. Except for a bird call or perhaps a barking dog he thought himself islanded in a deep natural hush, akin almost, he felt, to the divine calm that he had associated with the place in his boyhood. It had been a long, long time since he had been in such quietness. If he were prepared to pray, he thought, his very prayerfulness would have the majesty to be carried upwards on the silent wings of angels.

Then all he could think of to compare it with was the sound of the sea as he and Sally had been lying on the sand. Accompanying the thought was a reminder of his stupidity. Sally's smiles and laughter and the bold, open way she had offered him her love were such precious and demanding memories that he wondered madly why he should be here now. He had the panic sense that unless he did something very quickly he would lose her forever. She was the most precious person in his life, he knew that now with as fair certainty as he could know anything. The certainty emerged from the deep surrounding quietness and he felt it as surely as the heat of the sun on his hair once he had left the woodland. As for Rachel, he felt an even greater certainty about her, but it was a certainty of loss. One small nudge of fate and he could have been hopelessly in love with her. He had tried to persuade her to alter their relationship. Each time he had known it was against her will as much as his. And now he knew, as a fly buzzed close to his face with a defiling inquisitive persistence, that he had lost her and the ache of it was real.

A little to his annoyance he saw people ahead of him. They had most likely arrived in this area of bracken from the Manchester direction, he assumed. A man about his own age with a boy beside him was followed by a couple of younger children and a woman pushing a pushchair. The pushchair contained not a child but what looked like paper bags stuffed with things for a picnic. They said nothing to him as they passed and he said nothing to them, but he noticed the woman had red hair. Idly he looked behind him as he strolled farther along the path and he saw the woman also turn her head of full red hair to give him a second look. She was attractive, with her freckled, quite young-looking face, though it was her strong, rounded hips and shapely buttocks in tight jeans that he noted with a twinge of approval as her back passed from sight. She pushed the awkward little vehicle at arms' length, which stretched the blue material over her bottom even more tightly, and then called out to the man to help her. In fact, it was the boy, Jim saw, who ran back to take the pushchair from her. In that moment he looked away, practically at the moment that they all disappeared into the trees. The twinge he now felt was one of real loss, not for this casually encountered family group but for himself and the fact that he had no children of his own.

A life of commitments, he reminded himself. A life of good prospects. But a life unshared, a life without anchor. These facts buzzed in his head more loudly than surrounding insects as he wandered slowly down the pathway and into thicker woodland. Since he had not walked as far as this for at least a couple of years, he was surprised to find evidence of public amenities in what had previously been the wildest part of the whole area. The path also turned literally into a newly prepared sand and shingle walk lined with tree trunks sunk into the edges, with evidence that more such preparatory work was due to take place. A sign pointed to Toilets and there, sure enough, was an incongruous structure on stilts with silhouette figures of a man and a woman painted on the two doors. Adjoining it, through the trees, he glimpsed the shapes of cars parked in what he had always known as an unkempt area of bracken. There were voices coming from all round and he soon discovered why. The trees parted to reveal a brand new picnic area and playground with wooden tables and benches. A score or more of people were seated there watching a party of children noisily playing cricket. This was not *The Steep* he had known, not the quiet place where he had come so frequently as a boy.

He quickly turned back like a Crusoe who finds his island has been invaded. No matter how much he might want to recover the quiet of the past, he recognised that it was ridiculous to resent such an intrusion. He might be fretful at being driven away from what he had thought of as rightfully his, but none of it was justified. So he turned and followed the path upwards towards *The Steep.* In doing so he realised the family with the woman and the pushchair must have come this way. It was while he was thinking vaguely about this that a kind of chill of recognition swept over him. It was so strong that he was forced to stop. A couple of small boys carrying kites came down the path, calling out to someone down below: 'It's no good! There's not enough wind!' But Jim had started off, half walking, half running. He felt sweat break out on his temples and the back of his neck.

He had to find her, though to find anyone in this wide area of public parkland on a Sunday morning so crowded with people seemed impossible. Sweating badly, he ran along the path through the woodland towards the topmost part of *The Steep* and told himself she couldn't be far away, knowing well enough that in whatever time had elapsed since he'd encountered the family on this same path they could have gone to a dozen different places in the woodland and the bracken. The shouts and calls of those playing in the quarry returned to earshot. He came across two separate couples, one with a small dog, but otherwise the area of woodland appeared to be as deserted as when he had first entered it. As the trees ended he came out on to the ridge, walking fast now and breathing hard, and he saw the suburban panorama below him, beyond the frothy greenery of bracken. Flies buzzed round him annoyingly. Waving a hand before his face he looked carefully round at the groups of people who had already settled themselves at the bracken's very edge or partly under the shade of one or two rather stunted trees that lined the sides of the quarry.

Who was he looking for? The red hair should be enough, he thought. To be honest, though, who was he looking for? Was he looking for someone whom he had known ten years or so ago? Was he looking for the very first real ecstasy he had ever known? Did he imagine that by accident, on this very Sunday morning, he would meet her here on *The Steep*? And then he looked up and on the rim of the quarry, about twenty metres above him, he saw her. She was looking down at him. He had the sense that her eyes had literally drawn his gaze towards her.

Because she appeared to be alone now he felt the intimacy of their earlier relationship tauten his whole body. He waved, one quick flourish of his right hand. She smiled back at him and began descending a sheep-track of a path that slowly brought her to him, her red hair seeming to bounce upwards slightly at each careful downward step she took. He noticed how much her face had changed. She had grown fuller in the cheeks and her eyes had attractive little pouches, but her mouth and chin looked as sensual and assertive as when he had known her. The whole impression of her features had changed from prettiness to handsomeness. From that single impression he knew that she was happy.

'It's Jim, isn't it?' she asked. 'Do you still live in one of those houses down there?'

He nodded and said yes. Her accent had been more pronounced. Now it was the polite, almost accentless, Liverpool, with the sort of deliberately pure spoken English that mocked the pretentiousness of English differentiation by accent. He felt slightly in awe of it, as he felt in awe of her. 'But I'm just up here for the weekend. I live down in London now. How are you?'

'I'm very well.' It was as if she both saw through the politeness and at the same time respected his shyness, even liked it. 'I remember now, you said you were taking that job. Are you enjoying it?'

In that very question he acknowledged the true real distance between them. He was not even Manchester to her, let alone a university student, but London. That gulf was almost as great as the supposed social distance between them. He smiled a little sourly. 'I'm probably going to give it up. Are the others your family?'

'Yes, they are. We live in Chorlton. Kevin's a teacher. Emma's nine and Joan's five.'

These two children now appeared above them at the edge of the quarry and were looking down. The presence of the children and her readiness to mention them were evidence enough of her inherent pride as a wife and mother. She was being as assertive and strong-willed as he remembered in speaking about them. Suddenly, from a pocket of her blouse, she took sunglasses and put them on. Her eyes seemed blotted out from him. It indicated, and he read the message quickly enough, that there was something else she wanted to tell him, but daren't. In the short ensuing pause a girl's sharp, inquiring voice called:

'Mu-ummy?'

'All right, dear, I'm coming!' Then to Jim quietly, her lips becoming the centre of his attention: 'I'd never expected to meet you, you know. We've been here dozens of times year after year. Then I thought I recognised you. Could it be? I asked myself. You never answered my letters, did you?'

'What letters?'

'I sent you three letters when I knew I was going to have Robert.'

'Mummy!' one of the girls repeated, coming down the sheep-track. Jim could not tell what her eyes were saying to him from behind the sunglasses, except he knew that the anguish of an earlier time had long been overlaid in her life by some new happiness.

'Do you mean...?'

'Come here, Joan darling! Yes, I sent them to that house down there.'

'I never got them! Honestly!'

'Well, it doesn't matter now.' The girl ran down towards her mother and looked up intently at Jim. She leaned against her mother, who placed a hand on her shoulder. The other girl remained on the ridge of the quarry, looking down. Jim felt the shock of what he supposed she was telling him, that the boy Robert was his son. It was like a drop in temperature. He watched her lips closely. 'It doesn't matter now. I met Kevin when you went to London. So it worked out all right.'

What could she possibly mean? he asked himself furiously. He stared into the dark circles of the sunglasses and saw the ovals of her eyes behind them. A kind of annoyance was beginning to replace the first wave of shock. 'Do you mean that the boy you call Robert is…?'

She shook her head. 'No, I just wanted to tell you about Kevin, that's all.' There was another very brief pause. 'I think we'd better say goodbye.' She held out a hand.

'Who is the man?' asked the girl called Joan.

'Someone I knew, dear.' The hand was still extended, the lips moulding into a faint smile. 'Goodbye, Jim.'

He took her hand and held it firmly for a few moments. It occurred to him that he simply could not recall what such a formal act as a handshake had felt like, but now it felt as though his fingers were quite limp in her grasp. The hurt of their break-up, which had not really been either's fault, he felt sure, came back to him for a moment. They had not even so much as touched their hands together then. He had thought he was leaving just for a day or so, but he had taken everything with him when he left the flat in Salford and he'd never gone back. And the ecstasy of the relationship seemed completely inappropriate to this unscheduled meeting of their lives. Yet he asked, still keeping his hand in hers although her grasp had relaxed:

'You're happy, are you?'

'Yes, very.'

'Goodbye, then.'

It was time already, he saw, perhaps even a bit overdue, for the man he assumed was her husband now appeared on the ridge of the quarry accompanied by the boy. Jim shaded his eyes. He looked hard for more than a dozen seconds at the boy's features and yet apart from red hair similar to hers he couldn't tell from his scrutiny whose looks he might have. In any case, it seemed utterly out of place, not to say rude, to pry into what had been deliberately concealed from him. Still more important was the sense that he was nothing more than a stranger in her life and the life of her family. So he waved his hand and quickly went down one of the steep, narrow paths through the bracken. Dropping down the slopes of the path with a sensation akin to tumbling, he let the high surrounding fronds strike him in the face and engulf him.

At that moment, his was a mixture of shock and shame. The reality of it most annoyed him. In so far as he could think sensibly about anything, he suddenly resented the way relationships could reawaken and claim back something from you. They should remain in their tombs of memory. He was ashamed because he knew he had been put in the wrong, although it had all happened from ignorance. He was shocked because the implication of what he knew left a chill sense of his having wronged her or at least shown too little regard. At rock bottom of it all, he recognised, it was nothing so human as deception or ignorance or the failure of love that was the ultimate cause, but that mechanical, imperturbable force of class consciousness that dictated the hierarchy of their relationships. His arrogance sprang from it, the middle-class arrogance of the boy who thought of people, of *them*, as ciphers and deliberately excluded human figures from his drawings. It had taken the collapse of relationships, especially the breakdown of his marriage, for him to learn the first elementary lesson in the long process of becoming human, that, above all, it was people who mattered, their faces and their lives.

As the fronds struck against his face one after another and he descended *The Steep* drunkenly he felt his heart compressed into a growing ache of longing for Sally. The trite saying about absence making the heart grow fonder had the reality of a pain for him now. He yearned for Sally, saying aloud, as though the wiry, slightly barbed touch of the fronds were like a kind of punishment he deserved:

'Darling, I'm sorry! Forgive me, forgive me, forgive me! I love you, I love you, I love you!'

Then he was out of the bracken and in the open, walking across the grassland below the reservoir. A few people were still trekking towards *The Steep* and now he seemed the only one going the other way. He could tell no one what he now knew, even if only implied, that he was probably a father and had been a father for ten or more years.

He returned home to an awkward lunch during which his mother admitted she had intercepted letters 'from that girl you knew.' When he angrily asked her why, she said she'd never liked his association with her (her name, Megan, had never been used). She had simply thought it better not to forward any letters to his then London address.

'You told me, Jim dear, you didn't want to have anything more to do with her, didn't you? I thought it best not to send on anything. Really, I don't think it's fair of you after all these years…'

So he let the subject drop without mentioning any meeting that had happened on *The Steep*. It seemed a lot easier. The chief thing was that he had discovered quite by accident what he ought to do. He had to re-prime the canvas of the past as best he could, knowing that the under-painting was always likely to show through, but in due course a new picture would emerge and he could see the design of it already beginning to take shape in his mind's eye.

X

She put down the phone, repeating to herself that it was for Mum's sake she had given up everything, not because he had... not because he had... She had not completed that sentence to herself because he had said something else and now all she could remember him saying was 'I'm so sorry, let me explain, I should have told you right from the start about Rachel' and her own disgust at hearing this contrite remark, semaphored to the air of the kitchen by two raised fingers, but soundlessly, so he wouldn't hear how explicit was her reaction. She put down the phone and stared at rain falling into the artificial plastic pool under the trees. Her father had done no work in the garden since their Torquay holiday. Dead flowers needed taking away, hedges needed clipping and the vegetables by the far fence had an uncared-for look. All she had had time to do over the weekend was mow the grass. She looked down at her hands and thought how red they were and suddenly felt absolutely let down, absolutely deflated.

What deflated her was not the feeling that she had been 'used,' though that feeling was there as well, but a quite crazy sense that this very house, *The Cherries*, had really been the cause of it. Jim had reacted against it in precisely the way she had earlier. Its confinement and totally characterless respectability were among the features that made her hate it. Yet there it was. She was being irrational. You simply couldn't hate a house for itself. You hated it because of its associations. And even that wasn't right, because those parts of it associated with her mother, she loved. The air of defeat and resentment that her father had created in it was what depressed her and made the house so hateful. 'It's really, you know,' her mother always liked to insist, 'his own lack of confidence. He'll never admit it, but it is.' The same thing, she thought, was at the heart of Jim's problem. Maybe it was at the heart of all their problems. Now, more than at any time in her life, the lack of confidence in relationships seemed an overpowering truth. Especially now that Mum was in hospital.

That was what most occupied her. It was utterly absorbing, filling up everything she felt was hers – heart, mind, body, conscience – and leaving no room for anything as superficial, as insecure, as contentment, let alone happiness. Because it had been her fault partly, and Jim's fault, the fault of their relationship. All the time in the train from Waterloo, on the previous Friday evening, she had bitten back tears of sheer annoyance as well as of love and regret. She had been so shaken by the appearance of Rachel Wallace that she had been absorbed by it, and when she reached *The Cherries* she couldn't help herself, she'd told her mother everything. Then she'd dissolved into paroxysms of the most ridiculous tears during her account, relishing in a stupid way the bitterness of hating the Jim Nordon whom she had loved until only a few hours before. What she had not realised was how upsetting this might be to her mother. On every previous visit she had been so careful not to say or do anything that could have upset her mother. This time she forgot. During the night her father had woken her as he had done before.

'It's your mother. I think you'd better come.'

As if *he* could never do a thing by himself! But she'd recognised the symptoms instantly and called up the ambulance. It had arrived within fifteen minutes. That had precipitated the much deeper sense of the insecurity of all relationships, of which the most important for the time being was her love for her mother. She was likely to die, Mum was likely to die, and all because she had so upset her with her own tears and the sheer lack of control shown during the telling of her story – the silly, ridiculous, sordid story of how she'd been 'used'! And lurking under it all, as she'd confessed to her mother, was the apprehension that she might be going to have a baby. It would be Jim's baby, it couldn't be anyone else's, but she felt it was grotesquely unfair that what should have been a cement, a real bond, a link, the beginning of a family – call it what you will, and she flippantly waved her hand in the air, looking down at the suds in the kitchen sink – should very likely never be anything at all or, worse, should make her determined never to let *him* know that it was *his*. She would have her baby and keep it for herself. Very likely it would be the cause of her mother's death, but at least it would be hers. Unmarried mother and child – God, when she thought what her father would say!

Quickly, keeping herself preoccupied, she finished the remaining breakfast things, stacked the white plates in the rack, plonked the cutlery on the stainless-steel drainer, telling the dull, autumnal garden: 'I must get that man to fix the dishwasher,' and then opened the glass-fronted doors of wall-cupboards containing jars of preserves and sugar packets and flour and tried to think about cooking. There would be bound to be something in the freezer or the fridge, but she felt so deflated again, this time by the sheer neatness of her mother's arrangements. There was a calendar on the wall, something given to her father by a local building firm, with a picture of a tall blue iris against a blurred background. Her eye was caught by it, as it had been caught many times. Now, when she contemplated it, seeing it as a reality beyond the superficial appearance of such things as rainfall and falling leaves and an uncared-for garden, she felt herself reminded of the ecstasy Jim had given her, a deep sexual riot of the richest private feelings, momentarily made truly real as she pressed her tummy, her sex, against the hard Formica surface of the kitchen unit with a delighted little shudder. But the delight was then clouded by a feeling of outrage. The flower's suggestive shape called to mind something else, the time when John had insisted that she hold him by *that* part and he'd gone into a kind of giggly exultation and she'd deliberately made fun of the whole thing by running fingers up and down the shaft of the penis until suddenly, embarrassing them both, he had shot hot sperm over her hand. 'Well, isn't that what you'd wanted?' he asked, injured, a little triumphant. No, she'd never wanted anything of the kind, never! *He* had wanted it! It was illogical and unfair and rather sordid and rather fun. It made him seem very vulnerable and lovable and desirable, and she'd been deeply in love with him then. If only he'd been more secure and confident as a person, or even if he hadn't lived so close, perhaps there wouldn't have been such a strain in the relationship. Because he'd really been so immature, she thought, and as she thought this she realised it was the way her father would think and did think about John Rowlandson of *Timbercombe*. She wiped her hands. Heavy footsteps came down the short passageway from the stairs.

'What would you like for lunch?' she asked.

'Who was that? Was it the hospital? You'll tell me at once, won't you, if there's any news?'

'It wasn't the hospital.'

She waited for him to ask who it was, but instead he looked helplessly round the kitchen, made a kind of eating motion with his lips and then lightly fingered his chin. 'I must shave.'

'It was from work,' she lied, needlessly anticipating more of his questions. 'From the office. I told them I couldn't get there today.'

Her father screwed up his eyes and made another munching movement. She caught a whiff of the elderly masculine smell that she had noticed about him recently. She ascribed it, perhaps too charitably, to the anxiety associated with her mother's illness. She knew he was not as helpless as he pretended to be and simply wanted no more than the comfort of calm domestic routines that her mother always supplied.

'They'll let us see her this afternoon, won't they?'

He obviously hadn't listened to her lies. She folded up a teacloth and hung it in the proper place the way her mother always did, knowing she was acting a role he wanted her to have. 'Yes, two to four is the visiting time. If she's still in intensive care, you know, it is unrestricted for not more than two people.'

'We ought to find out, oughtn't we? I'll ring up right away.'

'The number's on the pad,' she called to his retreating back.

She *had* thought of the doing the very same thing that very morning, she reminded herself, but somehow or other after yesterday, Sunday, when they'd seen Mum and she seemed so much better, though still in intensive care, she'd not felt the same urgency about phoning the hospital, especially after Jim's call. That was the call she had wanted more than anything else. When he said he had been back to his own home over the weekend, which had apparently not been an outstanding success, and then started apologising, she again felt annoyed. Why did he have to be forgiven? she wondered. Why didn't he say straight out that he was a man who wanted sex? Why wasn't he hard-bitten and blatant about his urges? Until, of course, she heard her father's voice speaking to the hospital and then speaking to her:

'They say she is being moved out of intensive care this morning. We'll be able to visit her at two o'clock.'

'Nothing else?'

He raised an eyebrow at her question. The munching motion stopped. She recognised that her father had almost stopped listening to her questions and found them puzzling when he did register them.

'No, nothing else,' he said.

'We'll have an early lunch, in that case. Is there anything you'd particularly like?'

Again she expected him to overlook this, but instead he took enough notice to give a sharp reply: 'No, no, whatever you've planned. I'm not fussy.'

'About half-past twelve, then.'

He returned upstairs, presumably to shave. Despite being rather fretful at the way he treated her, she was glad at least that her father made no serious emotional demands on her. He was extremely anxious about Mum's health, she knew that, even though he hid the anxiety beneath an unemotional surface of short, tart statements. If he had been maudlin or self-pitying, she would have despised him.

The supposed summer weather was bad enough in its typical way. The soft drizzly rain made the untidy back garden look misty and autumnal and the sound of a steady dripping from some gutter or overhang made a surreptitious ticking noise that blended monotonously with the soft buzzing from the refrigerator. Each sound suggested vacancy and futility to her.

What is more, the suburbs were silent and unoccupied, it seemed, on this rainy Monday morning. If she had felt deflated emotionally by Jim's phone call, she now felt utterly by herself. On a morning like this normally she would have been facing her monitor in the small office next to Jim's where, so frequently in recent weeks, she had waited with tingles of pleasure for the summon next door, the plastic Italian chair and his voice dictating another section of the report. Before annoyance could return or any other eruption of feeling disturb her, she remembered something else and wondered how she could have forgotten. It was Jim standing like that, busily painting, completely absorbed, sure of himself, almost immune to her save as an object, however vital, to be conveyed as perfectly as possible to canvas. It made her feel jealous. He was self-sufficient at such moments, she felt, he didn't need her. All her annoyance, even her foolish jealousy, sprang from self-pity as much as from real hurt. Why hadn't she been aware of that from the start?

'Oh, Jim, Jim,' she said aloud, 'I shouldn't have, shouldn't have…'

Shouldn't have what?

No, she reminded herself, it was Mum who mattered. It was her duty to be at home now, to be ready to look after Mum when she was better.

That was *her* duty. Only…

****

'I am not aware of redundancy…'

Whatever that meant. Charles Ball was saying it, so it presumably meant something, Jim reflected and tiredly stared down at a smear of polish on the smart mahogany top of the desk.

'You are not likely to be made redundant, James.'

Charles Ball was the only person he knew who called him by his full forename. It was a managerial affectation. It also carried a whiff of reproof.

'Of course, if you choose to leave us, we will regret it very much. Your career has been successful so far. I think you could count on advancement – swift advancement – after the report. Which of course I await with interest. The end of this week, you say?'

Jim nodded.

'That'll be the end of Z10, then, won't it? So you'll be free of that.'

Jim knew exactly what Charles Ball meant. Very probably it would soon be common knowledge that he had been the principal author of the report emanating from the mysterious Z10, although there was the even more mysterious Plath & Siegfried Agency to be accounted for. No amount of advancement would ever take him out of reach of the acrimony felt by those whose careers had either to be terminated or effectively moved sideways. He had known that much from the start, despite Charles Ball insisting that the Council would only know it as coming from Charles himself.

'Of course we'll have to be thick-skinned. There'll be difficult times ahead. The prospects of promotion for someone who shows real ability, though, will remain as good as ever. I place you in that category, James.' Charles Ball sighed. He held Jim's letter in his right hand, rather deliberately between finger and thumb in the way Jim had noticed his mother always held her knife. 'But if you insist on resigning, I can only wish you every success. As for the issue of redundancy, I appreciate that it would be to your financial advantage. It *could* be arranged. It would make you seem an early victim of your own report, of course, that's one thing. There would be precedents to consider and we would have to agree an amount of, er, severance pay. But it *could* be arranged. Have you had an offer from somewhere?'

Jim explained briefly about a change of career.

'To what?'

Looking into the round pink face of Charles Ball and observing the light-blue, somewhat boyish sweetness of the eyes behind the reading spectacles, Jim felt that the question supposed him guilty from the start. How could he justify himself in front of those supremely disapproving eyes? They were innocent of the tedious passions and uncertainties of which he was full to the brim.

'I intend to become a painter full-time. It's always been my ambition.'

'Someone did say something, yes... Portraits, isn't it?'

Charles Ball did something with his fingers, twiddling them so that the ring on his third finger flickered sharp little rays.

'Yes.'

'Well, I must give you a commission. In due course. But before your fees get beyond my reach. Eh?'

A chuckle. He had received the news with the magisterial composure of an administrator who knows that no real power was ever yielded by a paint brush. They shook hands. From now on Jim knew he would be branded as starting on his shiftless way to professional failure as a painter or the alternative of casual art teaching for a pittance. Returning to his office, the sight of clouds over the city skyline taunted him with their reminder of Sally's absence, seeming as indifferent to his fate, let alone his recent courage in speaking to Charles Ball, as Sally herself had seemed over the phone.

He used his own smartphone, first to order flowers to be sent specifically to her at *The Cherries*. 'With all my love, Jim.' Second he rang through to Stanley Worthington and told him what he had just done. 'Good, very good,' came the reply. Then, to his astonishment, Miss Rhoda Jacobs put in an appearance.

'I wanted to remind you, sir.'

What he had not realised until that moment was the watchfulness of Miss Jacob's eyes. He had never found it easy to achieve any kind of relationship with her beyond the strictly professional. He had assumed that Sally's replacement of her had perhaps been resented but had not been actively opposed. Now she gave the strong impression of reclaiming what was rightfully hers. She seated herself in the plastic Italian chair, flicking open the pages of a pad and looking up, lips pursed. He had always respected her for her efficiency. Then she grinned. He had only seen her look like that twice before. Once when he had accidentally referred to 'Sally' rather than 'Miss Harris' and once when, to his own unmistakable dismay, he had discovered in her presence that his fly zip was undone. The effect was to squeeze up her round pale face into a crushed orange look in which the pallor became suffused with an orange shade of embarrassment. He knew then that this time it was a grin of triumph.

'You will be back from Deptford by five o'clock, Mr Nordon, won't you?'

'I suppose so.'

He had forgotten that the engagement was in his diary.

'It is rather important.'

'Why is it important?'

'I should be able to get all the correspondence done by five. I don't suppose you want me to p. p. them?'

'Ah,' he said. 'No. Of course.'

In fact, he never liked sending out "per pro" letters. It was a habit of his to ensure that all correspondence left his office with his own signature. The correspondence referred to had been left undone by Sally at the end of the previous week. They were a dozen or so letters to department heads and others explaining that a report on staffing, etc. was due to be completed shortly and sent to Charles Ball by the coming Friday. As for the report itself, that was virtually completed. All he needed to do was add all the data that Sally had collected. It would give the report the sort of weightiness that made it seem important, even if few if any of its readers would be assiduous enough to study the data in detail. No doubt Charles Ball would do his own editing of the text as he had done with all Jim's submissions. As for the visit to Deptford, Jim was grateful for the chance to get out of the office and away from Miss Jacobs.

The morning rainfall had stopped as he travelled by bus through characterless city streets. He was shown the site for the proposed new Borough offices. He was aware at once of the mundane sense of contrasting permanencies where water and land meet. Limehouse Reach northwards and Greenwich Reach to his right, Surrey Commercial and India and Millwall, they were the places where immanence and flux met, or used to, for there was continuous flux even in the immanence, and the surface of the Thames, hardly reflecting the craft on it, seemed to hold upon like a thought in its eye the watery, pearl-grey gouache of clouds above London's skyline, as though they literally animated each other and were in some deep sense communing. The wind blew into his face smelling of north-shore chimneys and a blend of inland waters and oceans, yet the spaces of the Thames itself did not look disturbed, only its edges where very rapidly splashing waves fought against the solid embankment just below where he was standing. The vigour of the wind and water urged him to respond to it, to act dramatically, but he was simultaneously consumed by the open neutral emptiness of the river reaches and the remoteness of life on the far bank.

Trapped against some wire-netting close by was an empty red and white cigarette carton that the wind continually shook and flicked about in a way that suggested it was given a kind of comic cartoon life. It made no noise, or none loud enough for him to hear it. Its almost mechanical dance spoke to him about the futility of his own failure to make up his mind, to do what he wanted to do, reminding him how much he danced to the tune of others, how little he really acted for himself unless he were drawing or painting and how that urge, like the wind, could now sweep him forward.

It did so at that moment. A stronger than usual gust dislodged the cigarette carton and it went jumping quickly over weedy concrete towards tall grasses. There it disappeared. That satisfied him. He would do what he wanted. He would risk his future. He would devote himself to cultivating his gift for portraiture. That would become his life.

For several evenings after returning from work he devoted himself to finishing the portrait of Sally. He concentrated on the features, the smile, the look in her eyes as she rose from the chair. If the remaining props to the portrait, such as the chair and the background, were suggested rather than emphasised, then he had achieved his aim. He let the portrait dry and drove down to Guildford, determined to see Sally and give it to her.

The September evening had a fragile brilliance. It had a pale, china-blue sky in which a pink sun hovered impressionistically near the horizon. Apart from a gusting wind that bent trees and slightly buffeted his car, the Surrey countryside resembled something that had been kept very carefully under glass, a faintly worn replica of summer hedgerows and smooth fenced fields and the promise of covert happiness in the deepening lily-pads of shadow forming under large trees. He thought obsessively both about Sally and Megan. He wondered if, had he known what he knew now, he would have had the courage to share the responsibility that Megan's letters might have suggested. Though they might have mentioned Kevin, as she had said they did, it was as likely they would have admitted her pregnancy and the cause. So he would have been a father, have married her, he supposed, and there'd have been no London, no Vicky, but Megan as his wife and their children growing up and, for him, games of golf, drinks in the bar, a hobby of occasional paintings and a very steady life. Perhaps his mother had actually changed it all for him quite by chance. But after the silence over Rachel, to tell Sally also about Megan would be what?

Impossible? Yes.

It was dark by the time he reached Guildford and he missed his way in the suburban streets. One looked exactly like another. After parking on a corner, he walked up one darkened avenue and peered at names like *Linton*, *Sunningdale*, *Bycroft*, *Woldingham*, *Southfield*, *Timbercombe*. In the dusk they all looked like *The Cherries*. Finally he learned from a woman walking a dog that there was a house with that name in an adjoining street. Somehow *her* street, Sally's street, seemed less pretentious and *The Cherries* when he reached it looked not only familiar but cosier, more welcoming, more tucked into itself. Though there was no light at the front, lighted slits in the curtains of a side window reassured him that someone was at home. He rang the doorbell, the large painting beside him on the porch step. After moments of doubt, the stained glass in the front door was lit up from inside to the accompaniment of subdued television noise. Sally opened the door and saw him.

He could not make himself say anything immediately. The sight of her brought a rictus of a grin to his mouth and a momentary choking sensation. She looked so fresh, with such a bloom on her complexion and the porch light so glossy in her hair. His body responded to her close presence with the sharpened alertness of a dog awaiting an adult's command. Her mouth opened on seeing him, not to smile exactly, but to say:

'Why, Jim, I...'

Then he stretched forward and took her in his arms. She did not fight against him in any way, though at first she did not yield either. There was a slight stiffening in her body's posture towards him, as if he were intruding upon its rights. They stood there under the porch light pressing stiffly against each other with her perfume rising excitingly to his nostrils. Suddenly there was a loud clatter. The portrait of her had been disturbed by some movement of his and now toppled into the hallway.

He stooped, picked it up and held it out to her. There she was, leaning eagerly forward, smiling. Her face, upon which he had expended most effort, seemed to rise directly out of it like a sudden remembrance of the past. She stared at it for a moment.

'Oh. Jim dear!'

He saw from the stern and withdrawn look on her face that this reminder provided too strong a contrast with the present. The air of *The Cherries*, even in the darkness, seemed to stretch out and hug her to itself. It wanted to claim her back from him. Again he had an instant sense of the sort of void that had filled the apartment after she had left. It was here now, and the talisman, the portrait, accentuated rather than reduced it.

'Take it. I want you to have it.'

He spoke in defiance of a growing certainty that the visit was in danger of being a mistake. He could tell not only from her reaction but also from alarm signals running along his nerves that it was no good, their love had suffered a wound, it would need time to recover. It was almost as if he wished to let nothing more be said between them, so that a sort of oblivion could wipe out the guilt associated with Rachel and his lack of honesty.

There was a silence penetrated by television noise. Presumably her father was watching it somewhere. Then he asked her about her mother,

'She's a bit better. She was sitting up when we saw her this afternoon. She insisted she was going to sit up for her tea. They think she'll be able to come home tomorrow. I'm going to have to look after her, you know that.'

He knew it, of course he did, and felt embarrassed at not being able to do more than nod when he earnestly wanted to express the hope she would soon be better. Front porches were not the place for intimacies, let alone genuine sincerity. He was secretly glad not to be invited into the house.

'I think, Jim darling, we oughtn't to… to see each other for a while. Not while I'm looking after Mum.'

She had the tone in her voice that she had used during earlier phone calls that week. There was the whiff of reproof in it similar to the one in Charles Ball's.

'I wanted to tell you,' he stammered out. 'I've decided.'

'What?'

'I've handed in my letter of resignation. Or perhaps I'm being made redundant. I'm not sure. Anyhow, I'm leaving.' The whiff of reproof now impelled him to speak in a rapid whisper. 'When I was back home last weekend I went up a place called *The Steep* and decided. I decided I would become a full-time painter. I decided I want you to be my wife. I love you very much. Here, please take this.' He handed across the smart little box containing the engagement ring. 'I'm not on my knees, I know. Please, Sally dear, take it. And now I'll leave. Oh, and I should say I've seen a place in Kew where we can live, where you can have the baby, where I think we'll be happy.'

He ran out of impulse, having blurted out these private things as if he had been unable to suppress them. It made no difference, though. She remained in the doorway, keeping the porch mat inset into the floor like a minefield between herself and the outer step of red tilework where he was standing. He made a move towards her and she instantly drew back.

'No, Jim, please.' She took the smart little box. 'Oh, no, you shouldn't, but thank you. No, I think we oughtn't to see each other.'

'Why not?'

'Not so long as I'm looking after Mum. Then, well, it'll be better.'

He recognised the imperative in her words, no matter how much he might resist them. He could not tell from the way the hall light was shining what her eyes were saying.

'How long, then, do you want us not to…'

The question was meant to have a sarcastic edge, but as he spoke a door behind her opened and her father looked out into the hall. Suddenly she leaned through the front door. Her voice was unusually sharp, even though no more than a whisper:

'Please, Jim, go away! Go away! Go away!'

She then closed the door and he could see nothing of her head through the stained glass of the front door window. A car's headlights swung their beams across the front garden as it turned and he felt exposed by them. Wind swept down upon the leaves of the cherry trees with a long hissing rustling in the darkness. They seemed to be shooing him away. He walked slowly, taking deep breaths, to where his car was parked on the corner.

XI

He had a vision as he drove back to London. It began to rain. The windscreen wipers swept to the right, swept to the left, swept to the right, swept to the left. Blobs of light enlarged, splattered and vanished with the approach and passing of vehicles. Overhead illumination or glowing shop fronts offered a brief winking brightness to the rainy dark at the edges of his sight. Suburban areas came towards him before he hit the A3 with the self-confident look of shrubbery and curtained windows. He had a vision of himself as he had been with Vicky, in the house in Harrow. In such houses, in all seasons, in a darkness like this, a man and a woman would be lying in each other's arms and would see the lights sweep from wall to wall and hear the long oncoming roar rising to quick throbbing to dying thunder of the vehicles as they came and went, through rain with a placid hissing and on dry spring or summer days, early, with a wistful excitement, and so their loving would be orchestrated in that front bedroom private as a womb, naked and together in a warm bed, with all the years scattered behind them in the long dying murmur of the traffic passing. And that, he thought, or something like it, would be the future for him and Sally once Victoria Mansions had been pulled down.

It was not resentment, nor was it pique, that decided him not to ring her back. It was a twofold sense that he had to be sure of his own future as well as of her willingness to accept his past before he got in touch with her again. In fact, much more simply, he was stopped by his own pride reinforced by a kind of panic. He had to find a job to replace his present employment. So he turned to Stanley Worthington, who had already made one or two suggestions. This time all he said was:

'You become a painter because you *are* a painter. You don't need courses or qualifications if you have the talent and can demonstrate it. You just need to go on working. Day after day, day after day. You mustn't get in a panic about your ability. You've got the ability. You've got to be determined enough and lucky enough to be able to demonstrate it. Then the world decides.'

Stanley waved a brush and hitched up his trousers as he spoke. He had been in poor health again over the summer. The art centre where he worked consequently needed some administrative help. Jim had readily volunteered to help at spare moments after the weekly class or at times when Stanley himself had to be absent. It was rumoured that a new administrative post was to be created in the coming year if the spring elections were to produce a new leadership of the borough council. Meantime Jim took Stanley's advice. He spent as much time as he could spare on painting, especially doing the initial preparatory work for Dora's new portrait.

On a Saturday he opened the front door of the apartment to find Mrs Rogers standing there. She had come up two floors, she announced, to get her money, since she mostly 'did' the apartment on Fridays while Jim was at work. She asked about Sally.

'Ooo, I'm sorry to hear about her mother. I suppose it'll take a long time, won't it? You don't have to tell me about heart trouble. There was my father's sister, that's my auntie, you know, and a cousin, I think it was, they all had it. My auntie died of it. It's a terrible thing. She's not young then, is she?'

'Who?'

'The girl's mother.'

'I think she's in her sixties.'

'Old really, in that case. To have a daughter that age, I mean.'

'Yes.'

Mrs Rogers had not entirely approved of Jim's association with Sally. She was too young for him, she had been known to observe, although the two had only met once, on a Saturday. In fact, her annual holiday, extended to five weeks that year because her daughter had needed help with a new baby, meant that she had not visited the apartment or even seen Jim very often recently. She had been calling much more frequently when Dave had been there. Seeing Sally, she made it plain that if she wasn't needed, it would be quite all right by her, she had plenty of other work in the Mansions.

'So she won't be coming back here?'

'She'll be staying in Guildford for the time being. Until her mother's better. And then of course they'll be pulling this place down, won't they?'

'Oh, you know, it'll be terrible for the really old ones here. They're so worried. Mrs Snowden in No 6, she is, and Mr and Mrs Ames in No 10, they say they can't find anywhere. Of course they'll all have to go. But Dora – she's a real character, she is – she says she's not going to move until they cut off the electricity and the water. Shall I come again next Friday, Mr Nordon?'

'Please, Mrs Rogers.'

'You'll be taking all the pictures and drawings, won't you? The ones, you know…'

The nude ones, she meant, particularly the nude drawing of Sally. Jim Nordon's 'nude period' had caused Mrs Rogers as much offence as his association with Sally. He assured her that he would take all his paintings and she needn't go into the second bedroom if she didn't want to. It had always been a rule of his that Mrs Rogers would never attempt to tidy his paints and materials. She waved her hand in good-natured rejection of what he was insinuating

'So I'll come in on Friday. I do hope you have better news then. You know, about her mother.'

It was not so much in the evenings or at weekends that he thought about Sally as during the daylight hours when he was at work. Her presence there had made the drafting of the report a lot easier than it might have been otherwise. To recognise her tap on the door, even the sound of her feet in the corridor, or to catch glimpses of her at various points in the Borough offices, not to mention the times she had sat in the plastic Italian chair, had lightened every moment of his working day . Now she was not there and the report had been submitted, his own routines had become concentrated on the tedious business of the dispersal programme (which would most likely come to nothing, though they had to go through the motions of planning it).

In the evenings and at weekends the yearning for her sometimes bore down on him strongly. The phone calls, not even the use of Skype, made much difference. He felt choked by her absence, knowing she was devotedly looking after her mother. Maybe she didn't love him any more? He put that aside by losing himself in painting whenever he could. There was a therapy in the odour of turps and linseed oil, not to mention oil paints or acrylics. It excited and lifted his spirits. To feel the challenge of colour and line and the yielding of such inert substances as the paints and the support to the task of making real, of representing the visible, became a controlled, disciplined and fulfilling joy.

Then he would think of her, expecting her to be there, or remembering a moment, a word, some smile or laugh. Worst of all was the long sexual ache for her, to which the recollection of her body beside his was like some memory of freedom forever lodged in the past. The imposition of such abstinence on himself was eased by his painting, but he knew he could not keep himself under such restraint for long. He knew it was treason even to think of Rachel, let alone stretch out his hand to his smartphone as he did more than once.

On the other hand, the memories of Sally that seemed most lasting and comforting were not sexual at all. They were memories of things she had told him from her childhood or her schooldays (usually, if they concerned her parents, involving her mother rather than her father), and of these one in particular stuck in his mind, chiefly because the source of it, a copy of Turgenev's *Sketches*, had been left behind in the apartment. Her mother had been reading it and had given it to her. One day Sally had been sitting on the chaise longue, her legs curled under her, when he had seen tears slowly pouring down her cheeks. The paperback with the black cover had been in her hand. She saw him and started incongruously smiling at him through her tears.

'I could howl! How silly, how stupid! I could howl!'

'What?'

'This story, this stupid story!'

It was the story of the paralysed Lukeria, the *Living Relic*. She held it out to him.

'*I walked in the meadows of green grieving for my life,*' she quoted. 'God, I could howl, absolutely howl!'

Suddenly she held out her arms to him. He bent down to her and they clutched each other. For whole minutes, he thought, they held each other, the noise from Southampton Row like some discordant indefinite rumblings, against which their very stillness together seemed a guarantee of love and understanding.

What he could not intrude upon, or ever fully know, was her love for her mother. He could not try to stand in the way of that love, no more than she could refuse the responsibility of such devotion. One evening after returning from Stanley's art centre he used his smartphone to ring her, hoping by using her mobile phone number to avoid speaking to her father. For some reason this didn't work. The gruff, testy voice told him to wait. Again there was the television noise, this time the Coronation Street music, the sad, brassy, evocative sound as the credits ran at the end of an episode that conjured up for him the feel of Manchester rain and grey streets. He could imagine that Sally had perhaps left her smartphone in the darkening hall of *The Cherries* along with the smell of polish. Then he could imagine she was perhaps saying to herself when she heard her father's summons: Should she? Should she let him, let Jim, intrude on her life? Or should she simply say no, she couldn't speak to him now. But the imaginings were cut off sharply by the sound of footsteps and then her voice so full and loud and a little breathless and, best of all, the frank gladness of it as she spilled out words of pleasure at hearing his voice and apologised for not ringing him and explained that her mother had had to go back to hospital for a couple of nights but was now better and in bed upstairs.

Better? Oh, yes, much better. But Sally was sure she had to have a lot of rest. It would be all right. It would take a few weeks.

When would she be coming to London? She couldn't say. Was she sure she was going to have a baby? Oh, no, she wasn't sure, not sure at all. But she didn't want to talk about it. The trouble was that she didn't like to leave her Mum for more than a couple of hours because her father always started complaining the moment she was absent for some reason. That naturally upset her mother despite whatever reassurances had been made. Should he come to see her at *The Cherries*? Oh, Jim darling, if you like to come, we'd love to see you. But no, that wasn't what he wanted. Instead he found himself saying in a shaky, frenzied way, as though fighting to remember badly learnt lines:

'I wanted to say I love you. Just that. I'm sorry about the baby. I hope, yes, I hope your Mum is better soon and I send her my love. But I rang to say… I rang to say I love you, I wish you were here, I want to hold you, I want to…

Oh, bloody hell, you know what I mean! Sorry, sorry. I just wanted to say I love you and I want you to be my wife.'

The embarrassment had moved downwards from his temples over his facial muscles like the spreading coldness from an injection and passed down his throat to lodge in the pit of his stomach. He switched off the phone, hearing nothing but an intake of breath from her before the noises of Victoria Mansions and traffic in Southampton Row surged into his ears with a roar like the sea.

'I shouldn't apologise. Why do I always apologise?'

In that way, despite his awkwardness, he felt nonetheless that he had made a flimsy bridge across the gulf created between them by Rachel's unexpected appearance. Also, in Sally's absence, talking to himself in the solitariness of the apartment had become something of a habit. He even found himself talking to the pillow in the old double-bed inherited with the lease of the apartment. Her warmth seemed there in a ghostly way beside him, a weight and solidity and gentleness filled with nothing but air and the noises of Victoria Mansions that had become all the more clamorous and pervasive since she'd left. And now when he'd spoken to her he'd only been able to blurt out a frenzied SOS of words and an apology before switching off the phone at the instant she was about to respond. He hoped she would call back, though relief at hearing that she wasn't pregnant came uppermost in his feelings if he were truly honest with himself.

In fact, there was a call. But it was Dora to say she was terribly upset at being unable to come for her sitting that evening, would he ever forgive her and could she come tomorrow evening?

He was glad enough to acquiesce. What else could he do, after all? She was paying him. It was her whisky he was drinking. She had insisted on leaving it with him so she could enjoy a drink during the sittings.

'Tomorrow, then. About half past eight.'

The phone calls to and from Guildford tended to become an evening ritual about as irregular as the visits by Dora Pratts-Morris. For this new portrait she wore what she called 'a town suit' and her looks were less 'county.' She tended to be smart to suit the tastes of Pacific Pallisades, which entailed make-up and permed hair, giving her whole appearance a shimmer and brilliance that Jim found very attractive to paint. Of course, she had to know about Sally.

'Poor thing! Looking after someone like that. Oh, that is a real problem. I'm so sorry to hear it.'

That was her first verdict. The mood of the sittings was always dictated by her. If she wasn't in the mood to discuss other people's problems, she liked talking about her own while sitting there in the spare bedroom, her hands clasped in her lap, looking serene and dignified, as Jim concentrated on the painting. He never pressured her to keep still or stop talking.

The problem of Sally's mother seemed at first to occupy a vacuum of ignored or neglected topics, but then he told her how he had gone up what was called *The Steep* and decided to leave his job. She tut-tutted at this and made a face but did not respond. Instead she said:

'I'm going to relax now. My neck's getting stiff.'

She moved her head and neck in a slow, easeful therapy and let her dignified pose yield to a more comfortable and relaxed sinking into the chair.

'I hope it doesn't last long – the looking-after, I mean. Interesting, though, what you talked about. My father always used to say that life was composed of steeps and slopes. The steeps sometimes out-numbered the slopes – an unhappy childhood, for instance, or serious illness, or an addiction, or an injury, or poverty, they were the steeps of life, but the worst, most lasting steeps, he always maintained, were those connected with love and with death, the ending or absence of love and the death of a loved one. Of course he had his own steeps. For the last years of his life he was virtually an invalid. Looking after him wore me out. He made me look after him though he could have afforded a whole array of nurses. It was his way. Well, how's it coming along?'

The portrait was growing slowly. As his first real commission Jim was trying to take the greatest possible care over it. He explained his problem and she nodded at it.

'When it's finished – and I'm sure it'll be lovely – I'm going to skedaddle off to California with your lovely portrait and spend the winter with Ted and Charlene. She's my sister-in-law. An idiotic name but a charming person. So if Mrs Rogers told you I'm staying here to the death, she's wrong. When they pull down our world, I'm just not going to be here. I think I'll have another one, a very small one, if you don't mind.'

Jim poured her another whisky along with some ice and soda. He knew there would be no chance of persuading her to pose longer once she had started on one of her monologues. This time she suddenly began talking about her wealth.

'Did you know I was rich?'

'Well, I knew you had money.'

'I have lots and lots of money as a matter of fact.' She preened herself quite blatantly, touching her hair and adjusting her pearl necklace. Often, when she wore spectacles (gilded, elegant things shaped to resemble large butterfly wings), she would delicately touch them, lift them, settle them again in place before speaking. 'Though I say it myself and I know how beastly show-off it must seem, I am a rich woman. I don't know why I stay here in our old Victoria Mansions when I could easily afford somewhere quite grand. It's my meanness. I inherited that from my father like I inherited his money.' She drank her whisky with relish and finished by shaking her head. 'Nonsense, of course. I stay here because of you, dear man. Well, now, what are your plans?'

Jim told her he had submitted his report and was contemplating the administrative post at Stanley Worthington's art centre, knowing, though, that it would mean he wouldn't have all that much time to devote to painting.

'Take it,' Dora urged in her sensible forthright way. 'Other things'll come along later.'

'Dora, I want to paint. I want the freedom to paint. The only reason I'm leaving my present work is because I want to do what I've been doing this evening *all the time*. I think I can. Going up *The Steep* made me determined. I think I've got the self-confidence to do it. Whether I've really got the talent I can't say.'

'Of course you have!' She was categorical and a bit scornful of his self-doubt. Her pouched friendly eyes appraised him closely. 'A good woman, like that charming girl you had here, the one with the sick mother, that's what you need. Excuse my silly bluntness. You'll find ways of painting, I'm sure, though God knows whether you'll find happiness.' She paused and looked away. 'I thought I'd found it with my dear Harry – and then what happens? He finds someone else. Years younger. I couldn't compete.'

Jim had known about Dora's husband, but he had never known she had been abandoned for a younger woman. No hurt showed in the elderly shapely features. He felt she must have become inured to it, though her mention of her husband's infidelity suddenly pierced him like a needle. In one of those awkward flashes of reminiscence that evoke the sharpest of feelings as well as the sense of past occasion, he remembered how he had once loved Vicky. He had been sure of his love then, sure of hers, sure of their happiness together.

'I know how you must feel.' The unsureness, the un-sticking, the crack-up of that love made his voice quiver. He found himself really unable to catch Dora's direct appraising gaze. He filled his own glass.

'Do you?'

'Yes, I, er...I'm divorced, you know.'

'Oh, of course, dear man! Aren't we here in our dear old Victoria Mansions for that sort of reason? That's why you and I are here. We have to keep together.' But he noticed her hand holding the glass of whisky shook as she spoke. 'It's part of being on our own little steeps, you know. Once you're on a steep place in your life, you're always tempted to look downwards at the past. You can't escape from it, of course you can't! Well, I can't!' She blinked quickly several times. 'Poor Harry's dead, you know. He was my second husband. All I really regret is not having been able to keep my first marriage going. It was years ago and it was my fault. I fell for Harry and he spoiled me. That was why my Leonard got a divorce. He was charming, quite the most charming man I've ever known. Very, very stupid of me. But I'll tell you one thing...'

The melting ice cubes in their glasses clicked bell-like almost simultaneously. Faraway traffic noises seeped into the quietness of the apartment and the noise of the lift door clangorously closing. Dora smiled a rather winning, courageous smile that made him realise how extremely pretty she must have been in her youth. A solemn, self-preoccupied, fresh beauty, like George Romney's 'The Parsons's Daughter', came to mind, though her smile was much more knowing and deliberate.

'You know, it's two things that are really dangerous. One of them is a kind of fifth column, do you know what I mean? It's always there in your life but you think it isn't.' She played with her necklace. Her cultivated voice, usually without stridency and softly accommodating in its tone, now made no attempt to be up-market. It grew harsh in its drawl. 'I think it's a kind of innocence, an innocence of the senses. You may know a lot about life and most people do. But when it comes to sensing the way things are going or feeling your way in a relationship – do you know what I mean? – you find you just haven't got the lines of communication other people have. It's a hell of a shock to you when it happens. It's not a lack of imagination. You can imagine all sorts of possibilities. No, it's not really knowing the language of the senses, being somehow too innocent, too naïve, too immature perhaps, when it comes to sensing the way others are feeling. Perhaps it's really a lack of true sympathy. But of course it's inside you, you're born with it and you don't grow out of it. Only when you need all the help you can get you suddenly find that this in-born innocence has let you down. I think that's one of our enemies.'

She looked slightly embarrassed at having confessed so much and practically finished her glass. She refused an offer of more.

'No, you know, dear man, there's a worse enemy,' she declared, waving a hand elegantly at him. 'The real enemy is envy.'

'Envy?'

'Yes. That's the real enemy in our lives.' She drew her lips firmly together over this remark as if challenging him to believe her. 'If you have what I call innocence of the senses and then you find yourself feeling envious, you're finished! Finished!'

'How?'

Dora pulled a little cape round her shoulders, seeming not to notice his question. 'No, I'm not serious. You're not finished when you're envious, you're just foolish. I've been foolish, my dear man, because of you.'

'Dora, that cannot be true.'

'It is perfectly true. I have envied you for living in what grandly calls itself "The Apartment".'

He burst out laughing and she joined in. It was true that the brass plate down in the street entrance, surrounded by *art nouveau* flowers and foliage, described the top as solely occupied by "The Apartment".

'Every time I go past it I envy you.' She laughed again. 'Silly of me, of course. No, I don't mean it.'

More seriously she confided that she'd decided that very morning to leave Victoria Mansions.

'They are going to pull our world down, that's for certain. And it's high time, as a matter of fact. Look at us here – bereaved, divorced, down on our luck, pensioned off, too old, I mean like Mrs Snowden or the Ameses, dear old people, but really on their beam ends. Each one of us here nurses something. And you'll be leaving, won't you?'

Jim was cleaning his brushes in the basin. 'I think I've found somewhere in Kew. I'll be renting a conversion, the ground floor and first floor of an old house converted into what's called a maisonette. Not as grand as an apartment, true.'

'You'll be getting married. That attractive girl...' She hesitated for a moment in search of the name. 'Sally, yes. So that's where you'll find married bliss.'

'Are you sure?'

She became very serious. 'You'll think me silly when I tell you this, I know you will.'

'Try me and see.'

'In this country,' she said in her artlessly aristocratic voice, 'you'll find married bliss mostly in suburbs. That's what they're there for. Suburban bedrooms.' As if the idea were somehow a trifle improper and quite silly, she added: 'And that's the best place for it. We all need to love each other a lot more. It's our crying need.' She was evidently a bit tipsy and recognised the fact. So she adjusted her cape more firmly round her shoulders with a kind of preening shudder, 'And in any case I'm sure you'll make your Sally very happy. So just for starters, if you've got nothing against it, I'll put up the money for an exhibition of your work. What do you think about that?'

They talked on for an hour or more until gradually it was clear she meant what she said. She wanted to be his patron. He could not deny that he wasn't flattered. He had done a good many portraits in the last four years, certainly enough for a reasonable exhibition. If Dora Pratts-Morris was ready to give him a start like that he was not foolish enough to refuse her out of hand. Her enthusiasm was not patronising, nor was it sentimental. Dora might seem stupid with her talk of married bliss in suburban bedrooms, but she was no spendthrift either with her money or with her ideas. In the course of their discussion, for instance, she had very sensibly suggested that he ought to set up a personal website. As for married bliss, if it existed in any quantifiable form it probably existed most often in suburban bedrooms, even if *Cotswold House* and *The Cherries* were not ideal examples. In the same way he felt justified in assuming that she was of sufficiently independent mind and judgement to mean what she said when she offered to support him financially. Still, that wasn't the main thing. The main thing was they were fond of each other.

'And I'm very fond of you,' were her last words when they said goodnight.

He had been on a steep, he thought, now I'm maybe on a slope. While he had such a thought he felt a little drunkenly that time was changing around him, stars moved, chemicals erupted on Saturn, winds raged on Jupiter. Flux, evanescence, changeability encroached on all he conceived as humanly stable. If there are steeps and slopes in life, they do not repeat each other. They are experienced once in one way, differently in another, and the differences only seem to have a pattern much, much later.

****

The usual communication from *Cotswold House* informed him that '*they never tell you anything in hospitals these days.*' As he had learned quicker by phone, his father had undergone tests and nothing organically wrong had been found. His mother's letter complained that '*he has a nasty persistent cough, but I think it's been a bit better recently.*' Then came the really important news:

'The apple crop was much better than we expected. So I am sending you a parcel of some fruit from the garden. There are also some tomatoes in a tin. Mrs Pollock, probably you remember her, at No. 117, has been very unwell, but she is now much better. I hear occasionally from Sam, Edwina's doing so well at school. We haven't heard anything about your plans, Jim darling. I was so hoping we'd be able to meet the nice girl called Sally-Anne. Your father didn't think we'd hear anything more and it seems he was right. Will you be coming to stay with us for Christmas? I must know now in order to make plans. Things always get so busy at this time of year.

'I often wonder whether the Labour people know what they're up to. We are having so many of them on television, aren't we? I suppose it'll mean we'll be having more strikes this winter. Now I must end.

Ever your loving mother.'

If the pattern of his own life might seem to be changing, the pattern elsewhere was reassuringly the same. As for Jim's anxious attempts to keep in touch with '*the nice girl called Sally-Anne*,' he had phoned every evening for a week and they had spoken. Sally's unwillingness to come up to London due to her mother's ill health was understandable and matched by an intuitively selfish reluctance of his own to go down to Guildford. He really did not want to meet her father again. He preferred to immerse himself in the day-to-day business of the dispersal programme, meanwhile waiting to hear what Charles Ball's reaction would be to his finished report and his desire to resign or be made redundant.

On a Friday evening he left work, took a bus to Southampton Row and crossed the street to enter Victoria Mansions. It was raining very lightly, as if a mist was being puffed into his face out of a scent spray. A little surprisingly the lift was working. It had been out of commission in the morning. He ascended slowly, the cabin jigging from side to side, revealing a vista of corridor then slowly withdrawing it like some elderly conjuror doing a laborious card-trick. All the time, through the usual grindings and squeaks of the old machinery, he was surrounded on three sides by mirror images of himself, pale-faced in a dark raincoat. The downfalling light made him look older, more forty than thirty, not that his complexion was any less youthful. He had a pale but nicely pigmented complexion offset by a good mouth with well-shaped lips of almost startling technicolour red. His features, as he easily recognised, were a mixture of his mother's chin, his father's cheekbones and a straight, quite pronounced nose. What would he look like in his late fifties? Perhaps dark-browed, lean-featured, with perpendicular lines in the cheeks like small sabre cuts. These cuts were not there at present, though the shading from the ceiling light made it seem so. Overall he looked like a quite neat, executive type who might never be supposed to have ambitions as a portrait painter. On the other hand, the beginnings of lines about his eyes and on his forehead, accentuated by the light, reminded him that, if he really wanted to change his life, he would have to do so soon, for he was certain (an access of hypochondria, this time) that his features would acquire the stiff, rather leathery, middle-aged, hard-bitten look he associated with his father.

The usual distant sounds from lower floors, those tunings-up of cooking preparations and early television that preceded the full symphonic first chords of an evening in Victoria Mansions, penetrated to him as he stood outside the door of his apartment and felt for his key in his pocket. Then the lift was summoned down again and went on its creaking way. Astonished, he found the door was unlatched. Panic struck him for a moment. Other occupants had reported thefts but he had so far been lucky. Perhaps Mrs Rogers had forgotten to close the door behind her or was still there (she had been late several times before). He pushed open the door. There was no light inside, only a fragrance, or a suggestion of it, that struck him as unusual. He switched on the light in the hallway and called out:

'Is there someone there?'

As if his voice, far from certain of itself, would instantly quell all resistance in an intruder or summon Mrs Rogers out from whatever unlikely corner she might be cleaning. He sensed rather than heard a movement from the bedroom. It seemed like nothing at all, like someone coughing loudly on the floor below or the slight expansion of a floorboard as the whole of Victoria Mansions admitted to the pressure of people returning from work – though, heaven knows, there were few enough of them in the building. As these fancies stole upon him he decided that the front door had simply been left open by mistake and, once inside, he deliberately closed it rather loudly. The sharp sound of the heavy door swinging into place had the effect of a barked command. It seemed to order the apartment to behave itself. With the door shut he felt he was in possession of this home of his. The sense of being where he belonged returned with an inrush of those smells of paints and turps that formed a background to the apartment's atmosphere.

The shock of finding the door unlatched dissipated at once. He took off his raincoat and hung it in its place. He knew how much he had ritualised his life by putting things in their places and following a routine of glancing in the kitchen and main room before preparing an evening meal. This time as he went into the kitchen to check what might be in the fridge he quite distinctly heard a sound from the bedroom. It was unmistakable. The panic flooded back. He went to the drawer containing the kitchen knives and pulled at it. Cursing the way it had always to be unstuck due to the warping of the cheap wood and simultaneously shivering, as if an ice age had struck and lowered the temperature to a point far below the ultimate zero, he felt that distinct crawling of the skin in the small of his back and between his shoulder blades that suggested the approach of some horror from the rear, a crazy masked gunman, a dervish with a knife. He struggled again. The drawer gave under his frenzied shaking. He seized a carving knife, knowing he would only be able to defend himself by sheer good fortune, not by any native skill, let alone by fear-induced desperation, and swung himself round to face the swing door between the kitchen and the hallway.

Someone was in the hallway. There was the sound of a footstep on the old piece of linoleum. He thought an intruder would be bound to make for the front door and leave at once. But there was no sound of the front door opening. Whoever it was had stopped in the hallway on the other side of the swing door. Perhaps it was Mrs Rogers after all. He knew she was a bit deaf and sometimes missed a word or two in conversation. Then involuntarily his hand holding the knife jerked backwards, as if he were preparing for the swing door to come inwards towards him, and it struck the opened drawer making the cutlery rattle loudly. At the same instant, in a fear-stricken voice that attempted to shout but emitted a sound more like a breathy whisper, he cried out:

'Who's there?'

It was a laugh. At least the sound was quite human and it came from the hallway. He thrust aside the swing door. In the brightly lit area immediately beside the front door he saw her. Her eyes caught the bright light, her lips were parted. She had about her what he thought was a fresh, desirable vitality, purposely heightened by the light-coloured dress, and if her complexion was pale it was not specially noticeable in the brightness. Her blue eyes, starred with her smile, were luxuriously brilliant as he recognised her and rushed towards her. It seemed as though the swing door, on the rebound, thrust him into her arms. For suddenly he was holding her, knowing the relief of feeling her suppleness in his embrace after so many weeks of separation and recognising the fragrance from her, the soft pressure of her lips and the total warm sensual invitation of her body. She began laughing and he laughed sporadically with her.

The knife fell to the floor, but it was really the knife that caused the laughter. She said it was so comic seeing him come rushing out into the hallway at her. He said he thought she was an intruder. Why hadn't she come out of the bedroom when he came in? She said she'd only arrived just before him and let herself in with her own key (he had forgotten she had her own key) and was making herself look nice. Then they stopped telling each other what did not need saying.

He felt such complete relief, it was as though there had been no gap in their relationship. He was returning from the office as he had done a month ago and they were in each other's arms. The only difference was the slight mutual hesitancy and strangeness. They had also lost the sense of the rhythm of Victoria Mansions, those many deep sounds from below that had orchestrated their love before and made them feel they were free. Now those rhythms did not beat up strongly. They were not driven by them as they had been. They stood there in the bright hallway, pressing gently against each other in a tenderness of renewing, reforming love.

'How is your mother?' he asked.

She said it was her mother who had insisted. She had insisted she come up to London. But she'd really not known whether… So she'd not rung beforehand.

'You don't mind, do you?'

'Mind! Of course I don't! I'm delighted!'

What was hanging in the air unspoken was the name Rachel, he knew that. She had been frightened she might find Rachel in the apartment or some obvious sign of her. The fact that she had gone straight to the bedroom seemed to confirm that fear. He said, speaking over her shoulder into the quietness of the hallway:

'I told you I loved you. Only you. There's been no one else. I want you to be my wife.'

He wanted to say much more, but she raised a hand to his face. That touch of fingertips to his cheek was overwhelming in its invitation and challenge. Suddenly, as though the rhythms were acting on them again, they were in the bedroom and he was lying facing her among a chill alpine scenery of white sheets. Her eyes shone at him with their blue clarity in a way that made her seem impossibly virginal and pure. He felt as though he were her seducer. But who was seducing whom? She had pointed at the drawing of her in the nude that he had done in the hotel room, the very first drawing of her. He had moved it into his bedroom before Dora's sittings.

'And I want us to be a family,' she whispered. 'I want a real baby now.'

So he knew her purpose. She raised her head from the pillow and smiled down at him. Her hair fell forward like a net and tickled his cheek. She appeared to be taking charge. This time she ran her finger over his lips in a sign that she wanted nothing said. He caught hold of her hand and held it. Her easily detectable, but light, sweet perfume came in little heatwaves. She let herself be drawn down on him, her body resting on him with a sensation of sensual lips and a deeper carnal luxury. It was hers, as sexually vital as ever, but now it was subtly different, altered in fragrance and tactile appeal. Their bodies rested against each other in their nakedness as they had done the first time, yet he knew that in each lovemaking there were so many fine gradations of the unusual in one body's awareness of the other. Because he had made love so frequently with Rachel, his body had grown used to this kind of treachery. It had become a habit of treachery, the body's treachery, that was far more unscrupulous than the treachery of the mind or heart. He knew that as surely as his skin surface knew the difference between hot and cold. His body had then made the overtures, accepted the light caress of her hand on his cheek, held hers in that known therapy, that familiar, gentle communication of bodily pressure to bodily pressure, their loving bondage to each other. Without more than the simplest words of agreement, they had held each other as though, if they once released, the world would fall apart and the universe shatter in pieces.

His right hand, holding and smoothing, ran gently feeling fingers over her shoulder blades, over the soft skin of her back; hers with expert and familiar gentleness touched into light like a torch his uprisen penis; his ran over her skin, over her breasts, over the fine budding nipples, then down, down, with sensual lightness. There was no frenzy, only a kind of excited softness as his fingers stroked and caressed and smoothed. He felt the literal uprush of her sensuality, her complete trustful abandonment to his gravely gentle, understanding, rousing seduction. It was all a prelude, but so sweet it seemed to rouse both of them almost beyond endurance.

Then the clasping, the urgent invitation, their lips pressed tight. Then the coordination of their limbs, as in some beautifully practised ritual, of which all dances were the imitation and symbol. Then the first long sustained anticipatory chord of the sensual entry of sex into sex. Then the pleasure of the ritualised act. The initial excited trembling thrusts, the easy encountering and matching, the desire mounting in waves of feeling. Then the dancing motion becoming fiercer and faster. Then a ritual at this stage in the very mutuality of their delight, in a kind of worship that they made towards each other and that greater pleasure that filled them in growing anticipation of some sunburst, some earthquake that would shake and melt their bodies in a flaming tower, an upward thrusting dome of light.

The flashes of this oncoming ecstasy ran through them. Then there came from all sides the thronging of cries and shouts in anticipation of the carnival's supreme climax. Then the breaking of waves, the crescendoing assaults of arrows upon the surface of a sea. Then the extreme trembling and the quivering and the finest control, as if a volcano were being summoned into activity by no greater force than the controlled movement of an eyelid. Then the eruption, the expended ecstasy and the breathless end of all carnival, the gentle withdrawal from coitus and the acknowledgement that their private experience was gradually receding into a generalised awareness of the commonplace, their surroundings and their relationship.

Her face lay in profile to him. He watched her closed eyelids quiver slightly, but she did not open them. She had fallen asleep. He let himself watch and listen. What she had not told him, though she had on other occasions over the phone, was quite simply how tired she was. Perhaps too tired, he imagined, even to think of coming up to London after days devoted to nursing her mother and sparring with her father. So her mother had insisted that she should have a break from her routine.

She meant that they should be married. Jim could legitimately suppose that much. It would be in any case what he most wanted. He would lie beside her as he was lying now and know that she would always be there. He would be successful if she were beside him. All his talent would be offered to her as a love gift. To delay saying that he loved her and wanted her to be his wife was like having to endure a diabolical wasting torture that seemed to shorten his life by as many years as the seconds ticked away with the words unspoken. But he could not make himself wake her. He had to let her sleep.

He let himself watch and listen. Just as the continually fluttering curtains of the bedroom window made sharp darts of light appear in series on the ceiling, the reverberations of Victoria Mansions below him were sounds that reminded of those points on a sea's blue surface where the continually appearing white froth of waves meant submerged rocks or promontories. The flickering in this case, due to the partly open sash window, seemed to be dissociated from the sounds. He watched it and felt entirely absorbed by it and under its hypnosis he fell asleep.

When he awoke the bedroom was dark and she had left him. His first feeling was one of panic. She had left him and gone. He jumped naked out of the warm bed, encountering the chill of the bedroom, and dashed into the hallway. It occurred to him that she might be taking a bath, but she was in fact in the kitchen preparing some supper. He pushed aside the swing door and found her as fully dressed as he had first seen her. He rushed to her, clasped his arms round her in a way that startled her at first, but she faced him and began to smile with a shining loving brilliance. He announced in a burst of words that he wanted to marry her. Would she marry him? Would she say yes, no matter how long her mother was ill?

She put down the spatula and let herself be hugged.

'Jim, my darling Jim, of course I will. But we don't have to talk about it. We *are* married – I mean, in every way that matters. And if you hold me much tighter you may do something terrible to whatever little Nordon might be on the way. So please let me get on with the supper. You were fast asleep when I woke up and I didn't want to disturb you. That's why I decided to get everything ready. Please go and put some clothes on. It's not the height of summer any more.'

Her common sense and practicality – mostly of course her loving concern – overwhelmed and curbed his naked love for her. He felt made naked by her, but not ashamed by her words. Instead he remained standing there clasping her. It was quite silly of him to stand there and feel the cold of the autumnal apartment create goose pimples on his bare skin. Then the phone rang. He felt shy of the peremptory sound instantly. But he went into the hallway and lifted the receiver of the phone beside the front door.

'This is Sally-Anne's father. I'd like to speak to her.'
The sound of that voice made Jim shiver.

XII

They waited outside the crematorium in the chill October stillness. It was as if through the trees and the layered cloud and the distances of space they could have heard people talking as far away as the moon. There was a bird making repeated shrill noises somewhere among the yew trees and far traffic could be heard from the motorway, but nobody spoke. Sally couldn't help herself. The tears were fizzing behind her eyes and in her throat and she could do nothing but hold a handkerchief and stare down at the mottled surface of the tarmac and her new black shoes. Her feelings were so mixed she couldn't be sure what emotion would be uppermost from one minute to the next. The service scheduled for an earlier funeral was delayed, which was why they were waiting and her father was fretting. Her father had fretted throughout the time they had had to wait for this space in the crematorium's schedules. When she and Jim had arrived down at *The Cherries* after his phone call and her mother had already been taken off to hospital, he had started the fretting. He had simply made the munching, chewing motion at the news that they were going to be married, nodding, not even smiling:

'In your mother's condition you oughtn't to do anything that'll upset her.'

It was a sorry, ungenerous, crushingly sensible thing to say, no doubt, but in his state of fretting she could hardly have expected anything else from him. Her happiness and her longing to share the news were like a tidal wave of feeling that simply struck the sheer cliff face of her mother's dying moments and her father's fear of death. Her mother had whispered to her in the hospital bed, 'You mustn't delay, dear, you really mustn't, not on my account.' It had all been over in such a short time, without her even being there to hold her mother's hand or help her in any way at all. They had told her late on the Saturday evening. She'd simply handed him the phone. All the time he had accepted the state of his wife's health as a personal challenge to his own decrepitude and sense of defeat. Though the doctors said otherwise, he insisted his health was deteriorating. He acquired the mannerisms of someone who demanded treatment as an invalid. So she couldn't tell him: 'Mum died about half an hour ago in her sleep, they said.' She had simply handed him the phone and dissolved into tears.

Her father heard the news and went to his room. He'd been saying his memory had gone. This was true, if only of the immediate past. He contrived not even to remember who Jim was, giving the impression that he mistook him for a colleague and complaining to him about the slights he had received from a superior. So he had made a habit of talking to Jim as if he were a third party: 'It's no good expecting sympathy from him, you know. He's not that type. He'll never have any sympathy for me. I've had to put up with slights from him all my life. It shows real lack of common charity on his part for him to start complaining about my state of health when my wife's in hospital. And now that my daughter's planning to get married to one of the departmental heads he'll have to take care, won't he?' But Sally knew her father wasn't wandering in his mind, even if Jim didn't. He knew perfectly well what the real position was. He played the role of decrepit senior citizen as a protection against the need to face the truth.

Now the truth had to be faced and he still fretted. She tried to think of the happiness she had felt as Jim drove her back on the Friday night, the happiness of knowing he really loved her, that she really loved him and trusted him. Yet, set against such knowledge, was the imponderable, marble cliff of fact, of life extinguished, things ended, the dead with their demanding silent look that could pursue one right through life and into eternity. Her mother's gentle, gentle eyes shining in the intensive care ward and her smile, like a little girl's trying to pretend the pain meant nothing, etched on the pale, somehow diminished face. That was the last sight of her, of darling Mum. The grief poured through her heart in a great torrent at the memory and nothing in the world could ever stop it.

John, her first love, had made her cry. She had cried so much then in her neat, well-dusted room, Mum's arm round her shoulders, Mum kissing her, Mum saying all the comforting things. Oh, John, John, John, it didn't matter if he never loved her as much as she had loved him, or it had been just sexual fun for him. To her he had been someone she could love so much she thought it would never stop. But her loving did stop eventually. She had even grown frightened of her own coldness at the thought of him. It was strange how one deep emotion roused another, how they succeeded one after another in driving their nails into her heart. She had not been able to escape the feeling that her love for her Mum might eventually grow cold as well. Because it vied with her love for Jim. Perhaps it claimed that part of her heart for a while. Now through all her grief she knew the warmth of her love for Jim was rising up again and would soon consume her life. It was her hope. More, she knew she had a gift for it. Even the clear, blank, uninhabited air of this October day seemed to fill with her conviction that she would be happy. She had a gift for it.

The undertaker made a *sotto voce* remark to her father. Receiving nothing but a glare of hostility, he turned to her instead. They could hear muffled organ music from the crematorium chapel. Apparently it was time for their funeral service to begin. She glanced behind her. Apart from P.G., as he was known, her mother's only surviving brother, there were several Harris relatives, including Auntie Mary and Uncle Donald from Torquay, and some of Sally's friends from school (one of them, Diana, gave a cheery black-gloved wave) and one or two older people who had been neighbours and acquaintances of her parents when they had lived in their other house. But there was no sign of Jim, though he had promised to be there. The service could not be arranged for any other time, but he said he was sure he could be there. Her father began fretting again.

'Come on. What are we hanging about for? We're late as it is.'

She nodded reluctantly. It was no good telling him that she wanted to wait for her fiancé, he'd be bound to do his incomprehension bit and start asking loudly who she meant. She nodded to the undertaker and they moved in decorous, silent procession after him into the flower-fragrant, sanitised atmosphere of the chapel. The interior was impossibly tidy, like a stately home opened to the public. No one could have imagined that another service for people entirely strange to them had occurred in the chapel only minutes before. The organ was invisible and its strains pervaded the austere interior like a pious muzak. They took their places in the pews, prayed, sat back and waited. The casket with the specially ordered wreaths and sprays stood on a kind of podium in front of cerulean pleated curtains. It was then that the anxiety over Jim's lateness gave way to another and more awful access of grief.

She could imagine Mum lying there very still in the darkness of the wooden casket. The sudden macabre imagining shocked her. Equally suddenly she found herself imagining that the embryo inside her, of which she was so certain, was dead like Mum, locked away inside her, but looking up the way Mum had looked from the hospital bed. The thought so startled her she gave a howl of grief. It was completely uncontrolled. She didn't care who heard her, who saw her crying. She knelt in the front pew and let the agony of the grief shake her. She wanted to cry out to all of them that she was pregnant, she was going to have Jim's baby. But he wasn't there and very likely he'd never come and she'd kill herself sooner than let the baby be taken from her. And the pious muzak went on in the background as the chapel was filled with the noise of her uncontrollable sobbing.

When she glanced round through her tears at her father he was doing nothing except sit beside her with his hands in his lap, making that slow chewing motion. She noticed Harris faces looking at her from pews on the other side of the aisle. When her Uncle Donald leaned over and asked if she'd like to go outside, she frenziedly shook her head.

'No! No!'

The tears grew worse momentarily. Then she gained some control over the quaking sensation that rose from inside here, as though the baby were itself joining in her paroxysms of grief. She clutched a handkerchief tightly to her lips to staunch the crying and tried to dry her eyes. There were tall white lilies in an ornate blue vase set just below the podium. She stared at them. They reminded her not of death but of the other Guildford house where they had lived before her father resigned. She remembered seeing her mother once holding lilies in her arms as though cradling a baby. Her mother had walked down the long path between flowerbeds one evening when the scent of the lilies had drenched the air with an almost anesthetising sweetness. How old was she then – eleven, twelve? It had been so many years ago and Mum had been well. They'd often played badminton on the lawn at the back of the house. Her crying stopped at the pleasant recollection. She turned and exchanged a smile with Di, her school friend Diana, her best friend. It was good to see her smile and feel her confidence coming towards her. Then she realised what was wrong. The tall white lilies had no fragrance. Looking at them closely, she saw tell-tale signs of dust on them. They were plastic! It so astonished her she felt ready to laugh.

Her thoughts returned to her mother's loneliness in the dark of the casket. She could imagine her loneliness there. The same loneliness touched her. The same weariness of the struggle with dying, with the inevitability of it, poured into her, leaving a sense that she had herself died a little. Her imagination was invaded by the vision of a wide calm sea and she was alone in a small boat gliding across it. The loneliness felt desirable. It seemed to comfort, to make no demands. The grief, like storms, had gone horizons away. She could look down into a sea clear as pure glass and hear from the depths the sound of voices. She rose hurriedly from her kneeling with the sudden panic feeling of having been left out. They were beginning the first hymn.

She felt the pressure on her cheek before she realised he was there. Jim kissed her and pressed her hand. He whispered many apologies for being late, but she hushed him, not minding at all. The way she felt herself glow at finding him beside her made the ragged singing instantly achieve a triumphant choral assurance and lent a tear-shine of brilliance to the illuminated folds of the cerulean curtains. She turned and looked directly at him, noting the line of his chin with its slight dimple and the firmness of his lips with their rosy colour accentuated by the natural paleness of his complexion, his straight nose that was like his father's, she felt sure, judging by his portrait of him, but meant to her all of Jim's true self, his niceness, his unsureness, his talent, his love for her, and then his eyes in silhouette, unaware at that moment of her scrutiny, with their hazel glow partly visible through straight eyelashes. Now, taking him by surprise, she returned his kiss in the middle of the hymn, pressing her lips to the middle of his cheek, fighting back tears of pleasure at her delight in him, her pride in him, and drawing from him a smirk rather than a smile, but in any case a crinkling of the eyes.

In fact he was annoyed. The meeting that should have taken an hour and half had prolonged itself to three hours and occupied most of lunchtime. Driving out of London, he had been caught in a traffic jam in Wandsworth and delayed by an accident on the A3. The sanitised, imitation air of the crematorium chapel with the horrible curtains and the organ music emanating from somewhere piled outrage on annoyance. He had the impression they were not attending the funeral of a loved one but an ignoble sideshow designed to hide the fact of death and cremation by deodorising and decontaminating it. Glancing round him, he saw rows of mostly elderly faces, most of whom returned his look with polite but curious interest. It troubled him that, when he would have liked to do something as simple and unaffected as cry at a funeral, he could find no emotion within him more affecting than annoyance. Thankfully the service was short. It concluded with prayers, a homily from the priest about Eleanor Harris's life and virtues and a final hymn. Then there was a muted mechanical whirring that sent the cerulean curtains into a decorous and slow withdrawal. A panel was revealed at the back of the podium and the casket proceeded to move from sight on noiseless runners. The whirring was repeated, the curtains slowly ran together. Pious muzak followed this little bit of mechanical theatre and they all trooped slowly out into the dull October day.

Sally, evidently in spirited defiance of the mood of the occasion, began introducing Jim to her Harris relatives. Her Auntie Mary from Torquay turned out to be thinner than he had imagined. She had an elegant, well-preserved face marked by characteristic Harris sternness, noticeable chiefly in the slate-blue eyes, but lightened by an attractively easy smile. Her husband – the Uncle Donald of whom Sally had often talked – was pink-faced and white-haired with eyes of such startling lucid blue they resembled the cerulean curtains. He seemed a lot more solemn than his wife Mary who, despite her stern look, appropriate of course for the occasion, found it hard not to show her smiling pleasure at meeting Sally's fiancé ('Believe it or not, I've heard all sorts of things about you, Mr Nordon.') She talked busily to him during the awkward interval between leaving the chapel and being shown to the marble-floored display area where the wreaths and sprays had been laid out for inspection.

He was also introduced to Philip Harris and his wife Marjorie who had come down from Birmingham; to their daughter and son-in-law, Celia and James Beckett; to their son Michael who was studying electronics at the University of Aston; to two elderly maiden ladies from Yorkshire who insisted they *were* maiden ladies – 'Herbie's cousins, you know'; to a Mrs Elizabeth Steadman who explained she was Herbert's sister; to Councillor Lawrence Childes and his wife Stephanie ('We've known Eleanor and Herbert for years'); to half-a-dozen other elderly Harris acquaintances; and to two of Sally's friends, Diana with the bright smile, who congratulated him and said she was terribly pleased, and to Melanie who was attending the funeral with her boyfriend Stephen. The introductions eased his tenseness and annoyance. The occasion, though, was permeated for him by an irreconcilable mixture of feelings, since he could not be sure how far to feel pleasure at the warmth of the congratulations or sadness at the condolences. Even if, on returning to *The Cherries*, the front room, Herbert Harris's study, the dining room and the kitchen became filled with guests talking busily, he could not feel sure there was anything to celebrate. He knew that at some point all the problems associated with death and bereavement would have to come to the surface, no matter how determined Sally seemed to be to put them aside for the time being.

Towards the end of what constituted a wake party, Herbert Harris introduced Jim to a thin, white-haired man with little worm casts of veins in his upper cheeks:

'My future son-in-law.'

'Herbert is jealous,' said the elderly man, twinkling a little through his spectacles.

'That is a damned lie.'

'Herbert's been jealous all his life. Jealous of other men's success. With him it's like a chronic disease. But I hear you're giving up your job. Is that right?'

Jim agreed. At that moment Herbert Harris grunted and turned away.

'And,' came the further question, the elderly eyes twinkling a little more brightly behind the rimless spectacles, 'you're having to do the right thing by dear Sally, aren't you?'

Jim thought he'd misheard at first, until the assertiveness of the voice intended that the meaning of the question should be understood. For a moment, as the embarrassment possessed him, he thought Sally's pregnancy must be common knowledge. That would account for some of the knowing looks he had received. So he couldn't deny the question's meaning.

'I am.'

'You don't have to worry, no one else knows. Sally has sworn me to secrecy. I don't think even Herbert is aware.' These remarks were spoken in an audible voice but close to a whisper and evidently in confidence. Though there were a dozen other people in the room, no one was close enough to hear the words. 'I should have explained,' said the man. 'I'm known as P.G. I'm Ellie's surviving brother. Eleanor, Sally's mother. I've always known her as Ellie.'

Then Jim recognised in those direct, twinkling eyes the look of Sally's mother and Sally herself. In the instant of recognition there sprang up a liking for this thin, white-haired man. Rarely entirely trustful of his own snap judgements about people, he occasionally had a strong intuitive sense of the kind of person he was meeting at first acquaintance. With this man who called himself P.G. he felt an unusual degree of certainty.

'I'm afraid I only met Sally's mother once.'

'She liked you, as a matter of fact,' said P.G. 'She wanted you and Sally to get married. But Sally had Ellie's problem. It's been very nearly a case of history repeating itself.'

In the pause P.G. smiled and nodded his head several times in a gentle acknowledgement of the wisdom of his own words.

'Like all of us – my siblings, I mean – Ellie was an army child, an army daughter, do you know what I mean? Loyalty, duty, they dominated our lives. She remained with our parents long after we, the boys – there were three of us – had left home for good. Out of loyalty, duty. I used to urge her to strike out on her own, but she felt she had to stay with our parents. Then along came Herbert Harris when she's in her forties and we all thought she'd stay a spinster all her life.' He lowered his voice and leaned close to Jim. 'The fact is she was desperate. I don't need to spell it all out to you. They had an affair and she became pregnant. And dear Ellie had a mind of her own. That may be hard to believe if you hadn't known her earlier. And of course Herbert wasn't the most pliable of men. So they had to get married in haste.'

Then he chuckled and swayed back on his heels.

'But it didn't work out too badly, did it? Dear Sally was the result. Ellie doted on her and Sally was very close to her. As for Herbert... The trouble with him was he left everything too late as he had a jealous, suspicious, cantankerous nature. He should have followed his own inclinations much earlier. When he was your age. Then he'd have been a lot better to live with. You're going to make a living painting portraits, I hear?'

Put like that, it sounded like little more than selling something door to door. Jim responded a little harshly:

'Believe it or not, I like painting portraits. And I'm rather good at it. I'm doing one now for a friend who wants to finance an exhibition of my work.'

'Congratulations! That's great news! Sally says you're very good. I'll commission you to do mine. Remind me about it. But do you see now what I meant when I said it's like history repeating itself? Sally was a love-child. She was Ellie's love-child. Do you get my meaning?' At that moment he gave a brief cry of surprise. 'Ah, my dear, they look very nice.'

Sally herself had approached with a plateful of hot sausage rolls. 'I forgot about these. They're freshly made. I popped them in the oven. Won't you have one?'

P.G. took one. It broke instantly and half fell on the floor. There was a commotion of apologies, people rushing with handkerchiefs and tissues and a brushing of flakes from his waistcoat. He protested at their kindness, loudly declared his stupidity and then seized Jim by the arm and explained that he, P.G. Mather, had been acting as solicitor for the Mathers and the Harrises for a great many years and would do whatever he could to help Jim and Sally with legal matters when they were married. With that he flourished a hand in the air and left. They had the rest of the sausage rolls for supper.

That evening Herbert Harris sat by the lively, glowing gas fire in the front room. He spoke rather sadly:

'P.G.'s always thought I was no better than a husk of a man eaten out by envy at other men's success. I'm not. It's a bit of an act. Sally knows it's an act, just as dear Eleanor knew it. I've used it as a way of countering the boredom of doing all the conventional things expected of me. I had talent. Look at this chair I'm sitting in. Sturdy, comfortable, durable, I made it, it's the real me.' An obviously well-made piece of furniture in light oak, it had a wooden frame and arms with the only sign of upholstery in the cushion-style seat. 'It's what I wanted to do from childhood on, but was never allowed to. I only had the chance when I retired. That's when I made this, along with the stool.' He pointed to where Sally was sitting on a low stool beside his chair. 'That's all bygones now and so it should be. There's a hole in my life that no one can fill. I loved dear Eleanor enough to fill my entire life. That's all I ever wanted. I had no other ambition. But of course I knew, I knew I would very likely outlive her. For the last two months or so I've been pretending not to think about it, but I've been thinking about it and, oh, I've been thinking. So I know now what I must do. I discussed it with her, yes, we discussed it. I'm selling this house and half of what it makes after paying off the remains of the mortgage will be shared between us. That's what Eleanor and I agreed. You, Sally dear, you will have half. I will then be going to Mary's and Donald's in Torquay. That was agreed when we were down there. I'll have enough capital and with my pension and the insurance money I'll be no liability to anyone.'

Sally clasped his hand in hers. 'Yes, I know,' she said. 'Mum told me.' She appeared to be looking at the jets of the gas fire but really she was absorbed in staring into space. Jim, who sat on the other side of the fire with his back to the curtained window, knew this and felt caught up in her absorption.

'Your mother and I,' said Herbert Harris, 'were good friends to each other, but we had our disagreements. You two'll have them as well. There's no knowing exactly what they'll be about. Practically all of them will disappear in no time at all and only the stupidest, the least likely, will survive. Such as my aversion to corduroy because your mother once bought me one of those corduroy caps. Or your name. There's a silly example. Your mother wanted you to be Sally, I wanted Anne. We couldn't agree and so we called you Sally-Anne. If we'd had more children, I can't imagine the awful problems we'd have had choosing names! But there it is – it stuck. You can blame us for that, my dear.'

A branch, perhaps one of the cherry trees in the front garden, tapped, tickled, scraped on the glass of the window and contributed to the simple converse between the faintly audible jets and Herbert Harris's monologue. The fact that there was no need to assert one's presence by speech made Jim feel accepted into this atmosphere of family confidences. He gazed at Sally's absorbed, unmoving face and the spots of reflected jet light in her fixed blue eyes, which seemed not so much blue as coloured by the general sun-burst effect from the fire. Her breasts, as she leaned forward in her contemplative pose, beautifully pushed out the folds of her black jacket. She had a rich feminine beauty in her look, in the slope of her shoulders and the firm lines of her formal, funeral dress, still looking sharp and new despite the recent party. All that lent intimacy to her pose was the loose, elegant hanging of her right hand from the wrist while the other held her father's hand. Herbert Harris said:

'You may have thought I was a grumpy old thing and you'd have been right.' He was talking to Jim, though Jim took a little while to realise the fact. 'It's a manner I have. Sally-Anne knows it. She makes allowances for it. Eleanor used to as well. Now that you're going to be a member of the family, you'll have to do the same.'

'I'll certainly try.'

'I thought I'd let you know, that's all.'

'Oh, I'll…'

This exchange disturbed Sally's thoughts. She looked up, smiled at Jim and shook her father's hand.

'You'll have to be nice to Auntie Mary, Dad, when you go down there.'

'I can be nice to her when I want to. I spent a childhood being nice to her, you've got to remember that. I'll spend an old age being nice to her. Oh, we get on well together. It was your mother and Mary who used to get on each other's nerves.'

'I know, I know.'

'There won't be any real problems. If there are, I'll just fall asleep. That'll soon put an end to them.'

Sally laughed. 'Okay, so there won't be any real problems. Just you go on falling asleep down in Torquay.'

Later that evening she told Jim when they were alone: 'I liked it, your maisonette. Thanks for showing me the pictures. I'm glad there's a bit of garden too. But I don't want to come back with you right away. I want to stay here by myself for a few days.'

'Why?'

'I want to sort out my feelings. And I want to say goodbye.' She saw the beginnings of misapprehension and disappointment in his face. To reassure him she leaned up to him and kissed him. 'You can understand, can't you? I've got to say goodbye. Mum's still too real for me to turn my back.'

She had been on her own steep place, he thought. Her love for her mother could not be extinguished as simply as the casket would be once the cerulean curtains had slipped back. There was certainty in what she was saying.

'Yes,' he said, 'I see that.'

'There's no need to look so bothered, Jim darling.'

Her father had gone to bed. They heard him moving about in the room above them. He could not erase from his mind what P.G. had told him. Would history repeat itself? Would they have their own love-child, their own *The Cherries*, their own *Cotswold House*, or would there be an exception in their case – perhaps, perhaps – and their love would be deeper, more fulfilling.

'You know what P.G. told me?'

'What?'

He told her. 'Is it true?'

She shook her head with a girlish, almost petulant, vigour. He realised at once it had been silly of him to ask such a thing. I should never have been told, he thought, that she was a love-child. He could only suppose that when their child was born, it would be a child of their love. The magic of that thought came with a momentary white brilliance from the fire as a sudden gust of wind caused an up-leaping flourish of gas jets that he noticed was mirrored sharply in her thought-filled eyes. After a few seconds she was aware of him watching her. Her lips drew apart in a smile.

'Yes, I suppose I was a love-child. Do you mind?'

'No, of course I don't mind.'

'I want to stay here, you see,' she said, 'because there'll be so many things to sort out. Di's promised to help me with some of the work. Before today, before the cremation, though, I don't know, I couldn't bring myself to do anything. Now first of all I've got to sort out myself. And I've got to do it by myself. I know Dad'll be a problem, but I can cope with that. Anyhow, he's made his plans, as you've heard. No, I've got to sort out my own feelings. In that horrible chapel, before you got there, when I thought you'd never come, I literally howled. I never thought I'd behave like that. Really. If I'd thought at all how I'd behave when it eventually happened, I'd sort-of imagined I'd be calm and collected, you know what I mean? But I had this terrible imaginary vision of the baby – well, I won't tell you exactly – but I thought it had died. Dead inside me, like Mum in the casket. And I howled. God, I feel awful when I think of it! Now, though, I seem to have become far too calm. That moment exhausted me. Afterwards, right up to now, I've been doing ordinary things, like talking to people, introducing you, listening to Dad, being a hostess, things like that, and now I need some time – I don't know how long really – but I must have time by myself to sort out my feelings as well as do all the things that'll have to be done here. I've just got to calm down. Then we'll get married? Does that sound silly?'

He shook his head. There was a pause. She stared at the gas jets.

'What I want to do is find out… I must find out, if I can, what my past is. I know that sounds silly. What I mean is, I want to find out whether there's anything among Mum's things that'll tell me – that'll tell me something I don't know. She always kept so many things wrapped up. I just wonder what there is there. And I haven't dared look before now. There's probably nothing at all. Do people have lots of secrets? I don't know. Mum wrapped me round. Her love was like that. I was her secret really. If Dad hadn't married her, she'd still have had me, her love-child, as P.G. told you, and have been an unmarried mother, because it was *me*, *me*, she wanted. It strained her. Her heart, I mean. But she had a great gift for being happy, that was her real secret. I've got it, too.' She yawned loudly. 'Oh, I'm so tired, so tired!'

When she looked away from the glow of the fire towards him, she was delighted to see him smiling at her without a trace of anxiety. It was a full, understanding, loving, candid smile of happiness. It quickly turned into a gentle laugh and she found herself smiling and laughing with him.

'It'll be all right, Sally darling,' he said. 'I know it will.'

****

The October night as he drove back to London had an intense, rich blackness. He felt he was going through black milk and his headlights were sticking pins into its thickness. He could see his own face looking faintly down at him in the mirroring effect of the windscreen. The night seemed to hold him in its huge cupped hands in protective wonderment at what he was doing. What he was doing was returning to London to arrange the wedding that he knew Sally would be too busy to arrange. He felt a mature certainty of the rightness of it. The report, with Charles Ball's emendations, had been approved at a recent Council meeting and it had been agreed he would terminate his employment in the Borough in the New Year. His life, now that he knew he had to leave Victoria Mansions by the end of November, had become a journey of discovery. The excitement of the knowledge was fed by the elation of his love, not only because it was right that he should love, but also because he was as deeply sure of the rightness of his decision to leave one career and start another.

The excitement of his love was matched by the excitement he always had when he held a brush and drew the one stroke that completed the line of an upper eyelid or caught the exact line of a cheekbone, a nostril, a lip. The human face had delicacy and depth. It had the bloom of a rose and the patinated, stippled hardness of stone. It was basically a rectangle formed by the edges of the mouth and the irises of the eyes. It was gradations of relationship, of eyes to nose and nose to mouth and mouth to jawline. These gradations were always subtly altered, enhanced or diminished by age and the angle or intensity of light. Oh, there was a host of other issues, of course, but all the vividness of a face, its enlivening character and its humanity were absorbed into and projected through the distinctiveness of the eyes. That was invariably the clue to personality in a sitter. That was what challenged him as a painter and ultimately excited him most of all.

Inherent in that excitement was the natural urge to visit the National Gallery or the National Portrait Gallery once every couple of months. More often when there had been special exhibitions. It was only through studying the masters that he recognised how much humility as well as daring was required to attain anything resembling their quality, not to mention their standard. And as he approached London and the night grew brighter from street lighting he felt the excitement, like his love, grow stronger and keener. He loved Sally because, without her, as he now felt certain, he was a lesser person. In being with her, he felt sure he could be the person he wished to be. The uncompromising intimacy between them rid their physical selves of shame and made them frankly, completely loving towards each other. The lights of central London were similarly dazzling in his eyes and replete with a twinkling ecstasy, covertly promising him that such ecstasy was always there for the taking and could go on and on, on and on, so long as love prevailed.

She heard the car go off and then went to bed. Windows gave a light rattling in an autumnal wind. Sleep overtook her almost at once after several nights of anxiety. She awoke to a 7.30 a.m. tinkling of milk bottles and revving of car engines throughout the suburb. A zest of autumn pervaded the gardens. It fitted her mood that was both happy and sad but chiefly full of a zest to live. Still in her dressing-gown she went downstairs into a slightly stale atmosphere of tobacco smoke and wine that still lingered though everything had been cleared away and washed up long since (and again she reminded herself about the dishwasher). The boy came with the daily paper, sending it gliding on to the front door mat. She read it in the slowly increasing warmth of the kitchen over two or three cups of coffee.

Her father came down after a time. They talked in brief fits and starts about the many things that had to be done. Otherwise the day demanded of them the fixed routine of meals, the preparation and cooking, much in the same way as it had during her mother's illness. That morning she did things automatically and mindlessly and it was only later in the day that she began to take stock. The sensation was very similar to recovery from illness, she had to admit. It was probably what she had meant when she had been so insistent on sorting out her feelings, except that the feelings were a good deal harder to sort out than were the practical matters that her mother's death and her father's departure for Torquay began to involve.

There were so many *things* left behind after the people themselves were gone or about to go. She vowed: 'I will not have so many things. I will try to travel as lightly as possible,' but it was an impossible vow to make, let alone fulfil. She knew she was as much given to accumulating things round her as her mother had been. She was also much less tidy than her mother. She found drawers and cupboards full of neatly folded garments and boxes with their contents listed on the outside in her mother's precise hand. None of these meant very much to her in an emotional sense. They were things that her mother had put aside because she'd probably not had any clear idea what to do with them. Much of the stuff, she thought, would do for charity. She unsentimentally disposed of them by thinking of them in that way.

When, late in the afternoon after much of the sorting had been done, she discovered a small cardboard box with the word 'Elsie' on it and opened it to find carefully preserved in tissue paper the very first rag doll her mother had made for her, its blue woollen eyes still looking out innocently from a rather worn and stained round face made from an old handkerchief (that she knew, because her mother had told her it was), she suddenly burst into tears, kneeling by the opened drawer of the chest-of-drawers, and muttered in the silence of the bedroom:

'Oh, Mum darling, you shouldn't have!'

Because her mother shouldn't have preserved this object of her doting childish love, which she had utterly forgotten, so that years poured back from nowhere, from the silent air, and riddled her with sensations from her girlhood and especially her yearning to have a baby of her own, a real Elsie.

'Oh, Mum darling, you shouldn't have!'

Because what her mother had done was in a very small way to challenge the mortality of human ways and habits by this persistent accumulation of things from the past. Sally wondered at it and felt a little frightened by it. There was almost too much of her mother in this house. She would never be able to occupy it as fully as her mother had, no matter how much her father might have resisted. So she literally swept away the tears and concentrated on the practical matters. From that day and the next and the next she succeeded in closing herself to sentiment as much as possible. She arranged for certain pieces of furniture, certain carpets, certain curtains and bed linen to go into store (in the hope they might prove useful for the new maisonette). Other things were sent to auction, yet others were to go to Torquay. The sale of the house was put in the hands of local agents and, to her father's almost indignant surprise, a satisfactory offer was made on it within a couple of days.

He, meanwhile, did not stop fretting. Having put himself into a state of near-dotage despite his claims to the contrary, he remained largely inactive, bothered by the prospect of transferring himself into his sister's world and yet quite happy to declare himself glad to be 'rid of all this,' meaning the day-to-day business of closing down *The Cherries*. He and Sally did not discuss their futures, but they had both reached a decision to go their own ways. Only her mother's refusal to admit her own mortality by playing down her illness had kept Sally buoyant while recognising that there could only be one outcome.

Yes, Sally thought, her mother had been the risky one, the impulsive one. It might have seemed otherwise to a casual observer. The Harrises had seemed outwardly such a conventional family. There was, true, little about them to give an impression of real eccentricity. But Sally knew that she, like her mother, was guided very much by her heart. Her mother, for instance, had believed it was a most sacred principle of living to respect and honour all emotions, provided of course they involved charity towards others. Sally had loved her for that emotional strength, even if a certain mythologizing had accompanied it. Her mother had made too much of *The Cherries* perhaps, had looked after it too assiduously. It had become a museum in some respects, filled up with the beautifully kept items of a private mythology. Yet the love remained, even after all the things had been taken away. This, Sally felt, was what she had to say goodbye to. It was not difficult. Her mother had spread love round them very easily; it had been her gift. Sally had inherited it. You carried that kind of inheritance with you wherever you went. There was never any need to wrap it up in paper and put it away in a drawer. She had to say goodbye to her mother's love of the place and take her own love with her.

So after a hectic week or two her own love reasserted its power over her and she knew she had to join Jim as soon as possible. All the time her thoughts had been about him. Everything she did had been in preparation for the time when she could close *The Cherries* and go to London. She had supposed that if they'd stayed together immediately after the funeral they would have become entangled by their separate emotional states. At least she had felt certain of the need to be separate then.

As soon as all the most urgent practical matters had been decided, she began to worry. Over the phone Jim seemed so close. She could close her eyes and see him in the setting of 'The Apartment' in Victoria Mansions as she remembered it, in the bedroom with all the pictures round the walls. She longed for that firm touch. She wanted to let his hands move with their gentle seductive touch over her skin. She wanted to kiss him. She wanted to hold him. She wanted the masculine smoothness and strength of his body close to her. She simply wanted the intimacy of being with him, of being completely sure, of knowing her love would encase him and protect him, of feeling his love and warmth close beside her, of sharing with him the tremors of new life inside her, of knowing again the sexual sweetness, the preparatory excitement, the urgency, the act of loving, the abandonment to it and the ultimate excited ecstasy.

NO.

She thought of herself as wanting Jim in calmness, like a calm flowing together of two lives. She loved him because he was precious. She loved him because whenever she was close to him she felt a little quick dance in the blood. She loved his smile. She loved his quietness. She loved his basic uncertainty about himself. She loved him because he'd shown her how vulnerable he was. She loved him for his talent, his devotion to his art, his sheer immersion in the processes and challenges of painting. She loved the mature handsome lines of his rather thin face and the usually solemn eyes. She loved him because she knew he loved her and she had never known that kind of assurance in love before.

YES.

I want to be married to you, Jim. I want to be your wife. I want to have your child. I want us to have a family. I want to make a home.

YES.

She fretted against the many things that were keeping her preoccupied for the time being. Then she heard him say over the phone:

'I've arranged it for the twenty-ninth. No arguing. You've got to be here. I can't get married by myself. And Miss Jacobs won't have me.'

Oh, she would be there! This is what Dad should have done, but she'd make sure he'd be there! She didn't know about other relatives, but there'd be friends, there'd be all kinds of people!

She caught the fast train to Waterloo some days later. It was cold, but bright sunshine and clouds looking like long thin fish filled the sky. A young man in a jacket with broad lapels and trousers that stretched skin-tight round his thighs sat opposite her. She felt like smiling at him because she felt like smiling at everyone. He smiled back and they exchanged a few words. She couldn't tell him: *'Look, I'm deliriously happy! I'm going to get married on the twenty-ninth! I'm in love with Jim Nordon and I'm going to have his baby!'* No, she sat there opposite the young man, who warmed to her and began telling her he was on the way to London for an interview for a new job. She sat there with her eyes glowing with happiness and wished him luck.

He said he'd need all the luck in the world to swing it. Then maybe he'd get married. He'd be able to afford a mortgage if he got this better job.

'You look so happy,' he said, smiling and slowly shaking his head in a kind of amazement. 'What's your secret?'

She didn't tell him. She just smiled at him and looked out of the window. Rows of houses flashed by, all of them looking more or less like *The Cherries*, and she thought: *'I'm going to be happy. I have a gift for it.'*

The Girl in the White Fur Hat.

by Richard Freeborn

(Dynasty Press, 2018) 280pp., pbk., £8.99 ISBN 978-0-955350764

Reviewed by Kate Pursglove

Intelligence reaches the CIA of a plot to assassinate the President of the United States as he stops over in London en route for a peace conference in Geneva; the Americans must collaborate with Special Branch to find the plotters and save the President. The plot seems to have its roots in Cold War incidents of over 30 years ago when a British diplomat in Moscow was caught in a honey trap, a Russian missile landed close to a British oil rig, and a Russian rocket scientist defected to the United States. So far, so airport novel. However, to place this book in such a category would be a serious mistake. It's a highly readable page-turner, with a swiftly moving plot and deftly handled switches between the present decade and the 1980s, but Freeborn's novel offers the reader far more even than this.

The quality of the writing, delicately evocative of place and time, is apparent at the outset. The leitmotif rainbow gives the impression 'for one brief instant that the whole – the rainbow and its reflection, however fragmented by the sea's movement, however shattered by wave-tops and the slow, longitudinal surge of cream-laced water playing in each *wave-wake – would make a circle uniting sea and sky. And it did. For one instant.' Spring in Moscow 'bursts into flame on windows just clear of frost, splashes sunlight down streets and squares in lunatic, gilded abandon. 'The forest outside* Moscow is 'a twilit cathedral of silver birches'. In a hospital intensive care room 'Save for an air-conditioning hum, there were no indications of life apart from the dancing movements registered on the monitor screen behind the bed ... The air was hot and static and pervaded by a prophylactic smell ...'

Characters, even minor ones, are drawn with depth and delicacy. Mr Thoreau, an American businessman who wants 'a hotline right into the heart of the Russian people', has 'lips with an aura of "Have a nice day" contentment' and a smile produced by 'a neat compression of his smile lines'. He thinks that the Soviet Union is 'an ideal place for golf... Undulant.' (His fondness for golf courses and his complete lack of self-awareness make us wonder if he is a possible future President.) Bob Jermin, the major protagonist, is, on the other hand, endearingly British. He is lured into a honey trap apparently by politeness. He knows that an invitation into a hotel room from a young and attractive woman whom he doesn't know can only mean one thing, but feels that it would be 'ungracious', even 'churlish', to refuse, and he keeps his socks on when he strips. He cannot refuse his grandmother's instruction to go to a Forbidden Zone, despite knowing that this could cost him his career and even his life. And he will not interrupt a dying man's last words to relay to him the questions of an insistent policeman.

The female characters have equal depth and immediacy, from Bob's grandmother bashing beetroot for borscht (while wearing a 'semi-decorative' hat) and interrogating him about his love-life, to Sophie who cleans his apartment and spies on him but at the same time feels maternally protective towards him. Grace Hampson, an American administrative assistant is 'power dressed to the perfection of milled steel' but we learn the reason for the armour in a love scene where her story is revealed; unlike many a thriller romance, this becomes a relationship of friends and equals. And the Special Branch officer charged with investigating the threat to the President is a woman.

The author knows the life of a junior diplomat in Cold War Moscow from the inside and the novel is as at home and as convincing there as in South London – the smells, the people, the language, the flat with the bath full of developing films, the constant surveillance and the things one may and may not do – being photographed naked with a girl in a white fur hat being clearly one of the latter, as was visiting a Forbidden Zone. The life and anxieties of Sophie and her kind are understood and succinctly conveyed; 'militiamen, the upravlenie, meat lines, poor-quality footwear, a surly husband, damp accommodation, leaky plumbing and mice'.

Freeborn is thoroughly at home in Russian 19th century literature, a key strand that runs through the story and gives it part of its depth. The novel is prefaced by a quotation from The Brothers Karamazov. It is Starets Zosima's address to his brother monks on the last day of his life and ends: 'Then each of you will have the power to conquer the whole world with love and wash away the sins of the world.' Brother Peter, the would-be assassin, who has left the monastic life and says he is 'rising from the dead' to 'do God's will' and regards his life as 'a sacrifice' repeats the words of the address to Bob when he meets him at a dacha in the Forbidden Zone in surroundings which might have come straight out of Dostoyevsky. The Forbidden Zone can be reached by bus, but Bob has to get there in a manner that echoes both Russian folk lore – an uncertain path through a dark forest – and the Bible – the crossing of a forbidding river. The girl in the white fur hat is 'an angel', though sometimes a wicked one. Thoreau, in many ways a figure of fun, has ideals which Grace shares and Bob admires – 'the ideal notion that human beings were precious and deserved to know more about each other ... that they were not to be classified and segregated and perhaps exterminated on grounds of class, social worth, racial theory, political expediency or religious hatred ...'. The rainbow, a biblical symbol of God's love for man, will appear again, not least as an inscription on the side of a ballistic missile. Love, both caritas and eros, runs through the novel, and Zosima's words return at the end in a surprising way, helping to explain how a honey trap, the firing of a rocket and an attack on the President can be seen as the outworking of love.

But for all its Dostoyevskian overtones the novel is never solemn or sermonising and is full of quiet humour. When Brother Peter delivers Zosima's address he is wearing striped Bermuda shorts and a sun hat. Thoreau (Freeborn has a cunning way with names) hears 'Liberty herself crying from the upper window of the Soviet Union and she needs intrepid, determined people like you and me to defy the flames and smoke and come to her rescue'. Bob and Grace, charged with the task of making contact with some of the 'real Russian people' decide to make some up, and to borrow their names from Chekhov. Thus Trigorin becomes a journalist and member of the Union of Soviet Writers who specialises in visiting collective farms but has 'marital and drink problems that could make him unreliable', and Arkadina is a ballerina who resents never being given lead roles and claims to have slept with Leonid Brezhnev and other members of the communist leadership, but whose ideas on Soviet defence policy are 'a bit haywire'. Even the honey trap, no laughing matter for poor Bob, will make the reader smile. And so this novel, which would not disappoint anyone looking for 'a good read' will also prove deeply satisfying to those looking for good writing, convincing settings and characterisation, wry humour, and an exploration of the depths of Russian (and British and American) soul. □